KISSING IN ACTION

LEXI GRAVES MYSTERIES

Camilla Chafer

ALSO BY CAMILLA CHAFER

CHAPTER ONE

I was sitting in my car, my camera in my lap, on a cold and gray morning when two strange women caught my eye. Both wore panama hats and trench coats that were buttoned to the neck with their collars turned up. One wore unfeasibly large sunglasses. The other had a mustache. The mustache was fake, and really didn't suit my mother. The Panama hat, however, did look good on my best friend-slash-sister-in-law, Lily.

Since I had no idea what the two of them might have been doing, I decided my best option was to call Lily.

"Hey," I said, when Lily answered. Through my zoom lens, I watched her lift the phone to her ear while she pressed her back against the wall. My mother leaned against the wall too, then opened her purse and retrieved a newspaper, which she held to her face. I repressed a sigh. Fortunately, she didn't cut eyeholes in it.

"Hey, you," I cooed, "Whatcha doin'?"

"Who? Me?" asked Lily.

"Um, yes." I frowned, zooming into the panicked look on Lily's face. She mouthed my name to my mother, now headless behind the newspaper. If she mouthed anything back, however, it was lost on me.

"Nothing. Absolutely nothing."

"Where are you?"

"Oh, just hanging out. Downtown."

I narrowed my eyes at her through the lens at her blatant lie. "I might just meet you. Do you want to get a coffee?"

"Me? No. No, definitely not."

"You don't have time for coffee?"

"I'm doing—" There was a long pause, during which, I watched Lily whip out a pair of binoculars from her trench coat and focus on something further down the street. I followed her line of sight with my camera. There was only one man on the street. He wore blue jeans, a black, zip-up hoodie, and a blue ball cap and carried a small, canvas gym bag. He didn't look familiar. "—Something really important," Lily finished.

"Yeah? What?"

"Just bar stuff. Um, new cocktail recipes. I'm also thinking of jazzing up the cocktail menu. Maybe even adding some snacks."

"I'd love to help!"

"No can do. This is highly specialized work."

"Okay. Well, maybe I'll call my mom and see if she wants to go out for brunch."

"Your mom's busy."

"How do you know?"

"I just saw her!" Lily shrugged and mouthed something incomprehensible at my newspaper-masked mother. "What is this, Lexi? Twenty questions? You private investigators! Always on the job!"

"So..."

"Great to chat! Gotta go!" Lily hung up.

"Weirdos," I said to my cell phone as I tossed it onto the passenger seat and took another look at the man in the ball cap. He scanned the area around him before entering the public library. I lost him for a moment, but saw him again through the long picture window over the main entrance. He took the stairs to the second floor and retreated into the non-fiction section, only to be lost from view. I refocused my camera onto my mom and Lily just in time to see them exiting the alley and hurrying along the street. They stopped outside the pharmacy, looking around, and appearing confused. There were some hand gestures and both held binoculars over their eyes as they scanned the street.

I grabbed my phone and called Lily again.

"Yeah?" she said when she answered.

"How's the cocktail menu going?"

"What are you talking about?"

"Your new cocktail menu."

"Oh yeah! That! Great! Just great! Listen, we'll have to catch up..."

"Are you following a guy in a blue ball cap?"

"No! No! Where did you get that idea? What a

bizarre thing to ask! Crazy! But just out of interest, did you see where he went?"

"The public library. He's on the second floor and just disappeared into the non-fiction section."

"Awesome, thanks, but no, I'm not following him. Crazy. Bizarre."

"I'm not going to ask, but that guy in the ball cap is now on his way out. Say hi to my mom," I replied before hanging up, and smiling.

I watched Lily and my mom speak briefly as they flapped around in a moment of heightened panic. Both of them collided, then darted to opposite sides of the library doors, concealing themselves just as the man exited. I noticed he no longer carried his bag. Apparently, Lily and my mom noticed it also because they both dashed inside. Through the viewfinder, I followed them upstairs and continued watching as they rushed around the library. After a couple of minutes, my mom reappeared, holding the bag aloft and they high-fived.

"It just gets weirder and weirder," I said out loud. Part of me wanted to call and demand to know what crazy thing they were involved in, but a bigger part of me didn't want to get roped into any of that lunacy. I'd had enough crazy in my life recently. After just completing a simple surveillance case: two full weeks of sitting on my ass in my VW while a shady employee stole and sold his employer's electronic products to pawn shops, I was looking forward to a nice little commission for the simple job and help put a bad guy in jail. Truth was, while some cases were complicated, and fully worthy of snatching every waking moment of my attention, I enjoyed doing the smaller jobs. They were safer. They didn't risk getting me kidnapped, or shot at, or anything else that might turn me into a nervous wreck, or force me to wear flats everyday in order to sprint faster if the situation turned scary.

Now, with my camera full of evidence on the seat next to me, and my mom and Lily out of view, I gunned the engine and headed back to the Solomon Detective Agency, ready to close another case.

~

"Sweetheart, I've got the best job in the world for you! It's not even dangerous!"

Considering some of the jobs I completed during my employ at the private detective agency I worked for, somehow, I doubted it. Nevertheless, I liked the enthusiasm of my boss-slash-boyfriend, Solomon. He was a terrific-looking man. Tall, handsome, closely-shaven black hair, skin like melted chocolate — and every bit as lickable — and eyes that sparkled when he was happy. He also gave me my first lucky break when I was at a crossroads in my life. Our current relationship developed later, but both facets of it were just as important to him. To some, working for your boyfriend might be a turnoff. To me, it was a bonus.

"No, really," Solomon continued when I merely raised my eyebrows before returning my attention to the online sale I currently browsed. "It's a dream job. Something you'd kill for."

"Is it posing as a mystery shopper with an unlimited credit card that never needs paying back?" I asked hopefully. At least seventeen pairs of heels had my name on them; and a job like that would have come in very useful right about now. I pushed my file towards him. "I closed the case and I'm ready for something juicy like that."

"No, but close. Quite close. Okay, nowhere near close," he admitted, taking the file and tucking it under his arm.

"Ugh!" I said, removing fifteen pairs from my basket.

"Lexi!"

I looked up again. "What?"

"Where's your enthusiasm?"

"I left it at home."

"You are going to love this case."

I had to wonder at Solomon's enthusiasm. He didn't usually get so excited about our steady influx of surveillance jobs, or crimes that the police couldn't solve. Whatever it was had to be juicy. That, if nothing else, now captured my attention. "Does it involve serial killers?" I asked, suspicion tingeing my voice. Three months ago, we solved a missing persons case that turned out to be a ruse by a prolific serial killer. He attempted to dupe us into seeking a victim who escaped, while he turned his attentions on me. I escaped too, and his prior victim got a book deal out of it. He got a jail deal: life. The case managed to earn the detective agency a lot of attention, as well as several new cases.

"No."

"Thieves?"

"No."

"Will I get shot, stabbed, or kidnapped?"

Solomon paused.

I sighed. "On a scale of one to ten, how likely are any of those things to happen?"

The corners of his lips twitched. "Between one and three."

I sighed again.

"Those are good odds!"

"Does it involve dressing up?"

"No."

"Oh, thank heavens." I breathed a sigh of relief. I was thinking back to an ill-advised decision a couple of years ago when my best friend, Lily, and I masqueraded as both ends of a plush pony in order to catch a bad guy. Since then, Lily married my brother and bought several other disguises, while I got duped by a master criminal, but managed to escape a serial killer. At least, I could never again say my life was boring. I couldn't say Lily's was either, not when I remembered what I caught her doing earlier.

"Unless you want to wear really nice clothes. We may have a budget."

My attention was all his. "Okay, what is it?"

"We're going to be working with the risk management team on our highest profile case yet."

I had yet to work with the risk management team, so that was very interesting news... and high profile? I folded the lid of my laptop, offering Solomon my undivided attention. "Go on."

"We've been called in by B4U to provide security and help with a..."

"B4U? As in, the hot, sensational girl band, B4U?"

"Yes."

"*B4U!*"

"Still, yes."

"As in the megabucks-loaded, after a super-famous meteoric ride to the top, platinum-selling B4U?"

"If that's what it says on Wikipedia, then yes."

B4U were the hot young sensation sweeping the country. Their uplifting beats and catchy lyrics, combined with gorgeous looks and all the latest fashions guaranteed them a skyrocket ride to success. They were assembled six years ago for a role on a kids' TV channel. It soon became a huge sensation, spawning two TV movies, one sellout tour, and three albums with several number one hits. My niece, Chloe, loved them. I tried but failed to get Chloe tickets to their concert for her birthday. Now I was about to become the best aunt in the history of the universe thanks to an all-access pass to the band. Screw serial killers, this was one hot gig!

"Why don't they already have a security team?" I asked. Actually, I knew very well they did after seeing a photo online of two of the band divas recently. They were on a shopping trip and surrounded by giants clad in black B4U t-shirts.

"They do. They need something else from us."

"I'm listening."

"It's not just a simple security job, although we'll be providing those services too."

"Alongside their security?"

"Possibly, in place of," Solomon replied.

"Sounds fishy. What's up with their people?"

"I'm getting to that!"

I paused, almost impatient for Solomon to begin speaking again. "Please continue," I said just as he opened his mouth. He gave me a look. I gave him one back. He probably liked it, but he didn't say.

"They are currently experiencing some problems and need an outside agency to help out. They don't trust their own team; so we're going to aid them while they're in town. Apparently, they're filming a new video here, as well as performing in a concert. They got here four days ago and will be on a layover for two weeks."

"Montgomery is going to be a heaving mass of teens screaming for the next two weeks," I sighed. "I'll probably be late for work every day. I think it's reasonable to let you know that in advance."

"Get up earlier," was Solomon's response. "And it won't be that bad."

"Have you seen their fans? They could break glass with their shrill screaming. I heard their fans blew out some windows at the last book-signing for their latest biography."

"I'm glad you know all this stuff because you'll be working directly with them."

"I've never been a security guard before. Will I have to wear flats? Also, I'll need a B4U t-shirt in a size small, along with four tickets to their concert."

"You won't be a security guard now either, and you can wear whatever you like. Why do you need tickets to their concert?" He paused, smiling, with a glint in his eye that he never showed my male colleagues. I was pretty happy about that. It would have raised some interesting questions if he did. "I'm very happy to supply you with a small t-shirt. I won't even ask why you need it for the job. I'm hoping you're just trying to blend in."

"The shirt is for my niece and it's a deal breaker if I don't get it. If my family should happen to find out I'm working with B4U, and I fail to use my powers to gain access to their exclusive merchandise, my niece will be devastated! I'll probably have to tell my mother and she might mention it to you..."

"Consider it done," Solomon said quickly. "I'll get you whatever you need."

"Four tickets and some signed CDs," I added quickly. "Perhaps a brief cameo in their video..."

"Don't push it."

"Okay. What will I be doing?"

"It's a simple investigation. All you need to do is find out who is blackmailing the band."

"Tell me everything!"

CHAPTER TWO

"Juicy!" said Lily when I caught up with her at the bar she owned. Her disguise was gone and she was dressed in a simple, white Lily's Bar t-shirt and black pants. She didn't mention what she was up to earlier and I didn't ask, although I was actually nearly desperate to know. However, having shared my exciting news, Lily spent the last five minutes jumping up and down while shrieking with glee. Finally, she settled down and placed a coffee in front of me. What I really wanted was a cocktail, but I had an appointment to meet the band later, and I didn't want to risk turning up inebriated.

"Who's blackmailing them?"

"Pay attention! That's what I'm supposed to be finding out. Solomon told me..."

"Who did he hear it from?"

"Umm..." I frowned. I had no idea. "I don't know. Their manager?"

"Okay. What did he say?"

"All I know is that B4U received threatening letters on every leg of their tour so far. Since they're staying in Montgomery for two weeks to shoot their video, they hope this might be their best chance to find the blackmailer before the tour, as well as the band's reputation, get ruined."

"Pfft," said Lily rudely. "Their reputations are so squeaky clean, they probably sneeze laundry detergent."

"They do seem nice," I admitted as I flicked through a magazine. As luck would have it, there was a paparazzi shot of B4U walking into a high-end store. Each band member was superbly styled in the latest fashions. I spotted at least one Vuitton hung on an arm, and three pairs of Louboutins. The rest of the clothing labels were lost on me, but each woman seemed to have invested several thousand dollars into their fashions, with everything utterly hip and desirable. Along with glossy hair and perfect figures, the band members had become role models and the latest paradigms for hundreds of thousands of adoring fans.

"Nice?" Lily reached for the magazine and turned it around. "Lauren Young personally donates ten percent of her salary every year to needy children. Amelia Toren is a mentor for inner city kids. Katya Markova escaped from Russia at age five, and came to America with nothing. She claims to be entirely self-made, and does motivational speeches in high schools for free. And Shelley Solis rescued a pug from a burning building before finding it a new home as a therapy dog for elderly citizens!"

"How do you know all this stuff?" I asked.

"Jord and I took Chloe to the park over the weekend and she didn't stop talking about them. I think I know everything a little kid needs to know about B4U, except how to get concert tickets."

"I told Solomon I needed concert tickets and merchandise, or I wouldn't take the case. Maybe I should visit Chloe and get some inside info?"

"She'll tell you anything you ask the minute you tell her you're working with them. You're going to be the all time number one aunt!"

"I already am."

"Number one biological aunt," Lily clarified.

"Whatever. Still number one!"

"Did I mention they had nine number one songs in two years?" Lily continued. Dragging a bar stool over and perching on it, she began blowing on her decaf coffee to cool it before taking a sip. "Not to mention, I love their TV show."

I took another look at the photo. "Who would want to blackmail four saccharine-sweet, accomplished, self-made, philanthropic young women?" I asked.

"Don't ask me. That's your job! One of them probably has a dirty, little secret. Maybe even a sex tape."

I frowned. "Really? Do starlets still fall for that?"

"Only the really stupid ones."

"I'll check it out," I said, making a mental note.

"When do you start?"

"Officially, tomorrow. They got into town last night and I'm going to meet them this evening. Tomorrow, I'll go through all the existing blackmail demands and keep an eye out for the source of the next one while Solomon works through their security issues."

"I want to come. I bet I could help. Also, I... No, I got nothing. I just want to meet B4U. Do you think they'll come to my bar?"

"I have no idea."

"Could you tell them that Lily's Bar is the hottest hangout in Montgomery?"

"I will."

"And will you also let me know if they plan to come, so I can tip off the press?"

"That would be wrong and possibly an invasion of their privacy."

"Fine, I won't tip off the press, but I might take a selfie. Can I still meet them too? I can take notes or something?"

"Sure, I guess. Solomon didn't say I couldn't bring anyone," I replied. He didn't exactly say I could bring someone either. In my book, that was as good as permission; plus, he usually didn't mind Lily so long as he didn't have to pay her.

"That's settled then. Hey, maybe the blackmailer is someone jealous in their crew? It doesn't matter how nice a person is if someone else covets what they have."

"I wondered that too. It would explain how the blackmailer always knows where they are staying. Solomon said they kept their hotel details under a 'for your eyes only' requirement so that the public wouldn't know in advance. Sometimes, even the band doesn't know until they get there; and they even go so far as to book in under false names."

"I would book under something really glam like Countess Esmeralda Blackheart."

I turned the page of the magazine as I raised my eyebrows. "No one would ever be curious over that kind of name."

"I know, right? Perfect! What did you say they were being blackmailed for?"

"Solomon didn't mention it. I don't think he knows. He said they are trying to keep it all under wraps so the press doesn't find out. It's strictly on a need-to-know basis. I can't even see the blackmail letters until tomorrow."

Lily blanched. "But you're going to tell me, right?"

"Maybe."

"How dare you 'maybe' me! You're my oldest friend and now we're related! Since when did we start keeping things from each other?"

"Since my job went on the line if anyone found out. I signed a non-disclosure."

Lily flicked another page, settling her gaze on a shirtless shot of Hollywood's latest heartthrob. "Hey, look at this. It's written by Shayne Winter."

"Who?"

"The *Montgomery Gazette* reporter who stalked us at the pony convention."

I had a vague recollection of the pretty, but pesky blonde reporter who was so determined to get a story. "She really made it to Hollywood? Good for her."

"Looks like the perfect job. Write fifty words, six of which are 'dribble' and get paid. Anyway, if you get fired, we'll set up our own detective agency. I bet we could attract loads of clients. I could give a free pitcher of margaritas as an incentive to pay up front."

"You sound like my mother. She's still trying to persuade me to set something up with my dad."

"Your poor dad. Did he enjoy the cruise?"

"He loved it, but you could have asked my mother that."

"What? How? I haven't seen your mother in so long. Not at all."

I narrowed my eyes. "Yes, you have."

"Have. Not."

"I saw you!"

"Where?"

"Outside the library, this morning. You were following a man. You were in disguise."

"Then how did you know it was me?"

"I called you and spoke to you!"

"Oh… yeah."

"I also watched you through my zoom lens."

"Stalker!"

"Hardly, I was wrapping up a case. What were you both doing anyway?"

Lily's nostrils flared. "I'm not at liberty to say."

"I'll ask Mom."

"Great! Now tell me how you intend to bring down the blackmailer, and keep one of the biggest, most famous, current bands safe, while not getting mobbed by the media? Do you need to borrow a disguise from me?"

I checked my watch, blanching as soon as I noted the time. If I didn't hurry, I would be late to meet the band. Judging by Solomon's excitement at getting the case, that wouldn't do at all. "We have to go," I told Lily. "Still want to come?"

"You betcha." She spun around on the stool. "Ruby, watch the bar... and all the people in it! Lexi and I are going to do something really cool!"

~

Solomon met us in the lobby of the Marchmont Hotel, which I visited a few times before and loved. The plush furnishings, the expensive curtains that pooled in front of floor-to-ceiling windows, the cocktail bar... It even had a pretty, walled-in garden where I attended a wedding reception the previous year. Yes, I could have moved right in.

"There are a few things you need to know before entering," Solomon told me as he rose from the leather wing chair he'd been sitting in. He kissed me first, then he kissed Lily on the cheek. "Lily, what a surprise," he said, sounding resolutely unsurprised.

"I know! Isn't it?!" Lily said, utterly delighted. I decided not to burst her bubble that Solomon wasn't even one iota surprised at finding me with my best friend in tow. "I just thought I'd lend Lexi a hand." She leaned in, lowering her voice. "I know a lot about B4U."

Solomon moved closer. "What does B4U stand for?" he asked.

Lily blinked. "I have absolutely no idea. Ask me an easy one."

"What do I need to know?" I asked, ignoring the question without admitting that I, also, didn't know what the band's name meant. Possibly, I decided, it meant nothing at all. Or maybe it was really crappy text speak from a sweaty, old, balding, music exec who thought it was "cool."

"For one, they are having a few issues right now," Solomon began, signaling for us to follow. We followed him to the elevators and he jabbed the *up* button.

"You'd probably be having issues if you were being blackmailed too," chimed Lily. "Have you no sympathy?"

"What she said," I replied, nodding to Lily, "but what kind of issues?"

"Personality ones," replied Solomon. "Don't expect them to be too friendly."

"Check. Anything else?"

"They're under a lot of pressure, just trying to keep the situation out of the media."

"No problem. We'll solve everything and get it under control," said Lily, stepping into the elevator as the doors slid back.

"Did I recently employ her and forget about it?" Solomon asked softly.

"I heard that. Get in! There's no time to lose!" Lily clapped her hands as she beckoned us to hurry. We stepped inside and Solomon punched the button for the top floor.

"The whole top floor is reserved for the band. There're three suites. The band have two, and their manager has the third," he explained. "We'll meet all of them together."

"I'm really looking forward to this," I said as the elevator began its ascent. "I've never met anyone really famous before."

"You might regret it."

I frowned. "Why? I know they're having a bad time, but like Lily said, that's why we're here. We'll get everything under control." I added, remembering my own stipulations. "Do you think they'll let us watch their video being filmed?"

"The manager has agreed to allow us total access while we investigate, so yes, I guess that would be okay."

"Me too?" asked Lily. "No one will see me, I swear.

Unless they want to, like if they offered us small, but pivotal roles with screen time. I'm happy to dance like no one is watching, although I have to insist on clothes, if that's a deal breaker... No, wait, we've talked about this stuff, haven't we, Lexi? Did the band make a sex tape? A naked, sexy-times sex tape?"

Solomon took a deep breath.

"What's your take on the manager?" I asked before Lily broke into an interpretive dance.

"Seems like a nice guy. He's been with the band since they decided to move from TV into the music business so... three years, I guess. He's got a solid background with a lot of successful stars. B4U is his biggest achievement to date. He appears to genuinely care about them, and it was he who came to the agency for help. He is very nervous of the magnitude and impact this could have on the band."

"It's only blackmail. What could possibly be so bad that there would be any fallout?" I asked.

"Their image is so squeaky clean. They can't risk damaging that when their stardom is built on it. Whatever they're being blackmailed about, we can assume it's something that they don't want made public. Their whole careers are based on them being everyone's girls next door. Without that, they're just like any other pop starlets," said Lily. The elevator glided to a halt and the doors slid back.

"What she said," replied Solomon as he stepped out. He greeted the two enormous security guards who rose from the stiff-backed chairs as we stepped into the corridor, and introduced us both.

The larger of the two nodded, and ticked off our names.

"I'm on the list?" asked Lily.

"I figured you'd turn up," said Solomon. "And took the liberty of adding you."

"Awww."

"They're waiting for you in Room One," said the man I nicknamed "Larger." He was huge, and at least twice my girth. His legs looked like tree trunks.

"How've things been?" Solomon asked.

The security guards glanced at each other and sighed. "The usual," said Larger.

"What's the usual?" I asked as we passed them, and walked to the end of the corridor, pausing outside a door. A scream pierced the air. I glanced back at the security guards, but neither of them moved.

Solomon opened the door.

A vase sailed through the doorway, clearing the narrow space between Solomon and me before colliding with the wall behind my head. It smashed, of course, and all the pieces dropped loudly to the floor.

Solomon closed the door.

"That," he said. He knocked even more loudly before opening the door again. "It's Solomon," he yelled over the screaming, hysterical voices. "With my investigator."

"And her best friend," yelled Lily, following us.

I had to stop and take in the scene. This was B4U, but certainly not the sweet, giggling, fun-loving B4U I knew from TV. Nor were they the perfectly poised women from the magazine articles. Sure, they were all gorgeously dressed, and their hair looked perfect, but Amelia and Shelley were screaming at each other, Lauren was holding her cheek, reddened from what appeared to be a recent slap, and the final member, Katya, was grabbing another vase to hurl from the credenza as we watched. She brandished it over her head, screaming horrible obscenities. The man in the center of them all, waving his arms and yelling somewhat ineffectually, had to have been their manager.

"Hello?" Solomon shouted. The band and their manager continued hollering.

Lily stuck two fingers into her mouth and gave one hell of a whistle, silencing the room. Katya turned her attention on Lily. She gave her mere seconds to dart out of the way before launching the vase. It bounced off the sofa and slid onto the floor. Lily picked it up and handed it back. "Better luck next time," she said. "I like your shoes. There is nothing on this earth like a pair of killer stilettos."

"Who the hell are you?" asked Katya, accepting the vase.

"I'm Lily Shuler-Graves, a big fan. Lexi Graves, who is taking the case, and her boyfriend-slash-boss, Solomon. Only Solomon. No first name."

"You're not single?" said Katya, addressing

Solomon. Her voice sounded silky, despite the former screaming, and she gave Solomon the once-over. She turned to her manager. "You said he was single."

"I said I didn't know if he were single, and I didn't care."

"What's the point of hiring a hot guy to do our dirty work if he's not single? Fire him and get someone else."

"Katya, I'm not firing him."

Katya pointed to me. "Fire her!" She fixed her eyes on me, mouthing, "Bitch."

I blanched at seeing the vitriol in her eyes and took a step back. I was tempted to take another step back and slide behind Solomon, but Lily was already edging in that direction.

"No one is firing anyone!" their exasperated manager sighed. "Ladies, sit down. These people are here to help us... to help you. Sit the hell down and shut the hell up!"

I was surprised to see the band slink over to the sofas, each sitting as far away from each other as possible. Thankfully, they did it quietly. Unfortunately, the shrill sounds of screaming still rang in my ears as I surveyed the room. Pillows were flung across the floor, and a side table was turned over. One vase was smashed in the hallway, and the other near victim sat on the coffee table after Katya put it there. Magazines were scattered everywhere. It looked like the fight must have been going on for some time.

Solomon, Lily, and I remained standing. I didn't know what Solomon and Lily were looking at, but I decided to assess the exits. There appeared to only be one, the door by which we entered; and fortunately, I was closest to it. However, it didn't appear that any more missiles would be flung in our direction.

"I'm Joe Carter, B4U's manager," said the man, cutting through the silence. "This is Amelia, Katya, Shelley, and Lauren. Sorry for what just happened. The girls are a little highly strung of late."

"I wouldn't need to be highly strung if that bitch would apologize," sniffed Shelley.

"Go to hell," screeched Amelia.

"Guess I'll see you there!" Shelley yelled back. She grabbed a pillow and walloped Amelia on the head. Amelia wrenched it from Shelley's fingers, and slammed it back at her fellow band member's head. All I could do was watch, while inhaling deeply, as the two attacked each other, grabbing and pulling hair. They rolled off the couch and onto the floor before Joe threw himself into the middle, prying them apart.

"You, over there," he said, pushing Shelley towards the furthest couch. He gave Amelia a lighter push, urging her to sit on the couch she just vacated. Amelia crossed her arms, scowling, and gave her hair a little toss. It settled perfectly into a satiny sheet that swung well past her shoulders.

"I hate her. I hate all of you," Shelley sniffed, her jaw wobbling as she stifled tears.

"Feeling is mutual," said Katya, shrugging one shoulder. "I hate your disgusting face. It ruins every album cover."

"You odious peasant!"

"Ladies, please! Be quiet!" Joe yelled, waving his arms over his head. "Can you shut up for ten minutes? Can you?"

"Ask Katya; she has the biggest mouth," said Lauren.

"And yet, you're the one still talking," Joe pointed out. "Zip it."

"Hah!" gloated Katya. "Better to have a big mouth than your huge nose, Lauren!"

"I said, zip it!" yelled Joe. "Ladies, this is Solomon from the Solomon Detective Agency I told you all about, and his associate, Lexi Graves and... I'm sorry, who are you?" He turned to Lily. Three more sets of eyes looked at her. The fourth, belonging to Katya, studied the buttons of her sweater, apparently disinterested, but I could tell she was listening. Her posture was a little stiff, and her head was cocked at an angle.

"Lily Shuler-Graves," Lily said, without explaining why she was there.

"Right," agreed Joe. "Like I told you ladies already, and I'm really trying to keep calling all of you ladies, the agency came here to help with our blackmail issue."

"Why don't you all tell us about it," said Solomon, "starting with the basics?"

Every member of the band started to talk at once, each of them suddenly focused and animated. I caught "secrets," and "I don't know what they're talking about," and "money," but I couldn't figure out a single individual story. It seemed like they were all talking about something different, and each girl wanted to get her word in over her band mates'.

"One at a time!" commanded Solomon, loudly. His imperious tone plunged them into silence. "Katya, why don't you go first?"

"Why her?" asked Shelley. "Is it because she's the biggest bitch?"

"No, it's because I asked," replied Solomon, barely glancing her way. "Katya, tell us what happened."

"I got the first letter after our first gig on this tour," Katya began. She was still picking imaginary lint off her sweater. "At first, I thought, 'Hey, this is stupid,' but then the same words were written in lipstick on the mirror in my hotel bathroom in the evening."

"What did the letter say?"

Katya pursed her lips and breathed harshly through her nose. "It said, 'I'll tell them about Russia unless you pay five thousand dollars by tomorrow noon.' It gave a bank number."

"What did you do then?" I asked.

"I paid, of course."

"What about Russia?" Solomon asked.

Katya shrugged. "I don't know."

"But you paid," pointed out Lily, "so you must have

known."

"Maybe, I don't know. I was five when I left Russia. We were dirt poor, but we made it to America, and now, I am big pop star! People are jealous. Not everyone gets to live out a dream, you know?" she said, her accent becoming more evident.

"Big pop star?" laughed Shelley. "You couldn't make it on your own!"

"Neither can you. You sing like a chipmunk," shot back Katya. " A drunken chipmunk. That's not surprising, because you're always drunk, yes?"

"Screw you!"

"What happened after you paid?" I asked, trying to prevent the girls from screaming.

"Nothing. Nothing happened. I forgot about it until I got another letter. Concert eight."

"What did that say?"

"It had a photo. It said something about my parents would be leaked to the press. Of course, it was a doctored photograph! This time, the blackmailer wanted ten thousand dollars!"

"Did you pay?"

"I told Joe."

Joe nodded. "That's when I asked the others and learned they'd all been receiving anonymous letters that threatened to blackmail them with supposed secrets that would be leaked to the press."

"I don't recall seeing any damaging photos in the press," Lily said. "It wasn't leaked?"

"That's because I paid. Again," sniffed Katya. "Now, they have fifteen thousand dollars of my money!"

"Did you all receive the letters individually?" Solomon asked.

Each woman nodded. "I have them all," said Joe, reaching for a box on the credenza and passing it to Solomon. "They got two letters each, all demanding money in exchange for protecting their so-called secrets."

"You said there were letters from every concert?" I asked, frowning.

Joe turned to me. "I don't know if the blackmailer found out we knew about all the individual letters, or if he changed tactics, but the ninth letter was addressed to all of them. It demanded twenty thousand dollars. Five thousand each, in order to keep quiet."

"Shelley, what did your letters say?" I asked.

"They said 'Remember ten years ago?' and asked for five thousand dollars."

Katya giggled. "Shelley is usually too drunk to remember even five minutes ago."

"Shut up!" screeched Shelley.

"Enough!" yelled Joe.

"Did you pay?" I asked, raising my voice in order to be heard.

"Not at first, no, but at the next concert, there was another letter and the price was raised to fifteen thousand dollars. And there was also a still from a video."

"You never told me that," said Joe, looking puzzled.

"I didn't understand it. It's me, but... I don't know how someone got it."

"What was happening in the photo?" I pressed. "Do you remember?"

Shelley rolled her eyes. "I don't know. Kinda. I don't want to talk about it."

"We need to know," Solomon pressed. "It could help us find out who did this. Your past is your past and we want it to stay that way."

"Fine, I'll tell her," Shelley said, pointing at me. She unfolded her long legs and strode across the room, bending to whisper into my ear. I raised my eyebrows as she gave the briefest of explanations.

"Did you pay?" I asked.

"Yes," she said softly before returning to her seat. She sunk into the couch and wrapped her arms around her legs.

"What about you two?" Solomon continued, moving on swiftly, while sensing Shelley's embarrassment. "Amelia?"

"It said, 'I know your secret.' It asked for five grand in the first letter, then ten grand in the second."

"You paid?" I asked.

"Yeah, I did."

"And you know what secret they're talking about?"

Amelia nodded.

"Can you tell me?" I asked.

"No. It's not very damaging though, and that's what

puzzled me," said Amelia. "I mean, I'm not embarrassed. It's just nobody's business, but mine. I just don't want it getting out. Not yet. Not until I'm ready. When I'm ready, I'll tell everyone, but not until then." She closed her mouth and refused to elaborate on anything else.

"Lauren?"

"It just had a name. Nothing else."

"What name?" asked Solomon.

Lauren sighed. "Michael."

"Do you know who Michael is?" I asked.

"Yes, but I don't know how anyone else would know."

"Who is Michael?" I continued. "Someone from your past?"

"Yes, but that's all I'm saying. Before you ask, yes, I paid. I don't care what the media does to me, but I don't want anyone from the press bothering Michael. That's not okay."

"You can't let someone extort money from you and keep paying to protect a guy," I said.

"He's not just a guy. Anyway, that's why you're here. Find the blackmailer and make whoever it is stop before we have to quit the band."

"You don't mean that!" said Katya, startled. "We're not going to quit."

Lily nodded, looking outraged. "She's right. You've got the world at your feet, Lauren. Think of the fans. They love B4U."

"Think of the money," said Katya.

"I'd sooner quit than let anyone else suffer," replied Lauren.

"Maybe we should throw you out of the band," Katya shot back. "Who needs her anyway?"

"B4U needs me more than any of us need you!" Lauren shot back before muttering something extremely rude under her breath.

Joe shook his head. "Okay, quiet. Ladies, it won't go that far. The detectives will get to the bottom of this, and the tour can continue without any further problems. It's sold out," he said, turning to us. "The fans can't get enough of them. They think they're the best band since... well, since ever!"

"Our fans are stupid, little kids," sniffed Katya. "Who cares what they think so long as their stupid parents buy more tickets and more merchandise?"

"You should care," Joe told her, turning around and fixing her with a furious look, "since you'd be nothing without them. How about showing a little humility?"

"Don't talk to me like that! We should fire you!" said Katya.

Joe dropped his head into his hands. "Why can't I get through to you?" he mumbled.

"We'll take the letters and..." Solomon stopped as Joe began to shake his head.

"Those letters don't leave this hotel. I can't risk having them fall into the wrong hands. We're trying to keep this out of the press! If anyone gets wind of it, the press will go crazy trying to uncover these so-called secrets. Who knows what kind of damaging stories they'll run? Even in the best case scenario, they'll hit on the truth. Worst, and they can make a bunch of stuff up, which is even more damaging. The band has a contractual obligation to do everything to maintain their untarnished image."

"Understood. We'll come back tomorrow and examine them; but Joe, you have to give us room to work."

"You can take my suite," said Joe. "You can have all the space you need."

Solomon shook his head. "That's not what I meant. We'll read the letters, sure, but we have to bring in handwriting analysts, and do fingerprint tests, and check for DNA. We'll need full access..."

"Sure, you can have whatever you need, but everything runs past me; and any specialist you summon comes to the hotel." Joe reached for the box containing the letters Solomon and I had yet to even take a cursory glance at. "Until then, these letters stay under lock and key."

CHAPTER THREE

Solomon and I were holed up in Joe Carter's suite by nine the next morning. Spread in front of us was every letter the blackmailer had sent so far, but we weren't looking at them. Instead, we listened to the screaming coming from next door. I could make out two distinct voices: Katya's and Amelia's.

"Do you think they're killing each other?" I asked, picking up my takeout coffee cup and taking a sip. When the lukewarm coffee hit my lips, I shuddered.

"I hope so," said Solomon. "A murder investigation would be a lot quieter than this."

"They really hate each other. You know, I watched their TV movie last night with Lily and they seemed like the best of friends. Their TV show ran for years!"

"They must be good actresses."

"I guess, but it's so disappointing. What else in the music world is fake?"

Solomon gave me an amused look. "What? Aside from voices, hair, breasts, and marriages?"

I laughed. "Okay, there's a lot fake about the music world, but I'm still disappointed. How do I tell my niece that her favorite band, the band that she and her friends aspire to emulate, are nothing more than a bunch of nasty, hateful bitches?"

"You don't. That's not our job. We're here to find a blackmailer, not to fix their PR problems."

"Phew! We don't have enough time to fix their PR problems."

Solomon handed me a pair of latex gloves and slid a pair on his own. While I pulled mine on, he sorted through the box of letters Joe handed over after insisting, again, that they couldn't leave the suite. "We have five piles," he said, pointing. "Here's Amelia's, Katya's, Lauren's, and Shelley's, two letters each, and this final pile has the letters addressed to all four of them."

"And what's this?" I asked, reaching for the handwritten sheet by itself.

"That's Joe's timeline of when the letters arrived and where."

"Shall we start with the first letter?" I asked.

"That's right. Katya's was the first." Solomon placed it in front of us and we studied it. It appeared exactly as she described, right down to the demand for money.

"Who was next?"

"Shelley got the next letter."

"Right. She paid up too."

"And so far, she's the only one who confessed to

35

knowing what the blackmailer was referring to."

"Uh-huh," I said, recalling the eye-popping secret Shelley confessed on the evening before.

"Which is..." Solomon prompted.

"Really interesting," I said, recalling Shelley's plea not to reveal it.

"I need to know. As your boss and besides, I'm working this case too."

"You are? I thought I was working the blackmail aspect solo?" I frowned, feeling puzzled.

"I'm helping you get started; then, while you investigate, I'll be working with the risk management team and keeping security in place. You won't see me much, but you'll still need to keep me in the loop."

"Are you sure you aren't hiding from Katya?" I asked, biting my cheek to keep from laughing. I recalled Katya's annoyance at finding Solomon with me.

Solomon shivered. "About that secret..."

"You can't tell anyone. I promised Shelley. No one at all."

"Can't promise that if it gets us to the blackmailer, but I'll be discreet."

That was good enough for me. "Fine. Ten years ago, Shelley had a fling that she wanted to keep covered up. Anyhow, someone found out, and got a video of them as true evidence. They sent her a still."

"That's it?"

"Yup."

"A sex tape?" guessed Solomon.

I nodded. It was disappointing that Shelley had fallen foul to putting her personal life on tape but she'd never intended it to be revealed. I felt sorry for her predicament.

Solomon paused, looking pensive. "Who was she with? Someone famous? Or was she compromised in some way? Also, wasn't she barely thirteen, ten years ago?"

I shook my head. "Turns out Shelley is a little older than we thought. She's actually twenty-six; so ten years ago, she was sixteen; and no, she wasn't with anyone famous."

"Huh. The blackmailer could run afoul of child endangerment laws if they ever distributed anything featuring Shelley at that age. No publication would risk running something like that," Solomon explained. "So what's the deal with this guy?"

I took a deep breath. "That's exactly it. Shelley wasn't with a guy. She had a fling with another girl. Shelley thinks the photo is from a sex tape they made."

"Whoa!"

"I know. No big deal, right? Except Shelley doesn't want her legions of teenybopper fans to know that she was once into, or still is into, women, and she doesn't want the tape made public. She's afraid the blackmailer might have it."

"We should find the other girl. Just to see if she knows anything."

"I asked Shelley, and she says the girl married an Australian guy and they recently won the lottery before moving to Melbourne. I don't think she needs the money."

"Check that out. I thought Shelley was dating a hot Hollywood stud!"

"How do you know that?"

"It was in your copy of *US Weekly.*"

"You read that?"

"Only for the purposes of this gig."

"Yeah, right," I scoffed. "Secretly, you're a pulp entertainment junkie."

We paused when something smashed against the wall that divided the suites and winced when there was another loud crash. "We should get in there," said Solomon, not moving.

"You first!"

The middle suite was a mess. We didn't have to knock; we simply walked through the open door and stopped next to Large and Larger, as I'd named the enormous security guards. Neither was doing anything. Instead, they just stood there, their arms crossed while Katya and Lauren glared at each other from opposite sides of the room.

"What's going on?" asked Solomon when no one spoke.

"I'm going to kill her," said Lauren.

"Can you do it more quietly?" asked Large. Larger laughed softly.

"Why?" I asked. "What happened?"

"She. Took. My. Shoes!"

"I didn't!" yelled Katya. "I would never take your nasty shoes. You have huge feet!"

"Take that back!"

"Huge, ugly, gnarled feet. I could go sailing in one of your shoes if I could stomach the stink."

"Argh!" Lauren screamed, reaching for the iPod dock on the bookcase. She wrenched it from its socket and hurled it at Katya. Katya ducked and the dock crashed against the wall, sliding to the ground without leaving a mark. "When will you shut up?"

"When you stop being such an evil bitch!"

"I wish I'd never met you! I wish you were dead! You are evil and hateful and vile!" screamed Lauren. "Everyone despises you! I wish you would go back to Russia so they could send you to the Siberian labor camp you belong in!"

"Lauren!" I gasped.

"I'm sorry," said Lauren. "That was mean."

"Apology not accepted," sniffed Katya.

"I'm not apologizing to you. I was apologizing to the Siberians. I hope you rot in a gulag until someone stabs you with a shiv. And stop sniffing, you stupid cokehead."

Katya started to sniff again, but stopped herself. "Screw you!" she yelled. "And screw your stupid shoes!" She pushed past me, almost knocking me over as she stormed out of the room. I made to follow, but

Larger caught me by the arm.

"Trust me," he whispered, his voice surprisingly high, almost like a whistling balloon. "Let her go. She gets nasty when she's in a mood."

"Does she get like that often?"

"At least three times a day, or we'd worry she's not well," he said, smiling, and revealing two very shiny gold teeth at the center of his mouth.

"Send housekeeping to clean up Katya's mess," instructed Lauren as she turned on her heel before walking out of the suite.

The four of us stood there, looking at the overturned furniture, the bouquet of flowers strewn across the room, as well as bags, shoes, and clothes draped over every surface. "Katya did all this?" I asked. "She's worse than a rock star."

"I'll send someone to clean up the flowers," said Larger.

"What about the rest of it?" I asked.

He shrugged. "Looks normal to me."

Solomon slipped his hand around mine. "Back to work," he said softly.

"They are destroying the illusion really fast," I said as we returned to Joe's suite and resumed our positions around the table. "I hoped last night was a blip, but I guess not."

"It could be the blackmailer. He could have set them all on edge."

"That's benevolent of you. Do you really think so?"

"No, but being threatened with past secrets wouldn't help their moods any."

With the suite next door quiet, Solomon spread out the letters, and silently, we read through each one. There were plenty of common clues that tied the letters together. For instance, the paper was the same size and thickness, suggesting it came from the same packet. The font and ink color used were also the same, and the ransom words sparse. Compounding that was each demand for money featured the same bank account number.

"Why don't we trace the bank account?" I asked. "The blackmailer might have opened it under his or her own name."

"I thought that too, but if so, he or she would have to be really stupid. They would, no doubt, expect the band to go to the police and start an investigation, in which case, they'd be found out quickly. Let me see those numbers again." Solomon pulled the closest letter to him and perused it carefully. "Thought so. This isn't a regular account. It's a numbered account in the Cayman Islands. Getting a name attached to it will be hard, if not impossible."

"So much for an easy solution."

"I need to talk to the security team; and I'll call Lucas about tracking that account. Can you take over from here?"

"Sure. I'm going to spend the next couple of hours going over the letters for clues before I interview the band and their manager."

"Do you want me to come back?"

"No. I know they're pretty horrible, but I hope that if I can speak to each one alone, I might make some headway," I said. I was wondering if some smooth words of female solidarity could pave the way. I figured Katya would prefer to get an offer from Solomon, but unfortunately, he wasn't on the table.

"Call if you need more help. Or a bodyguard," Solomon teased as he grabbed his leather jacket. "I'll be downstairs."

I agreed I would and took a moment to watch his rear end as he left. Sure, it was unprofessional, but it was worth it all the same. My job provided many bonuses.

Alone, I stared down at the ransom letters. All I could say for certain was that they all came from the same person, using the same printer, and with access to the same bank account. I also calculated how many tens of thousands of dollars the blackmailer received since the beginning of the tour. "Sweet gig," I muttered to myself. "Keep four secrets and make bank."

What I most wanted to know was: what were the secrets? Only Shelley was forthcoming about hers. Why she was less willing to hide her secret than all the others were, I didn't know, but I suspected when I dug into her background, I would find that her ex-girlfriend wasn't behind the plot. And despite B4U's mutual dislike of one another, it wasn't inconceivable that the band also knew each other's secrets. I had to wonder if it would be possible to extract those secrets from them, possibly by exploiting their mutual animosity, and using that to aid me.

"But how do *you* know their secrets?" I asked the letters. They lay there, blankly unable or unwilling to surrender any clues.

I grabbed my notepad from my purse and wrote *blackmailer?* in large letters. First, I added *superfan*, then *stranger,* then *known to the band.* It seemed rather unlikely that the blackmailer would be entirely unconnected to the band. It would have been very hard to learn the secrets of four band members who all grew up in entirely different areas of the country. For a start, B4U's management company was very careful to ensure, nourish, and cultivate, their squeaky clean image. Someone who was close to them would have to be absolutely convinced there was dirt before they went digging. It wouldn't be too far-fetched to imagine someone spending time and effort on one single starlet with the aim of blackmailing a big payday; but four women? No. That took an inordinate amount of time, effort, and access.

Crossing *stranger* off the list, I pondered *superfan.* B4U's target audience was the pre-teen, or "tween," and early teen crowd. It was almost a given that a child could not have orchestrated the blackmail. It was too careful, and too well planned. It had to be an adult, but what kind of adult would be a superfan of the teen-orientated sensations? Could a superfan find the time and resources to hunt for more dirt? If he or she were that big a fan, why would they want to threaten or hurt their beloved band? I added the word *deranged* along with a large question mark.

With the *stranger* and *superfan* ideas briefly considered, I had to turn to the people who were closest to B4U. Under *known to the band*, I added *friends, family, management,* and *crew* to my list. None of the band members were related as far as I knew. Although it was a possibility that their individual families might have known their secrets, it was highly unlikely that they knew all of the others', unless the band somehow mentioned them while gossiping. The same went for their *friends*, some of whom could have been mutual.

I ran my finger further down the list, pausing at *management*. To me, that meant Joe Carter. He was introduced as their manager and no one mentioned any assistant or team. I needed to talk to Joe to learn whom else he worked with, or who might have had any close access to the band. If anyone was hired to work on cleaning up B4U's image, perhaps they might know the secrets they were paid to hide.

Finally, there was the *crew*. I watched some footage of B4U's recent concerts on TV, as well as a few other photos in magazines, but I didn't recall seeing any familiar faces in the background. That didn't mean there weren't any. The footage was leaked via cell phone cameras, and consequently, of inferior quality.

From what I gleaned after watching the *E!* network, the band most likely had a team of dancers, personal assistants, stylists, hair and makeup artists, and musicians from the live band, not to mention the roadies who toted all their equipment. That was, of course, providing Katya didn't have them all fired on a regular basis. Nonetheless, it was still quite a long list of people who obtained regular access to B4U. Even if they didn't all chat, there had to be plenty of opportunities to overhear personal conversations.

I dropped my pen across my list and sighed. Instead of eliminating any possible suspects, I simply added dozens of more likely ones. "It's a start," I told myself. "Stay positive!"

I picked up the key card Joe gave us to the room, recalling his stern warning to not let anyone else see the letters, or even let them out of the room. I left the suite, pulling the door shut behind me, and listening for the automatic click of the lock.

Large and Larger were sitting in their usual positions, posted in front of the elevator. After mentally adding them, along with the entire security team to my list, I approached them.

"Hi! I'm looking for Joe," I said.

Large and Larger eyed each other before Large inclined his head towards the furthest suite.

"Awesome. Thank you!" I edged past their huge bulks and power-walked to the end of the corridor. The door to Amelia and Shelley's suite was open, so I ducked inside, hoping no air missiles would be hurled at me.

Fortunately, the suite appeared safe as I looked around. It was quiet and someone had obviously done a thorough job of cleaning. The broken pieces of vase were gone and the floor was freshly vacuumed. The air smelled like lemons; and the additional scent of fresh flowers managed to fill the room with a nice aroma. The two bedroom doors were shut.

"Hello?" I called out. After a moment, I called "Hello?" again.

No answer.

I knocked on the door closest to me. Soft footsteps sounded on the other side before the door opened, revealing Shelley. She had on a cute, cropped, pink leather jacket and tight jeans with heels. The purse slung over her arm probably cost more than two months of my salary. "Hey," she said.

"Hey, I'm sorry to bother you, but I'm looking for Joe."

"I haven't seen him." Shelley stepped outside her bedroom and pulled the door shut. "I have to go out now."

"Do you want me to alert security?"

"Why the hell would you do that?"

"So your assigned bodyguard can stay with you. To keep you safe," I reminded her when she frowned.

"Oh, right. Him. Yeah, whatever. I'm only going downstairs. I can't stay in this room another minute.

I'm bo-o-o-o-ored." Shelley stepped around me and swanned out of the room, without waiting to see if I had anything else to say.

I tried Amelia's door, but there was no answer. When I opened it, it was empty. I took a quick look around, noting how neat and tidy Amelia appeared to be. All her clothes were put away, and the wardrobe doors and drawers were neatly shut. There were a couple of books on the nightstand, which appeared to be of the self-help variety. I had no idea why someone of Amelia's status might need self-help books, but since I wasn't there to snoop — yet — I closed the door and retreated outside. Only when I paused in the doorway to the suite did I notice another door in the opposite wall at the end of the corridor. From it came a man's voice that was low and barely audible.

I moved towards it, hoping to find Joe. Pausing in the doorway, I saw him at the far end of what appeared to be a housekeeping room, with his back to me. Stacks of towels and toiletries lined the walls, along with large, empty bins, intended for laundry, and a couple of housekeeping carts. There was also a set of sliding doors that I figured must've been the service elevator, and designed for the exclusive use of hotel employees. I was just about to call Joe's name when he shifted to one side and I realized he was with a woman. She was shorter than him, with hair that curled at her ears. Their arms were wrapped around each other and they kissed passionately, completely oblivious to my presence.

I retreated back along the corridor without interrupting them. Given the location, the clinch was clearly something I wasn't meant to see. As I headed toward the security guards, I wondered if she were someone Joe was hiding from the band. She clearly wasn't one of them. The girls of B4U all had long hair, and this woman had very short hair. Maybe she was one of the hotel staff, or one of the crew, trying to have a secret fling. Given Katya's jealous outburst about Solomon yesterday — a man she barely knew — perhaps Joe had to conceal his relationships from the band.

The elevator opened as I reached it, spilling Katya and Lauren into the corridor. Katya lunged for Lauren's arm, grabbing and twisting. Lauren responded by hitting her with her oversized purse. "Get off me, you psycho bitch!" yelled Lauren.

"What's going on?" I asked the security guards.

Neither one made any effort to move. "That one just got into the elevator when the other one came running out and grabbed her purse," said Large, pointing to Katya and Lauren.

"Uh-hmm," said Larger.

"That's my purse!" screamed Katya, still attempting to wrench it from Lauren's hands.

"We have the same one. We all got one, remember? I got the gray, you got the black, Shelley got the tan, and Amelia got pink."

"I want the gray. We have to swap!"

"No, we don't. It's my purse and you're not taking it. You can't have anything you want, Katya!"

"I will tell Joe," Katya pouted.

"Do it. Maybe we'll get lucky and he'll fire you."

"He would never fire me. I know too much."

"What's that supposed to mean?" Lauren asked, stopping dead in the corridor.

Katya chortled a mean laugh and walked away. Lauren hurried after her and they disappeared inside Katya's suite. The sounds of their persistent bickering drifted out into the corridor.

"Can you tell Joe I'm looking for him," I asked the security guards. "Couldn't find him."

"Uh-huh," said Larger. Taking that as a yes, I gave him a grateful smile, wondering if they knew about Joe's closet activities.

A part of me wanted to pause and listen at the door to Katya's suite when the argument grew louder. I didn't know whether that part of me was the private investigator, a nosy person, or someone who was more than a little awed at being around four internationally famous women. I suspected I was influenced by all three.

Just as I slipped my key card into the slot outside Joe's suite, the sound of footsteps made me turn around. I was just in time to see Lauren storming out. She paused in the doorway to Katya's suite, turning. "I wrote three of the damn songs for our new album and Amelia wrote the rest, so you can forget trying to steal any credit for them, you talentless bitch. All the royalties are mine; and I'll fight you to the death to keep them!"

She slammed the door shut behind her and marched down the corridor. A moment later, loud music came on. Clearly, Katya wasn't upset at all, I concluded. Checking my watch, I sighed to find the hands reading eleven. It was going to be a very long day. Grimacing as I turned away, I stepped inside Joe's suite. I deliberately left the door open, in order to give me a clear view of the corridor. The letters were all right where I left them. Joe forbade any copying, but I couldn't work out how else I was supposed to study them away from the hotel without having copies. It wasn't feasible to create an office in there, despite Joe's insistence that we should. There were too many distractions, and too many people with personal motives who could stick their noses into the investigation. I needed to get close to them, but I also needed to maintain some separation. I couldn't have my mind clouded by a barrage of information and suspects, with the soundtrack of B4U screaming at each other. Before I could think it through, I whipped out my phone and began to snap photos of each letter. My task complete, I slipped the phone back into the hip pocket of my dress and hoped Joe wouldn't ask if I adhered to his rules.

Instead, I turned my attention back to my notepad. The people I really wanted to talk to were the members of B4U, but I didn't see any of them in the corridor. Unless I'd somehow missed them, Amelia still hadn't returned to her room, nor had Shelley. Katya was back in her room as of a half hour ago, and I didn't seen her leave again. After the argument, Lauren marched down the corridor towards Amelia's suite. I didn't think she returned to her room, and guessed she was probably lying low. Since Katya was closest, and I could still hear music playing faintly through the wall, I decided to visit her first.

As instructed, I went through the rigmarole of relocking Joe's room before I knocked on Katya's suite door. It was ajar and swung open a few inches when I knocked. "Hello? Katya?" I called, but only received silence in return. "Katya, it's me, Lexi Graves, the investigator Joe hired. May I come in?"

More silence.

My heart thumped as I pushed the door open further, but nothing crashed against the wall. I stepped inside cautiously, hoping Katya had either calmed down, or was so obsessed about hating Lauren that she might be persuaded to give up Lauren's secret. "What are you doing?" I asked, seeing her leg sticking out from behind the sofa. The leg didn't move. I stepped closer. "Are you okay? Katya? Is that a yoga position?" I asked, puzzled. With a sigh, and fully expecting some kind of nasty trick from Katya, I hurried forwards, determined to get our interview over with.

Katya wasn't playing any trick, or doing yoga.

A knife protruding from her back, along with the fresh blood, now pooling from the wound, indicated she was very, very dead.

CHAPTER FOUR

"Lexi Graves, you must be the unluckiest woman I know."

"Tell me about it." My oldest brother, Garrett, a long-serving detective on Montgomery's homicide squad, proceeded to do just that, However, I held my hand up after he mentioned the two thugs I found with holes in their heads. That was in the days before I became a PI.

"Enough!" I wailed. "I know, my life sucks! How could this have happened? I only just heard her arguing with another member of the band! And now she's..." I flapped my hand at Katya's body. It hadn't moved one inch. For me, that was a good thing since I bristled at the very thought of a zombie apocalypse; but for Katya, it was still very bad news.

"Dead," Garrett helpfully supplied as he pulled out his notepad, his pen poised. "Who was she arguing with?"

"Lauren. They were shouting at each other.

Something about a purse."

"Just shouting? What did they say?"

"Actually, they got kind of physical. Katya grabbed Lauren, and Lauren hit her with her purse. Katya was going to tell Joe — he's their manager — and threatened to and Lauren said something like 'Do it. He'll probably fire you' and Katya said Joe would never do that because she knew too much. Later, Lauren said she'd fight her to the death over royalties then she left."

Garrett looked around for one of the uniformed cops in attendance. "Go find this Lauren. I want to talk to her a-sap," he told him, quietly adding to me, "Also, well done for eavesdropping. This is helpful stuff."

"I wasn't eavesdropping. I was walking along the corridor when they got out of the elevator. Large and Larger can verify that."

"Large and Larger?"

"The security guards who always sit in front of the elevator. Can't miss 'em."

Garrett nodded. "I know who you mean. Where were you when Katya was stabbed?"

I was about to say I couldn't believe he'd ask me a question like that, when my name was called. I turned around, smiling, as soon as I saw who stood in the doorway. "Special Agent Maddox!" I grinned as he crossed the room. He gave me a quick hug then stood away, assessing my condition. Apparently, he must've found it satisfactory.

"Another body? Really, Lexi? How many does this make?" he asked, running a hand through his wavy, brown hair. He may have been my ex, but I wasn't immune to the glances he drew from the two female forensic investigators. I couldn't blame them. Maddox was a good-looking man who looked even better than usual, dressed in a dark gray suit and blue shirt and tie.

"Another one too many," I replied before holding up my fingers and physically counting. "What are you doing here?"

"High profile murder equals FBI interest. Since I have the best connections with MPD, I volunteered to come down here and see what was going on."

"We've got one Katya Markova with a knife in her back. She sings with a band named B4U. They're in town temporarily for a concert and also to shoot a video," explained Garrett, checking his notes.

"I have all those details," replied Maddox, walking over to the body and taking a long look. He glanced over his shoulder at us. "Anyone know why she has a knife in her back?"

"I was just about to ask Lexi the same question."

Two sets of eyes bored into me.

I threw my hands in the air. "I have no idea! I just found her."

"Let's get out of here and go someplace quiet to talk," Maddox suggested.

Garrett held up a hand. "Whoa there; we're not done."

"You're not seriously questioning your sister?"

"You're not seriously questioning your ex, and your ex's brother, who also happens to be leading the investigation?" Garrett responded, squaring his shoulders and looking annoyed.

"Nope. Just thought we'd put Lexi in a quiet room where she can get away from all this blood."

"Terrific idea," I agreed quickly, since he was exactly right. I have a strong stomach, but seeing the spray of blood on the wall behind Garrett made me queasy. Plus, it was different when you discovered dead bodies of people you didn't know. It was a lot different for me, finding the body of someone who was a living, breathing, albeit, bitchy person, only an hour ago. "Follow me," I said, edging out of the room before either of them could stop me. They didn't, and followed me to Joe's suite, waiting while I unlocked the room and let them in.

"Whose room is this?" Garrett asked, stepping in and looking around. "Yours?"

"I wish. No, this is the manager's suite. He's letting me use it while I work on the case."

"That's some foresight! Hiring you before the murder happened!" Maddox winked as I gathered up the letters, tucking them into the box and out of sight. "Why are you really here?"

"I'm not sure I can say right now," I told them as we took our seats around the table. "But I can tell you B4U's manager hired me to look into an issue with the band."

"Could this issue be related to the murder?" asked Garrett. "Throw me a bone here. What's going on?"

I grimaced. It was something I wondered myself in the minutes between stumbling into the hallway, yelling for help, and the arrival of the police. The blackmail notes were not physical threats, but several ambiguous ones warned about regretting one's actions if one failed to follow instructions, which I assumed meant releasing whatever secrets the blackmailer had. Plus, the blackmailer was getting paid to keep the secrets. Why would he or she kill one of the cash cows? It seemed too big a step to go from blackmail into murder. "I can't rule it out."

"You'd better tell us about it," said Maddox while Garrett nodded in agreement.

"You can't tell anyone. I signed a confidentiality order; and I'm breaking it just by telling you."

"Want me to flash you my badge?" asked Garrett. "And arrest you for obstruction?"

"Point taken," I said with a deep breath before pouring out the blackmail story.

~

"I'm lost for words," said Solomon. We were drinking coffee in the hotel lounge and Solomon didn't look pleased. "I leave you alone for two hours, and a corpse falls into your lap."

"Not exactly my lap," I said, grateful for the sweet, warm beverage; and even more grateful not to have a corpse in my lap. "She was in the next room."

"Knifed in the back," Solomon said, again, as if he couldn't quite believe it.

"Yep."

"You think Lauren could have done it?"

I shook my head, not to indicate *no,* but rather a confused *I don't know.* "I couldn't tell you. I saw her just as I got into the elevator downstairs. Two uniforms brought her to Garrett. She was wearing the same clothes she wore when she argued with Katya and there didn't appear to be any blood on her clothing. With all the blood spray on the wall, I would have expected to see at least, some."

"That doesn't definitely rule her out," Solomon said, echoing my private thoughts.

"Garrett and Maddox wanted to know if Katya's murder might be connected to the blackmailer."

"As far as questions go, that one is not way off base. I've been wondering the same thing."

"Me too. I don't see a feasible connection, but I can't rule that out. It's a big step, but maybe the blackmailer is sending a message." I paused, thinking. "So far, they've all paid up; so it can't be because they didn't..."

"I'm not so sure the latest blackmail notes were all paid," said Solomon. "Or at least, the next blackmail note almost certainly won't be. After all, we're here to find the blackmailer and end the demands."

"I was just looking for Katya to interview when I found her." I shook my head, almost hoping to dislodge the image of her. "I didn't have a chance to ask about her secret, or the others'."

"There's still time to find out."

I paused, the coffee cup inches from my lips, and asked in surprise, "We're still on the case?"

"Absolutely. Joe and I spoke already, and we agreed it's even more imperative now that there's been a murder. If the blackmailer turns out to be the murderer, the whole band could be in danger."

"So, we find the blackmailer, and we find the murderer?"

Solomon smiled. "That's the idea."

"What does Joe think?"

"Let's ask him," Solomon replied, raising his hand and waving to someone behind me. Looking over my shoulder, I spied Joe walking towards us. He dropped into a chair and ran a hand under his jaw while letting out a deep sigh.

"I can't believe it," he said. "I mean, if anyone asked me who in the band was most likely to be murdered, I'd have said Katya, but she's... she's dead... I can't believe it."

"Why would you pick..." I started to ask, but Joe carried on, talking over me, like he hadn't even heard me speak.

"And a knife in the back? Talk about poetic justice."

"Poetic justice?" I asked, a little louder this time.

The question in my voice caught his attention.

"Yeah, she was always the one who had no problem knifing everyone else in the back. Oh, metaphorically speaking, of course. She was pretty harmless, but she had a nasty tongue."

"I saw her and Lauren having a bust-up earlier," I said. "It looked like it was getting physical."

"That's Katya. She's all bluster though. Plus, the girls have always fought."

"I thought they were supposed to be best of friends? What happened?"

"Sure, that's the story we feed everyone. Truth is, they don't get on so well anymore. Been forced together too long, I guess." Joe raised a hand, signaling to the waitress. She came over, took his order for a beer, and departed quickly. "There isn't a person anywhere who hasn't been on the receiving end of Katya in a mood."

"She's not well liked?" I continued. I figured now was as good a time as any to interview Joe, even if I didn't make clear I was doing that. He appeared so forthcoming and willing to talk. It could have been the shock, or simply delight at Katya's rapid and untimely departure from the world, for all I knew.

"Hell, no."

"If you could pick someone, anyone, as the one most likely to want Katya out of the way, whom would you chose?" I asked. Solomon rested back in his chair, watching our repartee without interrupting.

Joe laughed. "That's an easy one. Everyone!"

"Including you?" I watched Joe's reaction closely. He didn't appear at all perturbed by the question and intercepted the cold beer from the waitress before she could set it on the table. He slipped a twenty-dollar bill into her hand and took a long swig from the neck of the bottle.

"Sometimes," he admitted, "she was really hard work, but these girls make me a lot of money. It serves my best interests to keep them together, and selling albums and merchandise. Plus, I wasn't anywhere near Katya's suite at the time."

"Where were you?" Solomon asked.

"Oh, I see. Ruling me out?" laughed Joe. "Checking out my alibi. Sure. No problem. I was in the library here in the hotel when I got the call. I went upstairs just after the police got here. So, you see, I was nowhere near the crime scene."

I exchanged a glance with Solomon. Anyone else wouldn't have noticed his slightly narrowing eyes, or his curiosity, but I knew him well, and he knew that I would have something to say about that.

"Can anyone verify that?" I asked.

"I don't know. I guess. There's probably a waiter that saw me."

"We'd like to investigate this new angle to the case, along with the letters you've given us," said Solomon changing the topic after another imperceptible glance passed between us. "It might help us find the blackmailer."

This time, Joe leaned forward, looking from Solomon to me. "You think there's a chance this could be the same guy?"

"Or woman," I countered. "But yes, we're working on a theory that the two crimes may be connected."

"So Solomon said earlier. You know, I kind of hoped Katya was the blackmailer," said Joe, surprising me. He continued without any prompting, "I know I said she was a blusterer, but she was still a mean person. I wouldn't have put it past her to blackmail the other girls for money. She would have loved getting one over them."

"Could she have known any of their secrets? They didn't get along," I reminded Joe.

"They might hate each other now, but at one time, they were tight. It's possible. Katya was a mega bitch; and it wouldn't have been the first time she cooked up a nasty scheme."

"Like what?"

"Oh, embarrassing the other girls in public, or sabotaging a costume. At their calendar shoot, she even turned up wearing something different just so she could be the center of their cover. Katya does not have any problems when it comes to trying anything to get ahead."

"Could money have been a motive for Katya? Did she have any money problems?" Solomon asked.

"You can ask the band's accountant, but no, I don't

think she was struggling. Katya's motivations weren't always clear though. She liked to play games."

"We'll add Katya to our list of blackmail suspects," I told Joe, not mentioning that she was already on it, along with dozens of other people.

"Guess it'll be easy to find out if it was her. No more letters will turn up!" Joe laughed. He took a long swig and returned the empty bottle to the table, having drained it in less than a couple of minutes.

I was just about to hit him with another question, when I heard his name being screamed across the room. The three of us looked around to see Lauren, shaking and sobbing. In front of her, three photographers shoved their cameras into her face, their incessant flashes making her blink as her hands flailed in vain attempts to push them away. The more she swung at them, the more they photographed her.

"Jeez," growled Joe, jumping to his feet, followed by Solomon and me.

"Wait here," Solomon instructed, trailing Joe.

I watched, rooted to the spot, as Solomon pushed back the photographers, allowing Joe enough space to wrap an arm around Lauren. He guided her away from the pack as the hotel manager and several bellboys hurried towards them.

"Get them outta here!" Solomon said loudly before giving one of the photographers a shove towards the nearest pair of bellboys. "Have you no respect?" he snapped at their parting backs before following Joe and

Lauren. "Let's find a private room."

"I'm so sorry," said the hotel manager, grimacing as he approached. "Mr. Carter, we have no idea how they got in. We've posted security staff on every door since you arrived, and we even doubled up our usual security procedures and officers to ensure your party wouldn't be disturbed."

"They must have got a hundred shots," wailed Lauren, mascara streaking her cheeks. "This will be in all the papers. They asked me if I killed her!"

"Hush," consoled Joe, tightening his arm around her. "Get us a room, would you?" he said to the manager.

The manager beckoned us to follow him. We left the lounge and a dozen watchful eyes before crossing a short corridor. Entering through a door he unlocked, we came into a small room outfitted with comfortable couches and a wall lined with old books. "The library is at your disposal," the kind manager told us. "I'll have complimentary drinks and refreshments sent to you forthwith."

"And I'll assign my guys to the doors," added Solomon. "No one will get past them."

I followed the manager to the door. "Is this room always locked?" I asked.

"Not always, but we've been renovating the past couple of days, so it's been out of use. Is there anything else?"

"No, thank you." He pulled the door shut behind him and I turned back to our party. I glanced at Joe, his arm wrapped around Lauren as he consoled her, wondering why he claimed to be in a room he couldn't possibly have been in.

"Thanks for getting me out of there," hiccupped Lauren before collapsing onto a couch. "I hate the paparazzi. They're... they're such vultures! And now they're going to publish photos of me looking a mess."

"Not a mess, honey. Devastated, inconsolable, at the death of someone who wasn't just a band mate, but a sister, and the paparazzi are just there to take advantage of your trauma. This is great PR for you."

Solomon and I exchanged WTF glances. As Joe spun the story, Lauren's tears subsided and her sobbing slowed to sniffs.

"You've had a hard morning," I said. "People will understand."

Lauren looked up, frowning when she saw me. "Who are you?" she asked.

Joe placed a hand on my shoulder. "This is Lexi Graves, the PI we hired. You met last night."

"Oh, right. I forgot. Hey."

"Hey," I said. "Are you okay to answer a few questions?"

"I already answered a whole bunch of questions that detective just fired at me. Hey, he was called Graves too. He gave me his card." Lauren patted her pockets, then reached for her purse, pulling it onto her lap and opening it, searching unsuccessfully.

"He's my brother and also a really great cop."

"He said I shouldn't talk about Katya with anyone."

"He didn't mean me," I told her, which was a lie. "He meant journalists and... umm... nosy people."

"Riiight," agreed Lauren. She screwed up her eyes, clearly thinking. "Am I supposed to have a lawyer? Joe, should I have a lawyer with me when I talk to the police?"

"Not yet," I said, before Joe could answer, "but call us if you like and we'll advise you. Also, we're not the police."

"So, I don't need a lawyer?"

"Is there a reason why you might need a lawyer?" Solomon asked.

"Like, no!" Lauren scoffed, batting her hand at him. "I didn't kill Katya. I told Detective Graves that, and he was all, okay. So, I'm innocent."

Joe nodded. "Then you don't need a lawyer, honey." He paused, looking worried. "All the same, if the police want to talk to you again, tell me, so I can call your lawyer."

"Okay," agreed Lauren readily, not asking Joe why. "Do I need a lawyer to talk to these people?"

"No, you don't. Joe hired us to look into the blackmail threats. We'd like to rule Katya's death out as having nothing to do with the blackmail..." I started, only to be interrupted by Lauren's squeal as she sat bolt upright.

"You mean the blackmailer killed Katya? Ohmygod, is he going to kill me too?"

"No, that's unlikely..."

"Ohmygod, ohmygod!"

"We just need to rule out..."

"It's like *Scream!* He's going to pick us off one-by-one! Ohmygod, Joe, he's probably already in the hotel. Get me a new suite! And I want someone to check under the bed and in the wardrobe! And I want a bodyguard and... and..."

"Breathe, Lauren, breathe," Joe repeated, taking Lauren's hand and patting it. "No one is going to hurt you," he added, glaring at me. "The investigators just need to ask you a few questions. I'll be here the whole time and then I'll assign one of the security team to look after you around the clock."

"Even when I'm sleeping? I can't have someone watch me when I'm sleeping. That's creepy."

"Whatever you want, honey. I promise you'll be safe."

"Well, okay, but I don't want to die, okay? Let's be clear on that. I do not want to die!"

"You won't die," Joe said. A gentle incline of his head indicated I could start questioning again.

"Lauren, can you tell me what happened between you and Katya this morning?" I asked.

"Nothing. We hung out at the mall, but then it got a little crazy with all these girls following us, so we came back to the hotel. We went to our suite and I left after we got into it over some shoes. I planned to go downstairs but then Katya tried to steal my purse and we went back to the suite. She wouldn't let up so I left to see if Amelia was in her suite."

"Did you see Amelia?"

"No, she wasn't there. I called her and she said she was downstairs."

"What did you do next?"

"I hung out in Amelia's suite, waiting for her."

"Why didn't you return to your own suite?"

Lauren sighed. "Katya was in it."

"You two were having a lot of problems?"

"Not really. She was her usual mean self and I didn't want to be around her. She keeps taking my stuff."

Joe nodded. "I had to speak to Katya a few times about not borrowing the girls' things."

"She doesn't borrow, she steals!" Lauren replied, her mouth becoming a cross pout.

"Did you have an argument?"

"No, we were cool, but I can't believe I got stuck sharing a suite with her. Anyway, I waited for Amelia and thought I'd take a nap on their couch, when I heard someone yelling. It was really loud and annoying, and I figured one of our fans must've gotten into the hotel, so I just ignored it. Then this cop came and found me and said Katya was dead." Lauren sucked in a deep breath.

"Was anyone else with you?"

"Like... when?"

"After you left Katya?"

"Ummm... no."

"What about Shelley?"

"She wasn't in their suite either."

"Who do you think might have wanted to kill Katya?" I asked, changing my line of questioning slightly now that it was clear Lauren didn't have any alibi.

Lauren laughed. "Seriously?"

I didn't think it was a laughing matter at all, but Lauren seemed to think my question was hilarious. I waited until her giggling slowed to a splutter as she held her sides, then repeated the question.

"Pretty much everyone hated Katya," she said succinctly. "Including me."

"You threatened to kill her last night," I pointed out. "And today."

"Did I?" Lauren shrugged. "I think I must threaten to kill her once a day."

"You said you hoped she'd be stabbed to death."

"Uh, yah, look, I don't know what you're implying, but I didn't kill her, okay? Like I said, I was taking a nap in Amelia and Shelley's suite." Lauren folded her arms across her chest and wrinkled her nose. I figured I had a small window of time before she got so annoyed with my questions, she refused to answer any more, probably forever.

"Do you know Katya's secret?"

"The thing she was being blackmailed about? About Russia?"

"Yes. What was worth blackmailing her for about Russia?"

"All I know is that Katya lived there until she was five or six before she came to America. She had this big story about her family escaping as refugees and making their way here to start a new life. She told this whole sad story about being an immigrant and having to learn English from watching the TV while her dirt poor parents scraped out a living, only I don't think it was all true."

"Which bit? That she came from Russia?"

"No, that was true. I just don't think her parents came here as refugees. I think they fled Russia, but only because they were powerful and later became targets for... oh I don't know! The mafia or the government or something. I just overheard something years ago about her parents betraying someone or other. Anyway, Katya's family were super rich and they brought a lot of money with them and they never had to scrape out a living."

"Is that the kind of thing she'd want to be kept quiet?"

"Wouldn't you? The press would have had a field day running the expose. It's not really the American dream when your parents are megabuck traitors, is it?"

CHAPTER FIVE

"He's lying, she's lying," I told Solomon. We were on the top floor of the hotel, sitting in Joe's suite, and far away from the overly interested glances of the other hotel guests. I couldn't blame them for their curious stares. If I knew I were staying in the same hotel as a hot girl band, and one of them had just been murdered, I would have been looking too, and not just to check out their fashions. Since our conversation in the library, Lauren had become increasingly louder until she finally dissolved into sobs. I didn't think she was that upset about losing Katya, but rather, feared she was becoming our number one suspect. Finally, Joe spirited her away to "rest."

"That so?" asked Solomon, glancing towards the door as if one of the band members might burst in at any moment.

"I know Joe was definitely not where he said he was. I saw him in the housekeeping closet, making out with someone."

Solomon turned his head quickly. "Someone? A woman?"

"Yeah, but before you ask, no, I didn't see who; and they obviously didn't see me."

"You sure it was Joe?"

"One hundred percent. What I don't know is why he would make up that story about being in the library."

"So we can put Joe in the vicinity of Katya, as well as Lauren."

I nodded. "At least, Lauren wasn't lying about where she was. She told us she was in the suite, alone."

"That doesn't help her since she doesn't have an alibi. You said she was lying too. What about?"

"I know Lauren admitted they were arguing, and they were pretty obvious about it. I saw them going at it too, and it was definitely getting physical. When she left their suite right before Katya was killed, she even threatened Katya. My opinion is they were anything but cool."

"Lauren is not making life any easier for herself."

I sighed. "I know. She didn't make any attempts to give herself an alibi. If it were me, I would have, but could she really have killed Katya?"

Solomon shrugged, which wasn't a lot of help, although it echoed my own thoughts. Sure, Lauren had motive, but the question was: how much? Was a simple fight over a purse, or shoes, or even credit for the lyrics enough motive to kill a person? Some women would have said yes, and while I busily contemplated which of my purses might be worth killing for, I also had to decide whether their arguments ran any deeper than that. Judging by what I'd seen and gleaned so far, I had to conclude that the band's problems must have been going on for a long time; and overall resentment was already established... but had it grown to the point of turning Lauren into a murderer?

I had a lot of problems with the hypothesis that Lauren was the killer. For one thing, while we interviewed her, she still had on the same outfit she was wearing when I saw her and Katya exiting the elevator that morning. Blood must have been splashed on the killer, yet there was none on Lauren's clothing. That didn't mean she hadn't changed her clothes, or even taken the time to change *before* the murder, and redressed into her former outfit afterwards, but it seemed rather unlikely.

Despite all of those contradictions, of one thing I felt certain. "I can't rule Lauren out definitively," I told Solomon. "Not when the facts are: she had motive, access, and opportunity."

"And Joe?"

"Potentially the same. It sounds like he crossed paths with Katya more than a few times; plus, he's lying about his whereabouts at the time of the murder, which is another red flag and mark against him."

"We need to interview them all."

"Regarding the blackmail or the murder?"

"Both. Let's find Amelia and Shelley and see what

they have to say."

"This is nice," I told Solomon as we rose simultaneously. "Working together, I mean. I thought I'd be on my own for the blackmail case, just staring at those same cryptic letters over and over."

"You have poor expectations of *nice*. Why don't I take you out to dinner later? Then I can show you what *nice* truly is."

"If you raise my expectations, you might be sorry."

Solomon smiled as he wrapped an arm around my shoulders. "Doubt it."

~

Amelia and Shelley were in their suite along with Joe. A tray of teas and coffees sat between them on the coffee table, along with another tray laden with sandwiches and snacks. Amelia was nibbling on a sandwich while playing with her cell phone and Shelley sipped what appeared to be a glass of champagne.

"How's Lauren?" I asked when we entered.

"Sleeping. She had a tough morning," replied Joe. He reclined his chair and stretched out his arms along the back. Amelia glanced at the hand closest to her, but made no move from the spot where her legs were curled under her.

"She had a brilliant morning," Shelley muttered. Amelia glanced over, raised her eyebrows, but said nothing as her phone beeped again.

"Shelley, have some sympathy," Joe said with an annoyed shake of his head. "I thought it best if Lauren relaxed a little. She had a rough morning, what with finding Katya, and talking to the police. Then that nasty incident with the paparazzi..."

"Lauren got her photo taken?" Shelley said, her mouth dropping open. "So, she gets to be on tomorrow's tabloid covers? Great!"

"Shelley," Joe warned before she shut up, and took a deliberately longer sip of her champagne. "The PR debriefing really wore her out and she's beat. I told her to take a nap in Amelia's room. Take a seat. Have some refreshments. What can we do for you?"

"We'd like to talk to Shelley and Amelia," Solomon said as we sat down. Shelley brightened. "The more we understand about the blackmail, the easier we can separate it from Katya's murder."

"I thought it was the same person," said Amelia, dropping her phone as her attention was visibly drawn. "I wish I could tell you more but I was downstairs when Katya was killed. I guess I was lucky. It could easily have been any of us alone."

"We don't know if it was the same person yet," said Solomon. "That's why we want to talk to you further. We've reviewed the blackmailer's letters and we want to talk to you about Katya's."

"I didn't see Katya's," said Shelley.

"Me neither," agreed Amelia. "But I heard about them."

"What do you know about the Russia secret?" I asked, wondering if their versions tallied with Lauren's.

Shelley and Amelia exchanged glances, but didn't say anything.

"C'mon," I cajoled. "Whatever it is, it can't hurt Katya now."

After a long moment of silence, Shelley shrugged. "Guess not. I heard Katya's rags-to-riches story was kind of suspect."

"How so?"

"Well, she was supposed to be dirt poor, but we bumped into someone who knew her at one of our concerts, some PR chick, and apparently, they went to the same private school. I looked it up online. It's super expensive and exclusive. You don't go there if your parents are scraping out a living."

"Do you know how they got their money? Could they have made it here?"

"Sorry, that's all I know, but I wouldn't put it past Katya not to have concocted the whole thing. She was a compulsive liar, you know."

"Really?"

"Totally! Everything that came out of her mouth was a lie! She'd tell her crappy life story to journalists; and they'd all print it as if Katya was some amazing success and prodigy! Anyone can be successful if their parents pay for their 'in.' The rest of us had to work to get into B4U. She just waltzed right into the final auditions and grabbed a spot."

"Is that correct?" I asked Joe.

"Before my time. I joined B4U as their manager once they wanted to take their TV career to the next level and break into music. I wasn't involved in the auditioning process," he told us.

I took a long, lingering look at the tasty-looking sandwiches before I asked my next question. "Did that create problems within the group?"

This time, Amelia answered. "Not at first. We all knew Katya was talented. She could sing, dance, act, and really, her story was an asset to the band… at first. We all had our own background stories, something that made us a little different from each other, so there would be someone special for every fan. We were supposed to be the people our fans might be. We were actually really good friends for the first couple of years."

"What happened to change that?"

"Katya," Amelia and Shelley chimed.

"How's that?" Solomon prompted.

Shelley fixed him with a perfect, white smile and I had to repress my urge to sigh. The last thing I needed was having someone in the band develop a crush on my boyfriend. On the other hand, maybe after a few more flashes of his sexy smile and smoldering eyes, and we'd have the case in the bag by the evening.

"She went from being a pain, to becoming a pain in the ass. Everything had to be about her. Everything was always about what she wanted; and if it didn't turn out that she was the star, she would try to sabotage the deal, or make some last minute change that always resulted in her getting the spotlight. You remember our last album cover?" she asked, turning to Amelia.

Amelia nodded, her mouth tightening. "We were all supposed to wear these little black numbers, but Katya's costume amazingly disappeared, leaving her with only a white dress. We were already three hours into the desert, and there was no time to get another costume, so the whole shoot had to be centered on Katya looking different from the rest of us."

"We looked like her backup singers!" snarled Shelley. "She did the same thing for our calendar too."

"She didn't even write a single song on the album," added Amelia. "Or sing a solo track. Lauren and I wrote them all."

"I'm not talented at songwriting," said Shelley, holding up her hand, "and I totally admit it."

"But you sang an amazing solo track," said Amelia.

"Were those things that Katya did the source of the bad feelings in the band?" I asked, only to be met with stony, *are you serious?* faces.

"Katya's antics didn't make anyone happy. She was a lot of work," interjected Joe. "But yeah, over all, she caused bad feelings."

"And that was only one thing," continued Shelley, finishing her champagne and banging the glass onto the coffee table. "Let's not forget how she messed with our costumes, and did not turn up for interviews! Then she'd call the journalist or whomever, herself, to make sure she got extra column inches, or even a solo profile!"

"Or that time when she told us our gig at an exclusive club was canceled before she turned up and did a solo acoustic set..." Amelia said.

"That was an administration error," started Joe.

He was temporarily cut off by Shelley's loud "Harrumph!"

"Sure, it was, Joe. We all knew it was Katya. Or when she switched the photos in our calendar two years ago so that she got all the best months! Or that time she made sure my dress was sent back right before the awards show I was presenting! And I had to borrow a second-rate dress from my stylist! Or that time she broke Amelia's guitar..."

"We get the picture," said Solomon.

"You have no idea," said Shelley, leaning towards Solomon. She tossed her hair and gave him a pretty smile, "But maybe if we got together later, I could go through a few other things with you..."

"I have plans later," said Solomon. "Let me ask you both a simple question. Did either of you like Katya?"

Amelia and Shelley exchanged looks again. "No," they both said in unison.

"Why didn't you ask her to leave the band if she was causing so many problems?" I asked.

"We wanted to, but we're under contract. It didn't matter what she did, and she knew it. None of us can leave," Amelia explained.

Shelley nodded. "We were stuck with her until..."

"Until now," Amelia finished.

"Now we're free," Shelley said with a high-five for Amelia.

"I don't see what any of this has to do with the blackmail," Joe interrupted as the pair of girls started to seriously celebrate their good fortune.

"It's all part of the investigation," Solomon said, smoothly glossing over our questioning. "Joe, how was your relationship with Katya?"

"Purely professional, I can assure you. Katya and I were okay, but like Amelia and Shelley already said, she was a difficult character. We had our run-ins; and yes, she caused problems, but she knew who was boss."

"Katya," said Shelley, and Amelia giggled. Joe ignored them.

"Could we take a look at Katya's contract?" Solomon asked him. "It will help us work out the dynamics involved in keeping the band together."

"I can't show it to you, but I can tell you the basics. The girls are all under contract to stay with the band. They can't quit unless it's for a very serious reason, such as severe illness or poor health. The band members were specifically selected and put together; and management wants them to stay together."

"Can they be fired?" I asked.

"Absolutely. If one of them causes embarrassment to the band, or the sponsoring management company, of course, they can be fired. That's why we need you to find the blackmailer. Everyone's job is on the line. If these so-called secrets get out, Amelia, Shelley, and Lauren could lose their jobs."

"Who would gain from that?" I asked.

"No one. No job is no salary; and no band is no salary for me."

"What happens if a band member is removed? Do the profits get split three ways?"

"No, it's more complicated than that. Part of their deal is salary-based, and part is based on profits from merchandising, concerts, and various other promotions. That's where the big money comes from. With Katya gone, her percentage doesn't go back into the band. They were set up as a four-girl group, so it's far more likely that the management company will appoint a new member, and that person will get a salary and profit share from future deals going forward. Katya's percentage for any deals up until her death will go to her next of kin."

"So none of us can benefit financially from Katya's death," Amelia concluded.

"Who is her next of kin?" I asked.

"I'd have to check the file, but I think it's her sister."

The bedroom door opened and Lauren appeared. "Is the bitch still dead?" she asked.

"Yep!" screeched Shelley. She reached for the bottle and poured another glass, drinking half of it in one gulp. I raised my eyebrows to Solomon in silent question at her alcohol intake. It was barely mid-afternoon and she already seemed to have consumed half a bottle.

"Joe, I need to ask you again where you were when Katya was killed," Solomon said, pretending to check his notes.

"I'll tell you where he will be," laughed Lauren, approaching the coffee table and poking at the sandwiches. She piled a few on a small plate, added chips, and plonked herself down next to Amelia. "He'll be partying with the rest of us later."

"There will be no partying. We'll stay at the hotel tonight. We need to show respect for Katya. Her body's barely cold," said Joe.

"Barely? She was always ice cold," scoffed Shelley.

"Can you hold down the fort?" Solomon asked quietly, leaning into me so he couldn't be overheard. "I think we need to separate them in order to get some straight answers."

I took a look at the band, who were giggling amongst themselves while they gorged down snacks and alcohol. "I guess," I said, feeling crestfallen at the very idea of trying to mediate between them. Perhaps without Katya throwing vases, it would be a lot easier; and if I were really lucky, maybe they would gossip. I could certainly glean some new information that way. "Can you find out who Joe was with, too? Maybe he'll tell you when he's alone."

Solomon nodded. "We've got locations for all of you

when Katya died," he started. "Lauren, you were asleep in this room. Shelley, you were downstairs in the hotel as were you, Amelia. Joe, you already mentioned you were in the library, also downstairs, but we have a witness that places you on this floor just prior to the murder."

"That's impossible. I told you I was in the library. Whoever it was must have been mistaken."

"My witness was very certain, and also said you were with a woman."

Joe laughed. "Really? I don't have time for women. I've got a band in the middle of a tour. Do you know how much work that is?"

"I don't want to embarrass you..."

"I'm not embarrassed, merely bemused. Like I said, your witness must have seen someone who looked like me."

"On this floor? In the housekeeping closet?"

"There's a housekeeping closet on this floor? News to me." Joe shrugged as he looked around at the band as if to say Solomon was talking crazy. "I don't think I've ever even seen the housekeeping staff."

"Me neither," said Amelia. "They're like elves. They come in and clean, but you never see them."

"Maybe because they're too busy making out in the closet," laughed Joe. "Listen, all I can tell you is I was nowhere near this floor when Katya got killed. Maybe your witness got the time wrong. I wish I could be of more help."

"Let me show you the hotel closet," Solomon said, "Maybe it'll jog your memory."

"Sure, if we must, but I don't how it'll help since I was never there. Girls, I can trust you all to cooperate with Lexi and answer her questions?" Joe said, rising and smoothing his jeans. "Which way?"

"Follow me."

"Your boss is a hottie," Lauren said when Solomon and Joe exited the room. "Is he single?"

"No, sorry," I told her. I was starting to find any girl in B4U fancying my boyfriend a little wearing. Of course, I could take it as a compliment that these beautiful, accomplished women found him attractive, and I must confess that part of me did, but I didn't like having to perpetually defend his honor.

"Damn shame. The things I could show him."

"Everyone's seen your things," said Amelia. "You should put them away before you get a reputation."

"Why hide perfection? Especially, when there's a party to plan," grinned Lauren.

"Party?" I asked.

"Nope, no party. We're in mourning mode right now," said Amelia, looking thrilled. "Hey, did you find the blackmailer yet?"

"Not yet. I wanted to ask you all a few more questions about that actually."

"Sure," said Shelley, "But can you do me a teeny-weeny little favor? Can you grab my sweater from my bedroom? I'm getting cold."

"Ummm," I paused, wondering why Shelley couldn't do that herself. Feeling slightly surprised, I thought, *what did it matter?* If I grabbed Shelley's sweater, maybe she would be grateful enough to help me find out whom Joe was spending his time with. "Sure. What color is it?"

"The striped, blue one. It's on the bed, through there." Shelley waved a hand towards the furthest door.

I walked over, pushing the door open and stepping inside. The room was dark and it was hard to make out anything in the untidy state she left it. I felt on the wall for the light switch, found it, and flipped it on. There was a huge pile of clothes on the bed, but no striped sweater. "I don't see it," I called back, making to leave.

Shelley appeared in the doorway, blocking my exit. "Try the chair by the window. Maybe I left it over there."

"Okay," I grumbled, audible only to me as I picked my way across the room. I rummaged through the pile of clothes on the chair, but again, no sweater.

"Did you find it yet?" she asked, going to the other side of the room.

"No."

"It's gotta be here somewhere. Keep looking!"

I turned to Shelley, to tell her that she was mistaken, but an arm reached through the doorway, and before I could even frown, the door was pulled shut and the light switched off. "Hey!" I yelled, stomping back across the mess in the dark. I gripped the handle and pulled. The door didn't move. I pulled again, but to no avail. Crouching to handle height, I could see why. Someone had deliberately locked the door! "Hey!" I yelled again. "Is this supposed to be funny? Shelley?"

There was a brief silence, then a small click. Beyond the door, someone giggled before saying, "See ya!" Another door further away slammed and I was left in silence.

"Shelley?" I asked again. "Shelley? Where's the light switch?"

I felt around the doorway for a light switch, but couldn't find one, so I groped my way over to the windows and pulled open the long curtains, flooding the room with light. No Shelley. I was alone.

"Argh!" I moaned. I felt put out at being duped so easily. I was locked in the bedroom and even more confused by Shelley's disappearance. Where did she go? How could I tell Solomon that the band gave me the slip after locking me in a bedroom? I needed to escape and see why they wanted me out of the way so desperately. Why would they pull such a stupid stunt rather than helping me solve the problems plaguing them? There was another door in the rear wall. I crossed over to it, not bothering to be careful about where I put my feet, and wrenched it open, hoping to find Shelley inside. Bathroom. Empty. "Damn," I grumbled as I turned back to the room. Everything I needed for my escape was in my purse: my cell phone, my lock-picking kit, and my Swiss Army knife.

Unfortunately, my purse was in the living room. "How else can I get out of here?" I asked no one specifically. "How did Shelley get out of here?"

It was an attractive room, decorated in a classic style with a super-king-sized bed (unmade), a large, antique wardrobe (doors open and flooded with clothes), a wingback armchair (more clothes) and a thick carpet (even more clothes and various unmatched shoes). As I looked around, I couldn't help feeling dejected. I was stuck.

Just as I wondered whether hollering would help my predicament, I heard male voices from the sitting room next door. Scrambling over, I hammered on it. "Hey!" I called out, figuring I'd deal with the embarrassment later. "Hey! In here!"

"Who's that?" asked a voice I didn't recognize.

"It's Lexi. Can you unlock the door?"

The lock clicked and I tugged the door open. Large and Larger stood in front of me, the confusion on their faces most likely matching my own. "What are you doing in there?" asked Large.

"I'll explain... oh, never mind. Where did they go?" I asked, looking around the empty room. No Solomon - great! But no B4U either.

"Who?"

"The band. Shelley, Lauren and Amelia. Where did they go?" I asked again.

"They went out," said Large.

"Uh-huh," said Larger.

"Yeah, I figured. Where did they go?"

"I don't know."

"Did they take a bodyguard? Did they call anyone on the phone?" I asked, my heart racing.

"They called their car service," said Large. "I think they went to a club."

I groaned. Why on earth would three supposedly grieving women want to go to a club mid-afternoon? Especially after receiving lockdown orders directly from Joe? It didn't make any sense, but I had to admit, they were hardly cut up about their friend's untimely death. Still, like Joe said, they were *supposed* to be upset. They had to appear like they were upset. Going to a club would not do that, and who would they blame first if the press got hold of the remaining members of B4U?

Me!

"Give me the number of the car service," I demanded from the pair, waiting while Large searched slowly through his cell phone before finally producing a number. I entered it onto my keypad, holding my phone to my ear as it rang.

"Marchmont Hotel Car Service," answered the woman on the other end of the line.

"Hi. I'm with B4U. Is the second car here yet?" I asked, bluffing.

"Second car?"

"Yeah, we sent for two cars. The first car just left and we're waiting on the second."

"I'm sorry, I don't have any record of two cars. Just the one."

"Well, fix it," I said, imperiously, as if were an irate member of B4U. "We're in a hurry!"

"Yes, of course, Madam. My apologies for the wait. We can have a car to you in five minutes. Shall I tell the driver to collect you from the rear service exit too?"

"That's right; and going to the same destination, which is... oh, shoot! Where did we book it?"

"The Blue Moon."

"Right. Yeah. Five minutes at the rear service exit," I confirmed, dropping my forehead into my palm. They couldn't have been heading anywhere worse. "Thanks." I hung up, aware that Large and Larger were staring at me. "When Joe and Solomon come back, tell them we all stepped out and will be back soon."

"Right," said Large as he looked around the empty room. "You and whom?"

"B4U," I said, as I skirted around them, running for the door before they could ask me anymore questions I didn't want to answer. I had a bad feeling, and a sense of urgency to get to the club and fast before B4U did something stupid.

CHAPTER SIX

The Blue Moon was pretty much the worst club I could've chosen to find B4U. And if it hadn't been for the two security guards, and the car service that provided the information, it would also have been the last place I looked.

The club was a seedy-looking joint. I was pretty sure Lily once held a job there. Fortunately, she wasn't one of the "hot topless dancers" the billboard next to the door advertised, but briefly worked as a bartender. I recalled the tips were good, but the clientele were not the kind of people you'd ever take home to meet your mother.

As I stared up at the flashing neon sign, my heart was sinking. This was a sleazy club, and why the band wanted to come here, of all places, I had no idea; but I knew it couldn't have been for anything good. As I decided what to do, I felt my phone vibrate in my pocket. I eased it out, checking the screen. *Solomon*. I let it ring out, since I did not want to explain to him why the band we were supposed to be protecting had ditched me to go to a strip joint.

I did the best thing I could under the circumstances. I called Lily.

"Hey," she said on answering. "I'm a little busy. Can I call you back?"

"I'll be quick," I promised. "What can you tell me about The Blue Moon?"

"The Blue Moon club? Nothing good. I mean, you know, I worked there a few years ago? Like, for a few weeks. I can't say it was my most favorite gig ever."

"Why's that?"

"Oh, nothing bad, it's just kind of sleazy. Remember Flames? That was a classy joint compared to The Blue Moon."

"Rough employees?"

"No, not really. They were pretty nice; at least, from what I remember. They just worked their shifts, made some money and went home. The customers were okay too. Not grabby, just kind of sad and lonely. Anyway, everything was all above board. Why?"

"I'm standing outside it."

"Did Solomon fire you? Honey, you can have a job at my bar!"

"No, he didn't fire me!" I replied hoping my indignation was obvious. "I have to go inside. Do you have any tips?"

"Only if you take your top off and work it." Lily giggled.

"Not those kinds of tips. How do I get in? I'm not exactly their average customer. I have hair."

"Last I remember, it was just a walk-in. The doormen won't give you any hassle, unless you start something. Don't start anything, 'kay?"

I promised I wouldn't and told Lily I'd call her back to fill her in later on the details of why I was about to enter the strip club. I just hoped the details weren't too tawdry.

Lily's memory served correctly. No one challenged me as I pulled open one of the wooden doors and stepped inside. I was immediately assaulted by loud music and the cloying scent of sweat and cheap perfume. A couple of guys looked over, then returned their gazes to the stage. If they were surprised at seeing a fully clothed female, they didn't show it.

I went to the back of the room. Stretching out around the edges were booths, with various tables and chairs dotted across the floor, punctuated by several podiums. Each podium was speared through the center with a floor-to-ceiling pole. A bar was off to the right and there was one barman on duty, which made sense, given there were only twenty or so patrons. Even that many seemed a little at odds with the time, as I expected it probably got busier later. A couple of scantily clad women were propped up at the bar, but nobody paid any attention to them. All eyes were on the small stage at the front.

My mouth dropped open.

Grinding around the poles on stage were the three

remaining members of B4U!

Only an hour earlier, they were wearing nice clothing. Expensive things. Fashionable, but nothing too "out there," and certainly, nothing that could alienate their legions of fans. Now their nice girl facade was gone. Lauren, Shelley, and Amelia were in various states of undress. Amelia looked almost conservative in an unbuttoned pair of denim hot pants and a push-up bra, her top purposely hanging open, whereas Lauren and Shelley were stripped down to thongs and bras.

Even worse was the song they were singing. "The bitch is dead," sang Shelley, "Ding dong!" Lauren and Amelia joined in, singing the chorus of their latest hit single, changing every few words to say something derogatory about Katya.

"Oh, shit," I whispered. If this got out, or if anyone in the club was smart enough to recognize the performers, the band members' careers would be over. And if Solomon found out they did this on my watch after giving me the slip, I could kiss not only the case goodbye, but my career too. That kind of thing had a never-ending power to cause embarrassment, which often followed a person around for years.

I peeled my shoes off the carpet and wound my way towards the stage, gathering items of clothing draped over chairs and tables that I recognized as belonging to the band. I folded them over my arms carelessly. A top flew towards me and landed on a nearby chair so I grabbed that too. I didn't care whose clothing I held, or what order I collected their things, just that I had them while I went to round up the band. I devised a plan to get them out of the club and into the safe confines of the hotel away from... oh damn! The man I passed held up a cell phone camera and snapped photos of them. Without thinking, I grabbed his phone and dropped it into his beer.

"Hey! he yelled, jumping to his feet. "What the hell?"

"Oops!" I said, holding up my clothes-laden arms. "My mistake!"

"That was no mistake, lady. That's a new iPhone. It cost me hundreds of dollars!" he snarled, towering over me.

"Yeah, about that... Um, let me give you my card and you can buy a new phone and we'll cover..."

"I want my money now! You see them—" He jabbed a finger at the stage before poking it at my chest. "That's my money shot! The photos I took will earn me thousands!"

"Well, not actually, because your phone is toast," I said, giving him a little shrug while checking around to see who might be listening. If this guy recognized the girls in the band, it wouldn't be long before others did. "But I will ensure your phone is fully paid for."

"I'm gonna sue, bitch!" he growled, jabbing harder at my chest until I stepped back.

On stage, B4U harmonized, "Still dead! She's still dead! Hurrah!"

"What's going on?" asked a deep voice behind my back.

I gave the newcomer a shallow glance, just enough to see whom it was while keeping an eye on the angry guy in front of me, as well as the band. The band was in my line of vision, the angry guy started turning red, and the newcomer turned out to be the doorman, and he didn't look happy.

"This bitch dropped my phone in my beer and I want her to pay for it along with all the photos she destroyed," said the angry man, grabbing his beer. It sloshed over his hand as he pointed to the soggy cell phone.

"What photos?" asked the doorman.

"Shots of them," angry man shook his hand at the stage. "Don't you recognize them?"

"Who?"

"Those girls! They're famous, man!"

"You dropped his phone in a beer, ma'am?" said the doorman, looking down at me.

I turned towards him, trying to keep my eyes on everyone at once, and wished I had another pair of eyes. Fortunately — or unfortunately — the band were still on stage. They ceased singing and were now each wrapped around a stripper pole. They were surprisingly good at it too. "Yeah, kind of. It was an accident, but I promise to replace it," I said as the angry man started to growl about it being no accident.

"Lexi Graves?" said the doorman, squinting in the

low light. "It's Lexi Graves, isn't it?"

"Uh, yeah." I gave him a weak smile.

"I saw your photo in the newspaper. You solve mysteries."

"That's right."

"Are you solving a mystery now?" he inquired.

"Kind of." I stumbled onwards, hoping he was somehow impressed. "Absolutely. Yes."

"Your brother arrested me for burglary. I did time for it."

My heart sank. This was not good. I needed to get B4U away from more guys with bright ideas and cell phones, especially now that we were starting to draw attention from the other patrons. I also needed to get away from the angry man whose footage I destroyed and the doorman incarcerated by one of my brothers. Carefully edging backwards, I was surprised when the doorman stepped forward, opening his arms. Almost reflexively, I folded my shoulders in, preparing to bounce off a blow before running in terror. Then, the strangest thing occurred. He hugged me.

"It was the best thing that ever happened to me," he cried, hugging me tighter. "Yeah, I got sent down for a year, but that turned my life around. I learned to read and write, and your brother helped me get a job here when I got out. My girlfriend came back to me and we just learned we're having a baby boy." He released me and pulled out a cell phone before jabbing the screen. It came to life, showing an ultrasound picture. "Isn't he perfect?"

"He's wonderful," I said, exhaling in relief. "I'm really happy for you."

"Dude, less happy reunion, more camera repayment," huffed the angry man. "Where's my money?"

"We don't let patrons take photos of any of the girls," said the doorman, pointing towards the door. "Out, and don't show your face in here again. You're disrespecting the women."

"Screw you!" said the angry man, pulling his arm back, and ready to hurl his beer glass in my direction. Before he could, the doorman grabbed him by the collar and marched him outside. I watched him get tossed out the doors with the strong suggestion that he never return.

"Sorry about that, ma'am," said the doorman, returning to me. "The name's Ray. You're really solving a case?"

"Yeah, and I need your help."

"Sure, anything."

"I need to get these three women off stage and into a cab while making sure no one took any photos or video footage of them."

"No problem," said the doorman. "You get the girls and I'll handle the rest."

~

"What the hell were you thinking, Lexi?" yelled Solomon. We were holed up in Joe Carter's suite, and my day wasn't getting any better. Solomon was pacing while I sat on the couch. I wished I were on my couch at home, my feet tucked under me, a pint of ice cream on my lap, and nothing but quiet echoing around me.

"Obviously, I wasn't thinking, 'Hey, I know a great place to show B4U while they're in town'," I yelled back.

We had been arguing for the past fifteen minutes, ever since my return to the hotel with three bedraggled band members in tow. I had to promise that I was sent to retrieve them for a huge, nationwide TV interview. I made it up, of course, but it appealed to their vanity and they redressed fast enough, each one wanting to snatch a few extra minutes of fame. My new friend, Ray Domingo, The Blue Moon's doorman, was true to his word. He made sure every last image of the band was erased from the patrons' devices and I felt confident that B4U's escapades would remain a dark secret from everyone, including Solomon. I repaid Ray's favor with two hundred dollars that I hoped the agency's petty cash would cover.

"A strip club!"

"I don't know who told them to go there!"

"Did you mention it?"

"No!"

"Not even a little bit?" Solomon held up his thumb and forefinger.

"Not even, oh, at all! I don't know how they got there; they gave me the slip, locked me in a room..."

"You were locked in a room?!" Solomon planted a hand over his eyes and stopped pacing at last. "How did that happen?"

"Shelley asked me to get something from the bedroom, and when we went inside, one of them pulled the door shut and locked it, and Shelley disappeared."

"I should have guessed they'd pull something like that. Joe said he's been trying to keep the security quiet so as not to spook the band any further; otherwise he'd have had more sets of eyes on them the whole time."

"See?! I told you it wasn't my fault! No one else even saw them leave... wait, no one? Not even Large and Larger?"

"Who the hell are Large and Larger?"

"The security guards who sit in front of the elevator."

"Those aren't their names."

"You're missing the point! How did they get out of the hotel without anyone calling Joe?"

Solomon's hand slid down and I caught a flash of confusion. I tried not to be too pleased about it, but it didn't work. "I don't know."

"It's not my fault," I told him again. "They should have been stopped several times before they left the hotel, and they weren't. They might have tricked me, but you can't pin that huge security breach on me also."

"They aren't prisoners."

"Too right. So, how do you think I could have stopped them? It was beyond me."

Solomon dropped onto the couch next to me. "Joe really chewed me out on this."

"It's not your fault either. Did you find out why he was lying?"

"No. He stuck to the story that he was in the library. He said our witness must have been mistaken and seen someone who looked like him in the housekeeping closet."

"You didn't tell him I'm the witness?"

"I decided against it. He's committed to his lie. I think we should try and identify the woman instead. She might be a member of the hotel staff, or someone in the band's entourage."

"Maybe he's protecting her?" I suggested.

"Question is why. Lying in a murder investigation is serious. We know he's lying and that makes him even more suspect. He could be protecting the woman."

"Maybe we could ask the band..."

"Not tonight," Solomon warned. "I think you should stay away from the band for now. Joe's pretty angry that they could have been exposed."

"He should be angry at himself. Not my fault," I said again. "He should thank me for getting them back to the hotel and making sure they weren't seen."

"Don't hold your breath," Solomon muttered.

"I won't. Listen, I'm not happy taking the rap for this. Yeah, they set me up, but I still found them and brought them back; and like you said, they're not prisoners. I can't stop them from going places. And you know what? It's not even a nice gig like you told me. The band was awful. Seriously awful, John! They're mean and rude and they're practically dancing on top of the grave of their band member who isn't even buried yet. Yeah, I know they hated each other, but they aren't even pretending to be upset unless someone promises them a spotlight and a camera."

"They're nothing like what I expected either," Solomon admitted.

"I'm this close—" I held up my thumb and forefinger. On second thought, I moved them even closer together, leaving bare millimeters between them, "—to asking to be taken off this case, and it's only been a day. I wanted a nice, safe blackmail, not murder and a bunch of nightmares in high fashion!"

"No can do. You're the only PI I want on this case."

"Ugh," I groaned. "Why? Why me? What did I ever do to you?"

"You keep solving cases, sweetheart."

"So do Delgado, and Fletcher, and Flaherty! I know they do. I've seen them!"

"They're all working on other jobs. Besides, it's better for the band to have a woman around. Sorry, Lexi, you're on the case; but for now, go home. Get some sleep and we'll start again tomorrow."

"What are you going to do?" I asked.

"Damage control," sighed Solomon. "And then I'm

going to review, once again, every security procedure this hotel and the band have in place. I need to put my team in charge before a real disaster happens."

I raised my eyebrows. "You mean it hasn't already?"

"Seems like you managed the situation rather well," Solomon replied, leaning in to give me the lightest of kisses. "Go home. Spend a day or two in the office working the blackmail case and looking for a connection between the letters and Katya's death."

"Does it help that I checked into Shelley and Amelia's whereabouts? Both were seen by staff downstairs prior to the murder," I told him, hopeful that he'd see the positive side of some of my recent activities.

"Not much but I'll look into it further."

I was too tired to argue. Besides, his instructions had a big plus: B4U wouldn't be my problem for a while and that would save me one massive headache. I was pissed at them and didn't want to see them, especially after they duped me. "You got it, boss," I said, springing to my feet. "A night in sounds relaxing. Who knows? Maybe an idea about the blackmailer's identity will even pop into my head!"

I kept up my good spirits all the way downstairs in the elevator, and picked up my car from the valet instead of walking through the lot. The paparazzi seemed to have frittered away and no one approached me as I left. I drove home, but truthfully, I didn't want a night in so much as I wanted a night out with my best friend. Halfway home, instead of heading to my recently purchased buttercup yellow bungalow, I hung a right and drove towards Lily's bar.

Ruby was tending the bar when I entered, and it was a little too early for the after work crowd. A few tables were filled with parties of twos and threes, but the real crowd wouldn't arrive for at least another hour. It was perfect for a catch-up, I decided as I slid onto a tall bar stool. I waited for Ruby to finish serving the two guys she was pouring beers for.

"Lexi!" she exclaimed, smiling as she approached. We'd met on my first accidental case and gradually become friends. When Lily opened her bar she'd offered Ruby a job. She occasionally helped me out on a case too and her surveillance skills were excellent. I liked her. "What can I get you?"

"A club soda and a Lily, please."

Ruby wrinkled her nose. "Lily left already. Was she supposed to meet you?"

"No, just thought I'd swing by. It's been a crazy day."

"Aren't all your days?"

I took a deep breath, wishing I didn't have to remember this day. "Not on this scale."

"Want me to call Lily?"

I pulled my cell phone from my purse and checked my reflection in the mirrors behind the bar. Despite all the crazy, I still looked good. Now, *that* was talent. "No, I'll call her." I tapped Lily's name and held the phone to my ear while Ruby dropped ice cubes into a tall glass, added a lime wedge and squirted soda to the brim, pushing it over to me as Lily answered.

"Heeelloo," she cooed, "what's happening?"

"Worst day over. Hate my job. Where are you?"

"How? Why? And shopping."

"What are you shopping for? Why didn't you call me?"

"Nothing, and thought you were busy being glamorous with the you-know-whos. What about the strip club?"

"There is nothing glamorous about them, believe me. Except their wardrobes, purses, heels, and hair. Everything else is awful. Just awful. I'd tell you more, but I'm at your bar and I signed a non-disclosure."

"Gotcha. You can break it in secret another time."

"I would never," I lied. "Where are you shopping? Are you at the mall? Want company?"

"Uh, no. I'm done. Didn't buy anything. Think I'll go home. Jord gets off shift in an hour and plans on making dinner."

"I'm having dinner alone," I moaned. "Solomon is working late."

"What are you having?"

"Hopefully, an epiphany."

"Definitely get fries with that."

"Let's meet up soon and hang out. I've barely seen you lately." I frowned. No, I saw her briefly at the bar, but before that, she was doing something suspicious that she had yet to reveal. The shopping excuse sounded a little thin too. "Except when I saw you with my mom, tailing that guy. What were you doing?"

"Nothing. Don't know. I wasn't there!"

"You were. I called you. We talked about that."

"Don't know what you're talking about. Don't interrogate me!"

"I'm not!"

"And I didn't buy anything at the mall. Nothing. No matter what rumors you hear, I bought nothing. Oh, I think I see your cousin, Siobhan. Gotta run. Catch up soon. Bye!" Lily hung up, leaving me staring at the blank screen. My best friend just gave me a runaround conversation, which made no sense, then hung up! All I wanted to do was rant about my day, give Lily some juicy gossip, and knock back a cocktail, or six. Why was that so hard to achieve?

My phone buzzed and I grabbed it, hoping Lily had a change of heart. Instead, it was an email notification from Ray, The Blue Moon's doorman. I opened it and read the brief message, closing my eyes when I saw the video attachment. *Found this on an employee phone in case you ever need it*, it read. *Don't worry, I scrubbed it from their phone.* The video still showed a clear shot of Shelley hanging upside down on a stripper pole. I sighed and closed the email without playing the video. While Ray probably thought he was being helpful, I really didn't need a copy of the video, just his assurance that he'd gotten rid of any other copies.

I half drank my soda, trying not to look as glum as I felt, before paying Ruby and heading back to my car. I didn't want to make dinner, so I drove over to Monty's and ordered a small pizza (with fries and ice cream), and took a seat on one of the chairs by the plate glass window while I waited. The smell of mozzarella and Monty's secret tomato sauce hung in the air while I sat there, making my stomach growl, thanks to a missed lunch.

Two feet came to a stop in front of me and I didn't even need to look up to know whom they belonged to.

"Why the long face?" said Maddox.

"Worst. Day. Ever," I muttered.

"But you're going to get the… Best. Pizza. Ever."

"With all my favorite toppings," I agreed, "but it doesn't make up for the job, the *you know who* complication, the *you know what* nightmares I have to interview, and pissing off everyone."

"Sounds like an average day in law enforcement."

"What are you doing here?"

"Weird day, dealing with crazy, famous people. Thought I'd grab a pizza on my way home." Maddox glanced over at the menu board behind the counter, calling to the guy serving. "I'll take a medium hot one."

"You're going to have spicy breath," I told him and he grinned.

"If I melt any plants, I'll let you know."

My order was called and I stood up to reach for the cardboard box and pay.

"You got a small? You eating alone?" Maddox asked.

"Yup."

"Where's the boyfriend?"

"Working late. I'm dining solo."

"Me too. Let's eat together. My place is on the way to your place, or we could go to your place, which is way past my place. What do you say? Did you get fries and ice cream? Say yes!"

I couldn't help laughing at Maddox's suddenly eager face. "Sure, but the ice cream is mine."

Maddox's box landed on the counter and he pulled out cash, paying before holding it up. "Follow me!"

I couldn't remember the last time I visited Maddox's apartment, but little had changed except for a large plant in a new planter in the entryway. I dropped my purse next to it before hanging my jacket on the peg, noting he added a couple more pretty pillows to his couch in the living room. We bypassed that and I followed him into the kitchen. He pulled out plates and a pizza cutter, placing them on the table and adding paper napkins and glasses, along with a bottle of mineral water. He sliced up my pizza, tipping it onto my plate and I divided half the fries, then poured the water while Maddox slid half of his medium hot onto his plate. He loosened his tie as he sat and undid the top button of his collar. I tried not to think about the time I delivered a pizza to him and what ensued thereafter on this very table before the cheese had time to cool. I shook off the thought since I had no business to think such things and concentrated on raising a hot slice to my mouth.

"I don't want to talk about work, but who do you think killed her?" asked Maddox.

I chewed and swallowed before replying. "I'm glad you started with an easy question."

Maddox laughed. "Sorry. Do you think it's got something to do with the blackmail?"

"Maybe. I don't know. I've only just started investigating. I can't rule it out." I opened my mouth for another bite, but paused, frowning. "Why the interest? Ah! You've taken over the murder case!"

"You got me. Due to the high-profile nature of the case, the FBI officially stepped in. We're trying to work it as a joint op but I'm treading on some of my old buddies' toes over at MPD."

"I bet you are!"

"Garrett gave me an earful."

"Sounds about right."

Maddox shrugged, chewing happily. Underneath his cheerful exterior, I caught sight of some strain around his eyes. For all that, he didn't seem to mind taking over the case, but I was pretty sure he minded annoying his former colleagues. "Looks like we're both working the murder case."

"Who says I am?" I countered, finishing the second slice in record time, and reaching for a couple of hot, crispy fries.

Maddox gave me a disbelieving look. "Sure you are. I know you. You can't stay out of this."

"Okay, I am, but unofficially. Officially, I'm looking into the blackmail connection and trying to work out if the blackmailer and the murderer are one and the same. As for who that might be, I don't know. My suspect list covers the rest of the band, their manager, their crew, security staff... the list goes on."

"That's some list."

I took a drink, washing away a little cheese and grease. I briefly pondered how useful it could be to have FBI resources at my disposal during my investigation. Sure, I had the agency's resident tech geek, Lucas, and a familial connection to the homicide squad, but it would have been useful to have an "in" with Maddox too. I didn't know what Solomon would say about me asking Maddox for help, but I figured since he knew everything, he probably already knew Maddox was working Katya's murder.

"Who is on your list?" I asked.

"Everyone." We laughed at the futility of our lengthy lists. "So, you want to put our heads together on this?" Maddox asked.

"Does that mean you want to see the blackmail letters?" I tossed back.

"Sure, but it would be good to get your thoughts too, since I don't suppose I can convince you to take a nice, safe case?"

"Nope, you can't," I smiled. I decided against telling

him I'd already tried to remove myself from the case and gotten shot down. "Okay. I'm going to head home, but I'll share the letters if you share the autopsy and forensic findings. Deal?"

"Deal," Maddox agreed. "Although you know, I could just requisition the letters without making any deals with you?"

I did know that, so I just laughed and began to clear my plate.

"No, leave it. I'll clear the plates. It was nice having dinner with you."

"Yeah, I enjoyed it too."

"Better than eating alone, right?"

I nodded, stepping past him to retrieve my coat from the entryway. I grabbed it from the peg, turning to pull it over my shoulders when I knocked a couple of envelopes to the floor. I reached for them, intending to return them to the small shelf. As I turned them over, the top item wasn't in an envelope, and I blinked in surprise as I looked at it. A booking for two at a romantic, little inn near Lake Pierce for the weekend. Hurriedly, I dropped the papers onto the shelf, and turned as Maddox stepped into the entryway.

"Don't forget your ice cream," he said, handing me the carton. "I'll call you tomorrow."

CHAPTER SEVEN

"How do you know it's a romantic getaway?" Lily asked. I was lying in bed, and the first thing I'd done upon waking was make a coffee, return to bed, and call Lily.

"I'll send you the website. It's gorgeous. Ten bedrooms all individually styled. Queen-sized beds. Freestanding bathtubs. Views either above the lake, or the gardens. Couples massages. Do I need to say more? I've been trying to get a free weekend with Solomon to go there over the last few months."

"Definitely not taking his mom," said Lily. "Did you ask who he is taking?"

"No! I put the papers back on the shelf and pretended I didn't see them."

"What happened then?" Lily gasped.

"He gave me my ice cream and we hugged and kissed..."

"Say what?!"

"On the cheek, Lily! And then I left and came home

and found four missed calls from Solomon."

"Did you call him back and tell him you couldn't answer because you were having an intimate dinner for two with your ex on the table where you once did it?" Lily asked breathlessly.

"No, I said my phone was in my purse and I didn't hear it."

"Oh. So, what are you going to do now?"

"Nothing."

"That's not much fun. I thought we could stake out Maddox and find out who his new girlfriend is. What if it's that detective? The one he may or may not have done the nasty with?"

"He swears he didn't and I believe him and... I don't know. What if it is her?" I asked, thinking of Detective Rebecca Blake. I hadn't heard her name in a while and didn't know what happened to her after Maddox joined the FBI.

"We need to find out."

"We don't. I don't. This is his personal business."

Lily snorted. "Sure it is. That's why we're analyzing it at seven thirty. Let's face it, I'm dying to know and so are you."

"I'm not stalking my ex."

"It's not stalking if he doesn't know about it. We all know that. I think it's the law."

"I'm pretty sure it's not."

"But are you positive?"

I thought about it. "Yes, I'm positive stalking

Maddox is not okay."

"So you're going to ask him instead?"

"No!"

"Good thing. You can never show casual interest in your ex's new smooch-partner. That *is* the law. I'm positive about that one."

"I agree. Do I tell him I saw his booking? Or pretend I know nothing and wait for him to say something? What do I do? "

"Beats me. You didn't agree to any of the fun stuff that would allow us to find out without asking."

"I'm going to pretend to know nothing."

"Kind of sounds like your case."

I stuck my tongue out at the phone.

"Saw that," said Lily. "Don't pretend you didn't do that."

I laughed. "I need to tell you more about the case. Crazy stuff happened yesterday, and now Maddox wants to work together."

"What can be so crazy about America's new sweethearts?" Lily asked. Just as I was about to tell her exactly what, she said, "Oh, gotta go. Got a delivery at nine and I need to get ready."

"Let's get togeth... Lily? Lily?" I asked, but it was no use. She had already hung up.

I tossed my cell phone onto the nightstand and reached for my coffee, wondering if the uncomfortable feeling I had that Lily was avoiding me was just that: a feeling. So what if she were hanging out with my mom and going to the mall alone? I did those things too. After a long sip, I decided I was just being paranoid. Lily had been my best friend for more years than I had fingers to count. She was busy running the bar, I decided, and enjoying her married life with the man of her dreams. I could hardly point the finger at her without looking inwardly. There were times when I'd blown Lily off in favor of a night with Solomon, or because I was working a case. That was grownup life, I decided. It might assist in the purchase of fabulous heels, but it played havoc with our social engagements.

After finishing my coffee, I showered, washed my hair, blew it dry, and dressed in my favorite blue skinny jeans and pink shirt. I finished off the outfit with cream flats and a cream leather purse that I hoped said effortlessly stylish. After a quick breakfast of yogurt and fruit, I made my way slowly to the agency office.

Delgado and Fletcher were at their desks when I arrived.

"Good morning!" I chirped.

"Who you gonna kill today?" asked Delgado.

"You're at the top of the list!"

Delgado spun around in his seat, smiling. He wore baggy jeans, a plain, navy t-shirt, and a gray hoodie under his leather jacket. There was a plain cap on the desk, and next to that, his telephoto lens and a thick file. Clearly he'd just gotten off a job. "Seriously, we leave you alone for a few minutes and a corpse turns up."

I refused to be any less chirpy. "I didn't kill her!"

"You were asked to do one simple job," Fletcher added. "Delgado, here, just took down a local drug dealing ring. I just filed a report on my mark, a guy with not one, not two, but *three* wives."

"Man is he going down in divorce court," said Delgado with a shake of his head.

"What's your point?" I asked.

"You get a blackmail case and it turns into murder!" finished Fletcher. "Our marks just stuck with the crimes we originally busted them for."

"Not my fault." I couldn't help pouting. I really never saw Katya's murder coming. Now, with less than twenty-four hours since her death, which hadn't yet broken in the national media, I was ready to re-double my efforts to find the blackmailer, in the hope that would lead me to the killer.

Delgado and Fletcher both had wide grins. "Just playing with ya, Lexi," said Delgado. "Could have happened to anyone. Need a hand?"

"No, I'm going to look into the band's past to see what I can find. Simple background checks today. All done in the office. Nothing dangerous for me today." As I said it, I shuddered. Yesterday, it hadn't occurred to me, but now it did. I was mere yards away from a murderer. I was on my way to see Katya. I could so easily have bumped into the murderer and wound up as collateral damage. Yet, I didn't bump into him, or her. In fact, from what I could glean, no one saw anyone leaving Katya's suite after Lauren left. How could that have happened? If there was no evidence on Lauren to connect her to the crime — although she was seen leaving the room after loudly threatening Katya — then how did someone else get in and out without being seen? That reminded me: how did Shelley escape from the locked room where I was trapped inside?

"You've got a look," said Fletcher. "I don't know what it means, but I know one when I see one."

"How could someone get in and out of a room without being seen?" I asked.

"What kind of a room? Katya's suite?" he guessed, correctly.

I nodded. "Lauren was seen leaving, but she denies being the killer."

"They all say that," interrupted Delgado, waving for me to continue.

"Let's say she didn't do it. How does someone else get in and out without being seen?"

"More than one exit," said Fletcher.

I put my palm on my forehead. *Could it really be that simple?* "I didn't see one."

"Doesn't mean it isn't there."

I picked up my desk phone and dialed Solomon.

"Good morning, beautiful," he said, and I guessed he was alone.

"Where are you?" I asked.

"At home. What's up?"

"Can you get blueprints for the hotel?"

"I have them already. Why?"

"Does Katya's suite show any extra exits aside from the main door leading onto the hallway that connects all the suites?"

"Not that I recall."

"I'm playing devil's advocate for Lauren. I think there might be another exit. Assuming Lauren didn't kill Katya, that's why no one saw the murderer enter or exit their suite."

There was a long silence. I was about to say Solomon's name when he said, "I'll get on it. Anything else?"

"No. That's it."

"Dinner later?"

I turned away slightly, dropping my voice to whisper into the phone. It was unprofessional to arrange a date with the boss, but I had an important question to ask: "Are you cooking?"

"Yes. Be here at seven."

"I'll bring wine. Any preference?"

"Victoria's Secret."

"I don't think they do... oh!" I smiled. "Okay. Later, John." I hung up, swinging around. Delgado and Fletcher stared at me with their arms crossed and silly smiles on their faces. "Oh, shut up," I said, but I didn't mean it.

Opening up my laptop, I set up four new files, one for each member of B4U. I needed to find out about their pasts, and not just the squeaky clean stories they fed to the media. What I needed were their real histories, the parts of their lives that would reveal the secrets the blackmailer already knew. At the moment, however, I was several steps behind that mystery player. I needed to get ahead. Even more pressing, I needed to find out if the murderer and blackmailer were the same person. Second, I had to pare down my suspect pool.

Somehow, I didn't think the band would agree to having their personal lives so closely scrutinized in order to find the blackmailer, but I tried to ignore the mild discomfort I felt at poking through their pasts. After all, I was doing it in order to help them. Since no one except Shelley would tell me any secrets, I had to find them out for myself.

The question was: whom to start with? I decided on Katya. *Could her secret have been the reason for her murder?* I wondered, as I started with simple searches. To save time, I put in requests for Shelley, Lauren, and Amelia's birth records, as well as their financials, DMV licenses, and details of their former residences. Some of those I could get by legal means; some of them Lucas could access. I never asked how he got them either. While I waited on those, I printed the photos I took the previous day of the blackmail letters and spread them out across my desk.

On a large pad of paper, I wrote *Katya - Russia?* Under that, I added: *Shelley - ten years ago.* I added *sex tape* to that since Shelley readily admitted what her blackmail secret was. Then I added *Amelia* and *secret*, the only clue offered in the letters. Finally, I added *Lauren - Michael?*

Calling up an internet browser, I began to type Katya's full name, but *auto fill* suggested "found dead", "murdered", and "tragic death" as the first three possible options. Clearly, her death had leaked to the press. I clicked the top option and scrolled through the news reports. All the national papers mentioned it as well as most of the gossip blogs. Some ran the story with photos of her covered body being removed from the hotel on a gurney before it was loaded into the coroner's van. It was gratuitous and served no purpose. The press, I noted, already had the basic information of the murder case. They all knew it wasn't a natural death, and the police were treating it as a murder. Their accounts differed as to whether there was a suspect, or someone in custody, or any suspects at all. There were a few shots of a distraught-looking Lauren, and more where she hid her pale face behind dark glasses. Fortunately, to my relief, there was nothing in the press about B4U's raucous afternoon escape.

I returned to the search page and typed Katya's full name again, adding "Russia" to my search query, before hitting *enter*. There were hundreds of pages. I opened the first one, an interview where Katya spoke at length about her early years in Russia, and her family's struggles to reach the US and settle here. The other pages I opened had the same or similar stories in varying degrees of detail. Very few of the articles carried any photos of Katya's early life, but that was easy to write off as her family being too poor to own a camera. It puzzled me, however, that there were no candid shots taken later from elementary or high school, or even from a yearbook. Katya often talked about school and her struggles to learn English so I knew she attended school. Surely someone had evidence to disprove her public story? Why hadn't they sold them?

"Got the birth records," said Lucas, tapping me on the shoulder and making me jump.

"That was fast. Do I want to know how?"

"No. Just know that I have my ways. I couldn't get Katya's, but I figured she was born in Russia, so that's no surprise. I'll reach out to my contacts there. I got her immigration papers..."

"How do you obtain this stuff?"

"Again, I have my ways. Here're the birth records for the other three. I thought they were all supposed to be teen stars or something."

"They started that way," I told him. "They're all in their early twenties now."

"Take a closer look at the dates on their certificates," Lucas said. "DMV licenses are here, but their financials are going to take a while. They've got high-level accounts. That means extra levels of security to overcome. They're probably used to hack attacks. Might be quicker just to ask them."

"I would if I thought they would give me access, but

I'm guessing, no. Will you keep trying?"

"Sure."

I shuffled the papers Lucas gave me, taking his advice to look closer at the dates on the birth records. Katya was twenty-three as widely reported. Lauren was twenty-five, but I was pretty sure she claimed to be twenty-three. Shelley was twenty-six. That was no biggie. Plenty of starlets lied about their age. I moved Amelia's to the top of the pile and frowned. Amelia would be thirty next month. Now that was entirely at odds with her claim. Just to be sure, I typed her name into the search engine, and sure enough, the band's Wiki named her as the oldest member of the band at a mere twenty-four. That meant while the rest of the band became famous at seventeen, nineteen and twenty — just young enough to pass for a faked younger age — Amelia was already twenty-three. Was her true age a big enough secret for her to hide it? If that were the case, why was her blackmail message so cryptic?

As I began contemplating that, my cell phone rang.

"Hi, Solomon," I said, smiling, wondering if he had any other requests for later.

"The story broke nationwide," he said.

"I saw online. What do you need me to do?"

"Nothing. Stay put. Press are arriving and it's going to be a circus here at the hotel soon. That's going to make our investigation harder. For now, I need you to stay out of the way so that all the focus remains on the murder and away from the blackmail."

"Got it."

"Where are you with the case?"

"Just running background checks. I think I discovered Amelia's secret. She's seven years older than she claims to be."

"Would you pay to keep that quiet?" Solomon asked.

"If I were a teen idol, maybe. Did you get the hotel plans?"

"Working on it, but I think you're right about extra exits. I went to the hotel and checked Amelia and Shelley's suite against the blueprints I have, and there's some kind of hidden access. I just can't work out how to get into it."

"Secret tunnels are so cool!"

Solomon made an unimpressed noise. "Where are you with the letters?"

"Since Joe wouldn't let us remove them from the hotel, I took photos. I'm reviewing them again while I run background checks. I'd like to continue interviewing the band."

"Could be a problem. They were supposed to start shooting their new music video today, but it's been called off for now, due to Katya's death. They have the time, but I insisted they remain in the hotel, and I've told you to stay out. Plus, their PR is here, briefing them on how to talk to the media in the days ahead. They're already talking about interviews and a real life story movie, made for TV," he finished wearily.

"I guess that's celebrity."

"Let me see what I can arrange with regards to access."

"Is Joe still mad at me?"

"He's too distracted to stay mad," Solomon told me. "Since yesterday, he's moved onto bigger issues, but he does want an update later on where we are with the blackmail letters. If they get out, on top of the murder, this nightmare will be never-ending for them all and our jobs will be a lot harder."

"I'm on it," I assured him. I spread the newly printed blackmail letters across my desk. After hanging up, and making my second coffee of the day, I got comfortable and assessed the letters from start to finish, arming myself with a big notepad to scrawl down my thoughts.

I started from the top. Katya got the first letter, with the second, third, and fourth, addressed to each of the other band members. The same cycle was repeated through letters five to eight. In total, each band member got two individual letters demanding a transfer deposit to the phantom account. Then, the pattern changed; letters nine to ten were addressed to the whole band with the same extortion demands.

The letters were all typed so it would have been impossible to get handwriting samples to match. The paper was thin and appeared to be a standard printer paper, although I had to recall that from memory since all I had now were the photos.

I wrote on my pad, *access to computer and printer.*

Next, I looked closely at the content of the letters.

They were brief and straight to the point. Each started by personally addressing the recipient, with a terse note about the secret the blackmailer knew, and then directions for depositing the ransom money. Unsurprisingly, it wasn't signed off with a name, which just told me that some blackmailers were undeniably rude.

Underneath my first note, I added, *find out who owns bank account*. It was an offshore account, according to Solomon, and I figured just about anyone could set one up so unless a personal appearance was necessary, that didn't rule out anyone so far. I added, *How was the account created?* and then, *How is it managed?*

I picked up my desk phone and dialed Lucas's extension. My biggest and best shot at a lead was to find out who owned the account. I could only hope the bank wasn't so mired in secrecy that Lucas couldn't get past their systems.

"Talk to me," he said on answering.

"Okay, since you insist, could you find out who set up the blackmailer's bank account?" I read out the numbers while he made a note.

"Solomon mentioned that. It's going to take more time than usual."

"I'm glad you're on it," I told him, which was a lot nicer than "Get started!" and hung up.

Even though I pored over the letters, just like I had the previous day, I had no success in narrowing down my enormous list of suspects. What I needed was a way to knock people off the list. Unfortunately, without talking to Joe or the band, I had no easy way of learning the answers I needed.

My eyes were getting tired, which was no good for my skin regimen, and I was getting frustrated. Shuffling the photos of the letters into a pile, I dropped them into a manila envelope, and had to admit defeat.

Besides, wasn't there a murder to solve?

Despite all my attempts, I couldn't shake the mental image of Katya lying there, dead. It didn't matter how many dead bodies I'd seen, each one was shocking.

The question remained: was the blackmailer I searched for responsible? Did Katya confront someone about the incessant demands and threats to reveal her secret? Did she threaten to expose them? I wouldn't have put it past her to get nasty and retaliate, I thought as I rocked back in my chair and stretched my legs, my mind racing ahead. It was conceivable that Katya might have even discovered who the blackmailer was. She might have had a vicious mouth, but she seemed pretty smart. As soon as I thought of her confronting the blackmailer, I discounted it. She hadn't gone looking for the creep, but died in her own hotel suite. Someone went there. Someone came to see her... or she must have summoned someone. Someone who knew how to get in and out of her suite without being seen.

That puzzled me. B4U had only been in the suite a few days before Solomon and I arrived for our meeting.

That could have given someone connected to them enough time to discover any secret entrances into their rooms. However, it seemed more likely that a hotel employee, or someone else who regularly serviced the rooms would have had that knowledge. That didn't mean it was an employee. An employee could easily have unwittingly passed on any access secrets to the murderer.

How did the killer know Katya would be alone? The killer must have approached her after Lauren stormed out. Did that mean someone was watching the pair? They had returned from an unscheduled trip to the mall, argued, and Lauren unexpectedly retreated to Shelley and Amelia's room. Their movements couldn't have been precisely foreseen or predicted.

The more I thought about it, the more implausible it seemed that the killer was an unknown assailant. Although no forensic evidence was found on Lauren, as far as I could see with my own eyes, all clues still pointed to her. She was the obvious person. She had motive and access. She shouted to Katya as she left and Katya didn't shout back. My only problem with it was: it was just too easy. That, and Lauren didn't even attempt to conceal her lack of alibi.

I didn't want to pin it on Lauren, but I couldn't help placing her at the top of list as my number one suspect.

More confused than ever, I deposited all my photos and files into my desk drawer, locked up and left. After grabbing my overnight bag from home, I was halfway to Solomon's house when Lily called me. "Why didn't you tell me Katya was dead! We've spoken twice since it happened! Ohmygosh! This is huuuuge! Who did it?"

"No idea," I told her truthfully.

"Was it a member of the band?" Lily asked, and I paused a fraction too long. "Oh, wow! Really? Which one? Who did it? Why didn't you tell me any of this? I had to find out from TMZ!"

"I was going to tell you yesterday when I came by the bar."

"I need to know everything now!"

"I'm on my way to Solomon's..."

"Meet you there," Lily squealed and the line clicked dead.

She was waiting for me on Solomon's doorstep by the time I turned onto his street, and searched for a parking space. Lily's turquoise blue Mini occupied the prime spot right outside his house, meaning I had to drive all the way to the end of the block before I found one. Grabbing my bag from the passenger seat, I walked back and let us both inside.

I told Lily everything while she cooed, gasped, and speculated on who the most likely murderer might be: Lauren, Shelley, Amelia, or, her wild card, Joe Carter.

I poured us both a glass of water after Lily refused wine and we perched on the bar stools at the island in Solomon's large, elegant kitchen. "Maybe I should tail them?" Lily suggested. "Pick one. Any one. Make it Amelia, she's my favorite."

I wondered if she would still be Lily's favorite if she knew Amelia's lies about her age. "No need. The paparazzi tail them wherever they go, and according to Solomon, Montgomery will be crawling with them soon."

"They would never spot me."

"True, you would blend in easily with their legions of fans."

"Exactly. Do you think they'll stay together as a trio?"

"I don't know. Maybe. I don't think they've decided yet."

"Katya didn't write any of the songs; and she only did a couple of solos ever. She's not the most valuable member. That's Amelia. She writes most of their songs. Maybe she could go solo?"

"I don't think any of them can go solo. I haven't seen their contracts, but I think they're obliged to stay with the band unless management throws them out."

"Or they die," Lily pointed out. "If the band breaks up, Amelia could make a lot more money as a solo star. Oops, gotta pee. Don't solve the case 'til I'm back." She slid off her stool, grabbed her purse, and hurried to the downstairs bathroom, slamming the door shut behind her.

I refreshed our water and tossed the empty bottle into the recycling can, thinking about what Lily said. Could Amelia make more money without the band? That had to be a strong motive for breaking up the band; and what better way to do that than by threatening to expose their secrets? I wondered if Shelley and Lauren could have similar greedy motives, but without their contracts or financial records, I couldn't definitively answer my own question. Assuming the theory that the blackmailer and the murderer were the same person, Amelia became the only name I could place as my number one suspect. She hated Katya and benefited the most from the band splitting.

By the time Lily returned from the bathroom, several long minutes later, I was still clinging to the thought that the band members could each have a lot more to gain by being ejected from the band, rather than staying together. All except Katya, who according to the anecdotes I heard, seemed to contribute the least to the band, but demanded the most. "I gotta go," Lily said, giving me a quick hug. "Something came up."

"What?" I asked.

"Uh, nothing. I mean, something. I'm running late!" She turned on her heel, heading towards the door, and leaving me no other option, but to hurry after her. "Oh, I meant to ask you, what was on the envelopes?" Lily asked, pausing as she pulled open the door. Before I could tell her I didn't know, and hadn't seen the envelopes, she hurried down the steps and vanished.

CHAPTER EIGHT

"How's dinner?" Solomon asked.

We were seated in his dining room, at opposite sides of the table, and I could tell he'd gone to real effort to pretty the table up, using expensive white china, glass votives with small flickering candles, and a narrow-mouthed vase of blooming white and pink roses.

"Delicious," I said, tucking the final forkful into my mouth. "You've outdone yourself."

Solomon smiled. "Another glass?" he held up the carafe of sparkling grape juice. It wasn't wine, but I had no complaints.

"Thanks."

"How're you feeling?" he asked next.

"Frustrated mostly. I cannot work this case out. Every time I find a new question to ask, it just opens up ten more. As for making a connection between..."

"I meant your health," interrupted Solomon.

I frowned. "I'm fine, thanks."

"Have you thought about taking supplements?"

"It hadn't crossed my mind, no."

"I thought I might go to the health store tomorrow and pick up some supplements."

"Okay. And then can we call Joe and ask him for the envelopes? I had an idea..."

"Do you want to take Victoria out at the weekend?"

I frowned. "Victoria?"

"Your niece," Solomon reminded me, a little unnecessarily. I knew who she was, I was just thrown by the question. Solomon was great with my nieces and nephews, having been present on more than a few occasions when I babysat, but he never volunteered before. "I thought maybe we could take her to the park or out for lunch. What do you think of her stroller? Is it a good model?"

"Uh... it's cute. Sure, I'll ask Serena if we can take Victoria out."

"Great. Delgado seems to be enjoying step-fatherhood."

"Victoria adores him. She thinks he's a jungle gym."

"She's changed him. She makes him happy. I never thought I'd see the day when Delgado became a family man."

"I never thought I'd see the day when my sister acted like a normal human being; so I thank Delgado every day for that," I replied, laughing. "And Victoria. Babies change people."

"For the better, I think."

"Absolutely. How did the blackmail letters get into

the hands of the band members?" I asked, switching topics, my mind still stuck on the case. "Don't they get screened by their staff first? Shouldn't a dozen people or more handle any letter before it reaches any one of them?"

"I'll ask tomorrow. Let's not talk about the case now. I don't want you to get tired. Do you want to change your hours? Do you need more flexibility?"

"No, I'm fine with working exactly as I am, thanks."

"If you need to, just say. If you want to come into work later, that's not a problem."

"Uh..." I frowned again, wondering if I misheard the dinner invitation. It appeared to be more like an appraisal session about my work. Any moment now, I expected Solomon to move the roses aside and produce his latest pension plan.

"And if you need to take breaks, just say so. I want the agency to be a good place to work."

"It's a great place to..."

"I was thinking of starting a company car program. Do you need a bigger car? More space in the trunk?"

"No, the VW has all the space for shoes and cameras that I need."

"Okay," Solomon agreed readily. "Just let me know if you'd prefer something bigger."

"Have you been reviewing employee benefits?" I asked, puzzled at his questions. "I can tell you I'm really happy. You don't have to worry about my hours or a new car."

"What about your health plan?"

"I'm healthier than I've ever been."

He narrowed his eyes. "Really?"

"Really!"

"Want some ice cream?"

"Yes, please."

Solomon insisted I relax in the living room while he cleared our dinner plates. I listened to him tidy away, loading the dishwasher and banging the freezer drawer shut. Meanwhile, I leafed through a magazine as I wondered what could have gotten into him. Normally, he loved talking about work, but this evening, he seemed to want to talk about anything else. Not that I minded him voicing his concern about my general health, it was just strange. As he dropped onto the couch next to me and handed me a spoon, I put it down to the stress of the case. Nothing had gone to plan, and nothing appeared straightforward. Even I wondered why on earth I wanted to talk about it. Really, I should have been enjoying an evening off with the man of my dreams and a large bowl of ice cream.

"Can I get you anything else?" Solomon asked, prying off the lid.

"What? Like a pickle?" I teased and he sucked in a deep breath. "Joking," I said hurriedly. "All I need now is a loving arm around me and I'll be set for the evening. I barely had to wait a second to get my wish.

~

Solomon and I awoke together, breakfasted together, and I convinced him, despite his warnings for me to stay away from Joe and the band, that we should go together to the hotel. On the way, I explained my confusion about the envelopes, waiting for Solomon to come to the same conclusion. If the letters were hand-delivered to specific areas where only the band members would find them, our suspect pool would have been substantially decreased. I could certainly check off superfans and strangers, moving directly to my list of band and crew.

Speeding past the front of the hotel, where a small number of photographers waited, we drove around the back to the employee parking area. Solomon flashed a pass for access and I followed him to the lobby and an elevator that only stopped at the top floor. "When we first visited, this accessed all floors," I pointed out.

"I tightened up security," replied Solomon. "Now, this elevator only services the top floor. It's easier to track all who enter and exit." Seconds later, we stepped out in front of Large and Larger before beginning our search for Joe as Large pointed in the direction of Joe's suite.

"Where are you on the blackmail?" Joe asked as we entered. He was sitting on the couch, a bunch of papers spread across the coffee table and didn't look angry anymore, which was a relief.

Solomon shut the door. "Lexi?"

"I'm following up leads, but there's nothing solid yet."

"I need it solved like, yesterday. My phone is ringing off the hook. Management are going crazy back in LA. I've got journalists from every newspaper, magazine, and entertainment show trying to get the inside word."

"All of that for Katya?" I guessed, knowing I was correct when Joe nodded. "So far, the blackmailer doesn't know we're investigating him or her. Probably thinks he or she is in the clear."

"To try again?" he wondered.

"Potentially," I admitted, "which means they won't be scared off either. Regardless of whether the blackmail and murder are connected, the blackmailer might try and use Katya's death to his or her advantage. To threaten and extort further since the band are now scared."

"Great. Just great. I thought you might have been the bringer of good news."

"Give us time, Joe," said Solomon. "Lexi's got an idea."

"When you gave us the letters, there weren't any envelopes. Can you remember if they were hand-delivered, or if there were postmarks?"

"I can do one better. I still have them." Joe got up and moved over to the desk in front of the balcony windows, pulling open a drawer. "I was going to throw them out, but then I thought about fingerprints. I meant to put everything together in the file, but I guess I've been a little distracted." Joe turned around, a plastic folder in his hand, and walked across the room, handing it to me.

I opened it, peering inside, uncertain as to whether I should touch the envelopes or not. Like Joe said, there could be fingerprints, and Solomon had access to a lab, but prints were useless without something to compare them to. What became immediately obvious was that each name was typewritten across the middle of the envelope and there was no postmark. Someone must have hand-delivered each envelope, which meant the blackmailer had to have obtained access to every place the band stayed.

"Can you tell me where the letters were found?" I asked.

"Either in the girls' bedrooms at their hotel or in the dressing rooms at the venue."

"The crew that tours with you all have access to the venue's dressing rooms?"

"Most of them, yes."

"Do the crew also have access to the hotel rooms?"

"No. Most of the crew stay elsewhere, so only a limited number would have access to B4U's hotel."

"Who would that be?"

Joe pushed out his jaw as he thought. "Me, security, wardrobe, their vocal coach, occasionally the dancers and choreographer are here."

"Have these people been the same throughout the tour?" I asked, rapidly narrowing down my suspect pool to the lower double digits.

Joe nodded. "They're all contracted through the tour, and we haven't had any replacements."

I pointed to the notepad he'd been using as we entered. "Can you write the names of all security staff who have or could have accessed the hotel, plus, the wardrobe staff, a vocal coach, choreographer and the dance crew?" A minute later, I had a list of eight, plus the names of ten dancers. I pulled a pen from my purse and added Joe, Lauren, Shelley and Amelia. Twenty-two names and one of these names had to be our blackmailer, maybe even Katya's murderer.

"Does that help?" Joe asked.

"Yes. I'm going to start talking to all of these people. Where can I find them?"

"Everyone will be at the warehouse."

"Preparing for the concert?"

"No, they're working on the video."

"I thought it got canceled?"

Joe shrugged. "It's postponed for now, but it might still go ahead. The guys above me want it reworked as either an homage to Katya, or a relaunch for the band as a trio."

"Kind of cold," I said, wondering how many hours had passed Katya's death before the management sent down their decision.

"That's the music business, honey."

"How are the band today?" asked Solomon.

"I think it's only just sinking in that Katya's really

gone. They're pretty cut up." Joe paused as a whoop sounded from the hallway. "They express their grief in different ways," he said, picking up his cell phone as it beeped.

"We'll head over to the warehouse," said Solomon. "And I want to take all the letters and envelopes for testing."

"I need to think about that," said Joe, reaching over and tugging the folder from my fingertips before I even realized what he was doing.

"Think about it fast," Solomon warned him. "Think about whether you want the blackmailer caught, or if you want another murder on your hands."

Joe swallowed. "I get your point, but I need some damage control too. Murder is bad for business," Joe added before we left and headed for the elevator.

"You were a little hard on him back there," I said to Solomon as the elevator doors shut, and we quickly descended.

"He's delaying. He's letting us see what he wants us to see, but refusing to take it any further."

"Why would he do that? What's he hiding?"

"What? Or whom?"

I frowned. "You think he knows who's behind the blackmail?"

"It's just a hunch but I think he might suspect someone."

"Why didn't you ask him?"

"Because I didn't think he'd say. He wants to be

wrong."

"Then it must be someone close to him," I decided, shaking my head at the pointlessness of my statement. "But he's close to everyone. He's the linchpin of this tour. He knows everyone and the entire schedule, including where the band can be found at any given moment."

Solomon pulled out his phone as we exited the hotel, heading towards his car. "Delgado, we're leaving the hotel and heading to a warehouse across town. Watch Joe Carter and let me know his movements." He hung up.

"Now you're having him watched?"

"Naturally."

I climbed in and pulled the seat belt around me. "I need you to drop me off at Warehouse Twelve on Westbrook Road."

"Drop you off?"

"So I can interview everyone on this list while you do whatever you're doing with security. That was your plan for today, right?"

"Plans change. You know whose security I am today?" Solomon asked, gunning the engine. "Yours."

Warehouse Twelve was a cavernous building with a beefy security guard at the door. Evidently, Joe called ahead because our names were on the list and we were waved in. At the far end, a set had been built complete with cameras and lighting equipment situated all around it. To the left of that, the dancers were practicing a routine. To me, they looked perfect, but the choreographer didn't seem to share my opinion. He repeatedly stopped them, shouted and signaled to start again. The dancers shuffled into different positions and struck poses. The choreographer counted them in, and again, they struck different poses to the beat before bursting into an energetic routine. Twirling, changing positions, and always remaining entirely in sync with each other, it was fabulous to watch and I wished I could have seen more.

"Let's start with wardrobe," said Solomon, pointing to the racks of clothing to our immediate right. I could hear the sound of a sewing machine running as we approached. Ducking around the rack, I found a tall woman with very short, very bright, yellow hair, holding up a PVC corset and squinting at it. A few feet away, another woman was bent over the sewing machine, carefully stitching a seam in place.

"Annabelle?" I asked, checking the list.

The yellow-haired woman glanced over her shoulder. "Yes, and you are?"

"Lexi Graves with the Solomon Detective Agency. This is Solomon."

Annabelle took a long look at Solomon and an even longer look at me. I couldn't help wondering what she thought of my outfit. With my pants and blouse, I was a lot preppier than the PVC corset she held. "You're here about the blackmail plot?" she asked, surprising me.

"Yes. How did you know about it?"

"Not many secrets here, darling. Plus, I was with Shelley when she got her first one."

"So you've seen the contents?"

Annabelle nodded. "I have. I heard there were more letters."

"How did Shelley react?"

"She was angry. Really angry."

"Did you see who left the letter?"

"No, it was already waiting in Shelley's room when we got there after that night's concert."

"How come you were in Shelley's room?" asked Solomon.

"Shelley was complaining that her top for one of their numbers was rubbing uncomfortably and I needed to do a refit that night. We had to restructure it before we got on the road for the next concert."

I nodded, like I understood. "You didn't have much time?"

"Barely any. There's only my assistant, Janette, and me working on this tour, and we're often overrun with alterations, refits and new costumes to keep it fresh." The woman whom I guessed was Janette looked up as she pulled the material from her sewing machine. "Is that finished? Oh great!" said Annabelle sounding considerably more pleased.

"We won't take up too much of your time," I told her. "I can see you're busy. We just need to ask you a few more questions about the letters the band received."

"Shoot."

"Can you think of anyone on the cast or crew who might benefit from blackmailing the band?"

Annabelle frowned. "They asked for a lot of money? So... everyone?"

"What about anyone who would benefit from embarrassing the band?"

"None of us! We're all relying on the band to stay together for our jobs. I don't know about everyone else, but I get a bonus for completing the tour, although I don't know what's going to happen now. The tour might be canceled."

"You still seem busy?" I said, pointing to the large stack of alterations on the rack next to Janette and glancing towards the dancers busily rehearsing. None of them looked like they were packing to catch a flight home.

"Joe told us we had to carry on as normal until a decision was made as to the band continuing as a trio. So we're taking a break from the concert clothing and focusing on the video. Joe wants a whole new look for the band as a trio, and that means rethinking the band's apparel, as well as ten dancers' clothing. Then there's footwear and coordinating with hair and makeup. It's a big job, and as usual, we have barely any time to pull it together."

"So if the blackmailer broke up the band, no one on the crew would benefit?" I double-checked.

Annabelle gave a firm nod. "We all need B4U to stick together. Many of us turned down other jobs to go on this tour, and our new projects are only booked to start when the tour is over. Sure, I might get another gig, but it's uncertain. Plus, in our world, no one wants to be 'resting' for long."

"Can you think of anyone who is close enough to the band to know the things the blackmailer appeared to know?" I continued.

"Not me, that's for sure. I had a purely professional working relationship with them. They're a bunch of divas, you know."

"I noticed."

We shared a smile and I wondered exactly how much Annabelle witnessed during the tour. Since she seemed to have no knowledge of the blackmail, I switched tactics and asked her where she was during Katya's murder.

"Am I a suspect?" she asked, looking unhappy as her eyes flashed from me to Solomon.

"No, we just want to build a picture of everyone's whereabouts," Solomon said.

"Oh, in that case, Janette and I were at a fabric wholesaler's."

Annabelle waved Janette over. She finished the seam she'd been concentrating on and joined us, sidling up next to her boss, Annabelle. Clearly, she'd been listening to our conversation, as she said, "Joe told us the girls wanted new dresses for their closing number so we were picking up our order. I think we got coffee after. I can show you the receipts?" she volunteered. "I keep all the records of our budget for accounts."

"No need for that now, but hang onto it for when the police come by," said Solomon.

"The police are coming by?" Annabelle repeated, looking even more uncertain.

"Standard procedure," said Solomon, reminding me of when I met him, back when he worked with the FBI, but not for them. I still didn't know who was responsible for loaning him. I wasn't sure anyone did. The only thing I knew was that he was disillusioned enough to leave traditional law enforcement and set up shop for himself. "Nothing to worry about."

"You didn't see anyone else from the crew between the hours of eleven and twelve?" I asked.

Annabelle and Janette glanced at each other and shrugged. "We got back here around eleven," said Janette. "We came through security, I think, and then walked over here and started cutting. I don't remember seeing anyone else."

"I think I saw the dancers come through a few minutes after, but we're kind of hidden behind these racks. I couldn't tell you exactly who was here," added Annabelle. "Is there anything else?"

"Can you tell us anything about Katya?" I asked.

Annabelle shrugged. "All I can tell you is that she was one mean girl. She treated the rest of her band like they were her backup singers, and the crew like dirt. As for guys, she just walked all over one after another. Honestly, I don't think she cared about anyone."

We thanked the pair for their time, and I made a special effort not to grab the clothes Katya would never wear again and make a run for it. Instead, my hands safely tucked into my pockets, we walked over to the dancers who were sprawled on the floor, catching their breath.

"The choreographer is Devon Heat," I told Solomon as we approached. "I looked him up on my cell phone on the way over, and he's worked with everyone who's anyone. I don't think his name is real."

"Never heard of him."

"You would if you had a life," I told him. "You need to go out more."

"I've been thinking about cutting back my hours," Solomon replied, stopping me dead in my tracks.

"Are you ill?" I stuttered.

Solomon turned back to me. "I've been thinking about the work/life balance. I need more balance."

"Does that mean I can finally lock you in for a weekend away?" I thought about Maddox's booking for the inn at Lake Pierce. Maybe not there.

"Absolutely. Where do you want to go?"

"Somewhere romantic and cozy."

"I'll book somewhere."

"With a roaring fire and snug blankets." I frowned at him.

"No problem."

"A freestanding bath, a variety of bath oils and scented candles," I added slowly, wondering why

Solomon was being so agreeable.

"Send me a list of what you want and I'll make it happen."

"Okay then," I said, half to myself as Solomon started towards the dancers with me hurrying in his wake. If this was the kind of balance he was looking for, who was I to complain?

"Devon Heat?" Solomon called and the choreographer turned around. He was a surprisingly solid-looking man with muscular thighs straining against tight jeans and very little hair left. He had nice eyes, thick eyelashes and I was pretty sure a sweep of blusher across his cheeks. I admit it was a judgment, but I judged well: the blusher made his cheekbones pop and I was tempted to ask the brand.

"Are you a dancer?" asked Devon.

"No," said Solomon as he crossed his arms, his biceps tugging against his jacket.

Devon gave him a very long look. "Shame," he snipped, turning away.

"We need a few minutes," said Solomon.

Devon stared at him wistfully. "I would, but we have a whole new number to rehearse and my dancers are terrible. *Terrible!*" he screamed at them. "Where did we find you people? The circus? Actually, that's where I found that one!"

A few of the dancers laughed and Devon flapped a hand at them. I breathed out. Apparently, the abuse was tongue-in-cheek. "Sure, what is it, doll?" he said, but he wasn't talking to me. Solomon gave me a look that was impossible to read, but I figured it was along the lines of never calling him "doll."

Solomon introduced us and Devon brightened, apparently more interested than when he thought he could add Solomon to the troupe. "Sure, I've heard about the blackmail. Those poor, innocent, little bitches," he said and the dancers giggled while he tapped a hand over his mouth. "Oops! Did I say bitches? I meant, poor dears."

"You weren't surprised they were being blackmailed?" I asked.

"No, lovey, I was just disappointed I didn't think of it first!" More giggles.

We went through our routine: did Devon know who might benefit from blackmailing the band or breaking them up, but his answers were virtually identical to those of Annabelle and Janette. In short, they all relied on the tour to continue to make their paychecks before moving onto new projects. Finally, when it was obvious we weren't going to get any new information from Devon, I asked him where he'd been the previous morning.

"Sweetheart, a knife in the back might be poetic justice, but it wasn't me. I took this group of monkeys to run an exclusive dance workshop at The New Montgomery Dance School downtown. We have thirty witnesses. Or, at least, we would have if they acted even half awake. We were all there."

"Except Don," piped one of the dancers. "He had that leg injury."

"Right, except Don. Don, did you kill Katya?" Devon asked. I looked in the direction of Don, my eyes settling on a dark-haired man with a square jaw and a closely cut crop of dark brown hair. His zipped vest over a thin singlet revealed muscular arms and solid pecs.

"Sure, you got me," said Don, dryly. "In between getting my knee checked over at the hospital and hailing a cab to the dance school to catch the last of the workshop."

"Was anyone with you?" I asked.

"The doctor at the hospital and a nurse. Oh, and the cab driver. I got a cab receipt," he said, digging into his vest pocket and producing a small card.

"Oh, honey, how many times have I told you to change your clothes from day to day," sighed Devon.

"Dude, I did. This is a vest. It's cold in here," said Don to a chorus of agreement.

"What happened to your knee?" I asked.

"I twisted it getting out of bed so I decided to get it checked out. If I dance on an injury, I could wreck my knee and lose months of work."

"We're already surprised Don gets any work," sniffed Devon. "Yet, here he is. Fortunately, uninjured. Hip-hip-hurrah, no new dancer for me!"

"You're a mean jerk," said Don, smiling, and not nearly as cruelly as he could have said it. I got the feeling they were all used to moaning and complaining at each other, taking the insults and tossing them back as fast as they came.

"Who is still employing you," Devon pointed out as he turned back to us. "Do you need anything else? A signed confession, my phone number?" he produced a card and passed it to Solomon with a wink.

"That's all," said Solomon.

I thanked Devon for his time and we backed away with Devon shouting, "Call me!" after us.

"What do you think?" said Solomon, deadpan. "Should I call him?"

"Sure thing, doll."

Despite searching for the vocal coach, she wasn't at the warehouse, but that didn't seem unusual since the band weren't here for her to work with. That left our final port of call with the security man on the door. When we found him, he was sitting on a wooden chair, a lit cigarette in hand, and regarded us both with more suspicion than when he let us in. I wasn't surprised; he'd probably seen us interviewing others and wondered why we were approaching him now.

"Call me Dan. Yeah, I know what you're here about," he said, as I started to tell him why we wanted to talk to him.

"What's that?" asked Solomon.

"You want to know where I was when that woman from the band died," said Dan, taking another long drag and flicking the ash onto the ground. He puffed out a thick stream of smoke and Solomon narrowed his eyes at him. "I was here on shift. You can ask anyone who came in and out. Or check this." He passed us a clipboard with several sheets of names. Solomon flicked through them as I asked, "Do you recall hearing anyone threaten Katya?"

"That her name? No, not that I recall. I remember she was loud and always reamin' someone out over somethin'. She had a real nasty mouth."

"Any of that recently?"

"Pretty much everyone, every day since they got here." He barked out a sharp laugh, then coughed before placing the cigarette between his lips, talking as it waggled. "Look, I'm standin' at the door. I don't always see much."

"You'd be surprised," said Solomon, turning the pages flat again and returning the clipboard. "Did you get any unexpected visitors here? Say, from when you were hired for the job up until Katya's death?"

"I'm employed by the warehouse so I've been here for my shift since the band booked the site. I don't recall anyone gettin' in whose name wasn't on that list. We've turned away a few fans tryin' to sneak in. Nothin' unusual."

"You've never done security at the hotel? Or for the band?" I asked.

He shook his head. "Like I said, I come with this building. If you want to speak to band security, that guy on the phone over there is your man." Dan pointed to a short, balding man standing by a Porsche.

"I recognize him," said Solomon. "Thanks for your time."

"No problem, man. Hope you catch the guy that did this."

"Guy?"

"Figure of speech. It's always the wronged boyfriend, isn't it?"

Solomon shook his head. "If she had one, he would be the first person I'd ask." He nudged my arm, indicating I should follow and as we walked over to the loud, short man.

"Why didn't you ask about the blackmail?"

"No letters were reported being found here, and the guy doesn't have access to the hotel."

"Maybe he heard something?"

"It's unlikely, and I don't want him starting rumors," Solomon said as approached the Porsche. "This is Josh Alvarez. He's the head of security for the band, but I haven't had a chance to talk to him yet."

"I thought you'd gone over security with him already?"

"With his team, yes, but this guy was always absent."

"Isn't that weird?"

"I thought so. Josh Alvarez?"

Josh held up one finger and turned his head away, yelling at someone about not drinking on the job. When he finally hung up and turned around, he appeared startled to see us. "You can write to the band for signed photos," he said, attempting to step around us.

"We'd rather have a minute of your time," I said.

"I wish I had more time, cutie, but some of us big boys are busy. Try hanging around the warehouse door, and you might strike it lucky for an autograph or a selfie."

"I don't want an autograph or a selfie."

He peered at me "You want a job? Do you dance?"

"Uh..." I paused, wondering how to answer that. I thought I could dance, but I suspected wine had a lot to do with that. The real answer might have been no, but I was enthusiastic, and didn't that count for a lot?

"Will you go topless?" Josh persisted, his eyes dropping to my bust line.

"Joe Carter hired us to investigate the blackmail threat to the band," said Solomon, squaring his shoulders as he stepped in front of me, forcing Josh's eyes into staring at his chest instead. As far as sights go, I wouldn't have complained, but Solomon was more my type than his. "We're looking into Katya's murder too. Let's find some time for a few questions."

"Right, Solomon, our private dick. Ah! Sure, fire away. Joe said to answer any questions."

"Where were you at..."

"The time Katya was murdered? Here. I was going over the security schedule for the video shoot."

"Did anyone see you?"

"Sure. That guy over there on the door and

signed me in. There were a few other people in here too. Oh, and Shelley."

"Shelley was here?"

"Yeah, she left her purse or something and came to pick it up. I think that was eleven-thirty?"

"It was definitely her?"

"Yeah, it was her! I said hello and she told me to kiss her ass. I'd love to, but there're rules about that kind of thing these days. Anything else?"

"Do you know where I can find the vocal coach?" I asked.

"Home on bed rest. She got the flu three days ago so we sent her home rather than exposing her to the band and getting them sick. I gotta go. I have meetings. If you and your secretary need anything else, call me," said Josh, handing Solomon his card. He climbed into his Porsche and sped away, leaving us watching him.

I turned to Solomon, trying not to steam. "Secretary?" I asked.

"An honorable profession," said Solomon.

"Secretary!" I muttered again as we made our way to Solomon's SUV.

"Focus on what we found out, not his stupid comments."

I mentally pulled myself together. "Okay. So, Shelley left the hotel and she came here. She's definitely got an alibi."

Solomon nodded. "Shelley is not our killer."

CHAPTER NINE

The front entrance to the hotel was surrounded by journalists, photographers and fans, with people spilling all over the sidewalk onto the road as they jostled for a good view. Solomon slowed to bypass them while some turned to stare into our windows, probably hopeful of seeing a band member. I wasn't sorry to disappoint them.

"This is going to get crazy," said Solomon.

"Going to? I think it already got crazy," I said, taking a long look at the bank of video cameras. In front of one stood a superbly coiffed woman speaking into the camera and gesturing to the hotel at her back. Clearly, the news had brought the national press in. "When did they all get here?"

"Late last night after the story broke. They're either camping out, or rotating in shifts."

"Can't they just wait for a statement from B4U?"

Solomon shook his head. "That's not how the media works. They need to be on the ground and working contacts to get a story. If there's no story, they need photos to guess a story. If they're not getting a story, they're regurgitating each other's stories."

"Sounds like they'll try and get into the hotel again."

"Not going to happen." Solomon pulled into the rear service road and rolled to a stop at the security gate. A guard stepped forward and waited as Solomon produced his pass before buzzing us through a moment later.

"The gate and guard weren't there before," I said, looking back over my shoulder as the gates closed behind us.

"Installed yesterday. No journalists sneaking in the back entrance."

"And no B4U sneaking out?"

Solomon smiled. "That's an added bonus."

"What if the media get wind of the blackmail too?"

"How about they don't?" said Solomon, without any trace of amusement. "This has to be kept quiet."

"I don't know why. Maybe with all eyes on the blackmailer, they either stop, or we have a whole bunch of eyes working out who it is."

"Or we have a whole bunch of eyes digging for dirt on the remaining band members." Solomon turned the car into a parking space and cut off the engine. We didn't move from our seats, choosing instead to admire the concrete wall view.

"So it's out in the open. The blackmailer can't continue."

"Joe paid us to keep this quiet and the band don't want their secrets in the open. They just want the blackmail stopped and the culprit caught. Listen, Lexi, it doesn't matter if we agree with the client; if they pay us to do a job that we take, we complete it to their satisfaction. If this gets out, it's not just a case of the blackmailer getting caught, it could mean their careers are ruined anyway."

"So, we keep on quietly digging?"

"Exactly." Solomon climbed out, and walked around before opening my door, and offering me his hand. I took it, hopping down, only for him to catch me mid-hop and gently lower me to the ground. His hands were warm against my waist and I rested my hands on his shoulders, enjoying the moment to kiss briefly before remembering we were professionals.

"John, I have very little to go on to find this blackmailer. All I can do is knock the people off my list one by one, and that's going to take forever," I told him as we walked towards the hotel.

"Look how many suspects we've eliminated today. I still think that if we find one, we'll find the other. Let me get that," Solomon added, reaching for the door before I could grasp the handle, and opening it for me.

"Thank you. Now we can rule out Shelley, I want to talk to Lauren and Amelia again. Maybe Joe too. Until I know the identity of the woman I saw him with, and find out why he lied, we can't rule him out as Katya's murderer. He was in the right place at the right time;

plus, she's still our mystery woman. She could be connected."

"I agree."

"I love it when that happens."

We rode the elevator silently, stepping out onto the top floor opposite Large and Larger. Neither moved from their usual watchful positions in front of the elevator, but Large nodded to us. As I placed my foot on the carpeted corridor, a scream pierced the air.

Solomon and I took one look at each other and broke into a sprint towards the furthest suite. Behind us lumbered Large and Larger.

Solomon burst into the suite ahead of me, his arm protectively holding me back. Naturally, I slipped under it, expecting to see a corpse. Instead, Shelley, Amelia, Lauren and Joe all stood frozen in the room and each one of them was alive and breathing.

Lauren looked up first. Holding out an envelope, she said simply, "We got another one. Another blackmail letter."

~

Solomon and I sat with Joe in Joe's suite. It took an hour to calm down B4U with each of them unable to coordinate their hysterics with the other band members. Amelia started first, flapping her hands and shrieking that she wanted to get a new hotel, then just as she calmed down, Lauren started in, claiming someone was out to get her. Finally, just as we assured her — and probably not correctly — that no one was out to get her *right now*, Shelley screeched, "What about me?"

Finally, we took the letter and slipped out of the room, leaving Joe to orchestrate a cool down. We huddled at the end of the corridor near the housekeeping closet.

"Let's look at the good news," said Solomon. "The blackmailer still thinks there's money to be made."

"I need to show you the dictionary definition of 'good news'," I snipped, reaching for the letter.

Solomon laughed, flashing a perfect set of white teeth. "The good news," he continued, "is that the blackmailer doesn't think the murder is a reason not to pursue the primary goal: cash."

"Um... yay?"

"Also, we can rule out Katya as the blackmailer."

"She's still dead!"

"It also tells me that the murderer and the blackmailer probably aren't the same person."

"How? Murderers need money too!"

"Look at it this way... A murderer would want to lie low. He wouldn't want to attract attention that could bring the police to his door. This blackmailer isn't thinking that way. If he knows about Katya's murder, and I'll bet he does, he thinks that not only is everyone's attention diverted, but also that the band will be scared enough to pay up quicker."

I took another look at the demand for fifty thousand

dollars, a price tag that was far higher than any of the other demands. "It's a big payday."

"It's a final payday," decided Solomon.

"Yeah, looks that way," I agreed, "but what makes you think there's any 'if' about knowing about Katya's murder? Montgomery never had so much media attention. They know."

"Even better. While everyone is looking for the murderer, we can focus on smoking the blackmailer out."

"We?"

"We," Solomon said firmly.

I slid on a latex glove and reached for the envelope, turning it over. The three remaining band member's names were printed in computer type on the outside. It was also not postmarked. Whether there were any fingerprints was a matter for our lab guys. I returned the envelope to the plastic baggie Solomon produced and picked up the letter. The message got right to the point.

Shelley, Lauren, Amelia.

Remember, I know all your secrets.

None of you are safe.

Only Katya's secrets are safe.

$50,000 in 24 hours and you'll never hear from me again.

Ignore this and your secrets will be revealed.

The account details were printed below, but unfortunately for us, there was no return address or signature. Either was too much to hope for. Solomon was right though; this was a final blackmail note and our final opportunity to catch our perp.

"Doesn't the bit about Katya sound like a threat to you?" I asked.

"I think it's supposed to. Wouldn't it make you want to pay up?"

"Yep," I agreed, taking another look at the ominous print, "but I'll need a pay raise. Do B4U have fifty thousand dollars?"

"I think that's irrelevant. They've paid enough to keep their secrets safe. We've got twenty-four hours left before their secrets might be spilled to the world."

"Nothing like pressure to focus a person," I said and Solomon nodded slowly. "I asked the security guards if anyone came onto the floor in the couple of hours before the note was found and they both said no."

"I've been looking into your idea about secret passageways. They don't show up on the blueprints I was given, but I'm convinced the plans don't match up to the rooms. If someone else knew the passageways were there — and we go with the theory that someone else snuck onto the floor, unseen, to kill Katya — then the blackmailer could know about them too. That could be how they were able to place the letter in Shelley and Amelia's suite without being seen."

"That theory just makes it sound even more like the blackmailer and killer are the same person."

"Or it makes it sound like two people know about the secret passageways."

"If that's the case, who's to say there isn't someone standing in the walls, listening to everything we say right now?" Even as I said it, a cold chill ran down my spine. I wondered if that's how B4U felt with their every move being watched. It was a creepy thought, and made even creepier in that Solomon and I both froze. I, for one, was listening for anything in the walls, but all I could hear was my rapid heartbeat. "Can we find this passageway before I give myself a heart attack?" I asked, while trying not to chew my lip or throw myself into Solomon's lap.

"You got it," said Solomon in a low voice. I wondered if he wanted to throw himself in my lap. I wouldn't have said no. Well, not for a while. "Let's get the access route to the suites closed off as a matter of priority."

"If you want, we could hold hands," I suggested.

Solomon gave me a doubtful look. "Scaredy-cat."

"That's got nothing to do with it!"

"Really?"

"Hardly anything to do with it," I muttered.

"Are you sure?"

"Mmm-hmph," I whimpered as I sidled up, almost pressing myself against him. He stuffed the blackmail letter and envelope into his jacket's inside pocket. There was a lot to be said for being brave, but I preferred to be honest enough to admit the idea of someone creeping around behind the walls was pretty scary.

"Let's start in Shelley and Amelia's suite since we can be sure the blackmailer got in through the tunnel there."

"Yeah, and Shelley definitely got out of her room somehow when they locked me in."

Shelley and Amelia had already vacated the suite by the time we got there, along with Joe and Lauren. That made it a lot easier to crawl on the floors of the living room on our hands and knees looking for openings. I could just imagine their faces if they watched. As I plucked a thick shard of glass from under the credenza, I could quite easily imagine, had Katya been alive, what fragile object she would be using to throw at us at that moment. I could easily imagine her stepping over me, or even on me, to get to Solomon who currently lay prostrate, next to the wall, sectioning Shelley's room from the living room.

"I don't know why I'm lying here," he said after a long moment of me frowning at him. "I know there's no secret passageway in this wall because the doorway is too thin."

"I did wonder."

"You didn't say anything."

"I was enjoying a moment of superiority."

"Do you want to enjoy some filing later?"

"Only if that's a euphemism."

"Let's check inside the bedroom."

I winked as Solomon rose. "I knew that was a euphemism but... in someone else's bedroom?

Solomon!"

Solomon laughed. Wrapping an arm around my shoulders, he guided me into the bedroom and over to the bed, pressing lightly so I sat. "Take it easy. I'll crawl around the floor."

"Mind the..." I started, but Solomon had already tripped over a stray shoe before righting himself.

"What a dump," he said, shaking his head. "Where's housekeeping?"

I looked around the room, noting the smaller number of items draped over the furniture and strewn across the floor. All the drawers were shut and the bed was made. "I think they've made up the room already. This is clean compared to when they locked me in here."

"If I ever have a daughter, I'll make sure she knows how to tidy her room." Solomon moved over to the doorway and ran his hands gently across the wall.

"A daughter?"

Glancing towards me, he shrugged. "Or a son. I don't mind."

"So long as they're tidy?"

"Tidiness is important. Kids need boundaries and discipline."

I planted both hands on the bed as I fixed him with a confused look. "Huh."

Solomon stopped. He ran his hands down the wall towards the floor, then began to move them around, pausing as his fingertips drummed back and forth across a vertical portion of the wall. "I think I found something. A concealed doorway. This the right place for one too."

I crossed the few paces towards the wall and crouched next to him. "The pile of the carpet is ruffled here, and again here," I said, pointing to where the carpet met the baseboards.

"That's consistent with a door opening. I don't see any obvious handles. Maybe the entry mechanism is concealed." Solomon got to his feet, moving toward the lamp on the credenza. "Look for any kind of lever or..."

I leaned against the panel and pushed. The doorway slid backwards on well-oiled hinges.

"...Or feel under the furniture for a button or a trigger of some kind. Maybe there's a... oh! How did you get that open?"

"I pushed." I concealed my smug smile by biting the insides of my cheeks.

"Cool." Solomon stepped through the doorway, turning back to face me. Just as he did, the door began to close. He shifted his shoulder against it and pushed back. Seconds later, a light flickered on. "There's a light switch here," he said, "and the door is on a timer. Must be so housekeeping won't forget to close it behind them."

"So where does it go?" I asked.

"Let's find out." Solomon took my hand and led us forwards as the overhead lights flickered on ahead of us. Behind me, the door closed.

"There's a little hole in the door," I said, stopping to

peer at it. "Like a spy hole."

"Must be so housekeeping can check the room is empty before they enter."

"Or so they can spy and hear secrets," I countered.

"If all the blackmail notes arrived here, I would agree with that theory and start looking at hotel employees, but the blackmail started way before the band got here. Look, here's another spy hole. I'm guessing, but I think this is Katya's room. Put your gloves back on." Solomon pulled on a pair of latex gloves before pushing on the door, which slid backwards. We stepped into the room and Solomon pressed something on the electronic panel inside the passage. "There's an option to keep the door open until it's manually canceled," he explained. "I've seen this model before."

I walked around the room, being extra careful not to touch anything. As far as I knew, it was still a crime scene, and having never had any cause to be in Katya's bedroom, I didn't want to add the notion that I was in it. I figured that was why Solomon prepared us with latex gloves. "This is Katya's room. These framed photos are hers and I recognize that leather jacket. And those heels. They aren't even in stores yet."

"How'd Katya get them?"

"Could only have been a gift from the designer."

"Why would they do that?"

"B4U are huge. If they're seen wearing something new, it sells out in hours."

Solomon frowned. "Really?"

"That's celebrity. If B4U wears it, their fans want it. Katya might even have been paid to wear the brand in an endorsement deal."

"How much is that worth?"

"The sky's the limit."

"We're in the wrong business."

"You want to be paid to wear a high heels? There are definitely people who will pay for that," I said, barely holding back my laughter.

"I like those cute ballet pumps you wear sometimes."

"They don't come in your size."

"Would you like another pair? In another color?"

"Yes, in all the colors."

"Show me the ones you want and I'll get them for you. They look comfortable and easy to balance in."

"Said no women ever when picking shoes." I reached for the door handle and pulled the door open only to find myself at eye level with a gun barrel. I slammed the door shut. "Solomon! Gun!"

The door was flung open and the gun poked through. Solomon grabbed his gun and aimed. "Put down your weapon!" he yelled.

"Put your weapon down!" yelled the other man.

"Maddox?" I yelled over them.

"Lexi?" Maddox sighed. "Solomon?" He holstered his weapon and rolled his head back. "I could have shot you."

"Unlikely," said Solomon, lowering his own gun.

"I feel left out. Should I point at something when I stop hyperventilating? Maybe my finger while I shout at you?" I asked Maddox.

He looked chagrined. "Sorry."

"What are you doing here anyway?"

"I just got here and was looking over the crime scene when I heard someone moving around in Katya's room. Since I just left her room, I knew no one was in there. You two spooked me! How did you get in there anyway?"

"Secret tunnel," said Solomon casually, like he used one every day.

"You'd better show me."

Solomon inclined his head as he turned away. "This way."

We trooped after Solomon, the three of us entering the tunnel. "That way is Amelia and Shelley's suite, where we entered," Solomon said, pointing back the way we came.

"What about this way?" asked Maddox.

"We haven't gone that far yet."

"Let's go."

The passageway continued for several meters before we stopped. "Here's another exit," said Solomon, his voice soft. "I can see Joe Carter in his suite and the band."

"Keep going," replied Maddox equally softly.

We continued silently, reaching a dead end. "Let's go

all the way back," Solomon said.

Without space to pass each other, we turned around. Now that I was in front, I could see the long tunnel stretching ahead of me. The lights flickered out and my heart pumped faster until I was sure it must have been audible to the two large men behind me. The lights popped back on, revealing no assailants, which was fortunate since I was the only one without a gun. I decided I'd just duck if it came to a shooting match.

"Sorry about the lights. They must be on timer or some kind of sensor too," said Solomon. "Lexi, go all the way to the end, past Katya's suite."

We retraced our steps along the length of the passageway, counting the exits to Joe's suite, Katya's room, past Shelley's, and finally exiting into the housekeeping closet. "This tunnel could conceal anyone who wants to move around this floor unseen," I said.

"And all they have to do is get into that elevator and leave," said Maddox. "Why did no one tell me about this? I spoke to the hotel manager and the security team."

"We only just found out," I told him, deciding to skip over the moment my suspicions started. "I suspected there was a secret door somewhere, but not as extensive as this. That could explain how Katya was killed and no one saw a thing after Lauren left the room."

"It also doesn't rule out any member of the band, or their manager as the blackmailer. Or anyone who could have found out about the passage," said Solomon as he pulled out his cell phone and hit a button. "Delgado, get someone up to the band's floor. I need a guy to monitor a secret door. Yeah, a secret door. Now."

"I'm going to fingerprint," said Maddox, grabbing a kit from his pocket.

"You just happen to keep that on you?" I asked.

"I have all kinds of emergency stuff in my pockets. Penknife, string, notepad and pencil, gum..."

"You're a regular Boy Scout."

"What do you have in your pocket?" he asked.

"A manicure loyalty card."

"Solomon?" Maddox asked.

"Yeah?"

"What do you have in your pocket?"

"Seriously?" Solomon faced Maddox, his face impassive. That, I knew by now, was his version of stony.

"Seriously."

"Get fingerprinting."

Maddox gave me a little eye roll and stepped back into the passageway, reaching for the lights. A moment later, the door slid shut behind him. I ran my hand around the doorway, impressed at how well concealed it was. I couldn't even see the lights that I knew must be on the other side.

"We should get the band's fingerprints for comparison with anything Maddox finds," I said. "Perhaps you could ask him when you're feeling politer?"

"What's that supposed to mean?"

"The way you just spoke to him!"

"How?"

"He was just making a joke, and you cut him down."

"We're here to solve a blackmailer running into tens of thousands of dollars that ended in a murder."

"That's not Maddox's fault, so there's no need to be an ass."

Solomon raised his eyebrows. "Did you call me an ass?"

"I'm going to step outside for some fresh air," I decided. I knew how easily this could become an argument and I didn't want to participate, so instead I turned towards the hallway, walking right into Amelia as I stepped out of the small room.

"What are you doing in here?" she asked. "Isn't that the housekeeping closet?"

"Following a lead," I told her. "But I'm glad I ran into you. We need to take your fingerprints."

"What for?"

"We're checking the fingerprints in the rooms and on the envelopes and letters," I lied, "and we need to take yours for comparison."

"The police already took them when they found Katya."

"We need some too."

"Well, sure. No problem," Amelia agreed. "Anything I can do to help, but I guess my fingerprints are on everything. I think I touched all the letters."

"There's a kit in the car," Solomon said, stepping behind me. "I'll get them."

"No, it's okay. I was stepping outside anyway. I'll get it and be right back," I told him, stepping around Amelia and heading for the elevator before Solomon could stop me. I needed the fresh air, but I needed the space more. It wasn't just Solomon's rudeness to Maddox that puzzled me; it was his recent behavior towards me. He'd been remarkably attentive and more than a little pissed when guys spoke to me. I understood that. Josh Alvarez objectified me, while Maddox was my ex. Although I thought Solomon's concern about me was sweet, some of his comments confused me. As I stepped out of the elevator, I figured Solomon must be on some weird kind of health kick that he wanted me to participate in. Perhaps it was affecting his mood.

I passed a couple of hotel employees on my way to the parking lot, smiling as one face looked familiar. The maid nodded and looked away quickly, rushing forwards as my step faltered.

"Hey!" I turned, calling. "I know you! You're not a maid!"

The fake maid broke into a faster walk and I doubled my speed until I could grab her by the arm.

"Excuse me!" she squawked, pulling her arm back. "Get off me! I have rooms to make up."

"You're Shayne Winter. The journalist."

"I'm not. I'm..." She peered down at the nametag

sewn onto her uniform.

"You are not Juanita," I told her.

"Damn it," Shayne sighed. "It nearly worked. I know who you are too. You're Lexi Graves. Here's the deal. Tell me what you know and I'll print your comments as an anonymous source for my paper."

"I'm not telling you anything!"

"Why not? I put you on the front cover of the *Montgomery Gazette*. I made you famous."

"The *Gazette* does not make you famous."

"Semi famous. In Montgomery."

"I don't want to be famous anywhere. And I'm not letting you break into B4U's floor."

"You don't have to let me. Be my inside source instead." Shayne pulled a small recording device from a pocket and shoved it under my chin. "What are the band doing right now? Are they devastated? Are they planning Katya's funeral? What are they wearing? What was Katya wearing when she died?"

"I'm calling security."

"Just a few words. Who cried the most? Are they going to regroup as a trio? Have the police nailed a suspect yet?"

"Um, let me see..." I waited as Shayne's eyes widened in anticipation. "Oh yeah, not telling," I teased.

"How about I tell you something and you tell me something," Shayne said, playing her trump card.

"What do you know?" I asked.

"Something juicy. What's it worth?"

"Tell me first."

We played standoff for a few minutes, staring at each other, then blinking when it got too hard not to. Shayne gave up first. "Fine. Amelia got married last year and you'll never guess who her husband is. I'm breaking the story in tomorrow's edition."

My mouth dropped open. "Who?"

"Your turn."

"I can't tell you anything."

"Then I'm not telling you who her husband is."

"You've told me enough." I raised a hand to Delgado as he stepped through the glass doors, flanked by two security guards. "Security! Get this journalist out of the hotel and don't let her in again."

"Hey!" Shayne yelled, breaking into a run. The two security guards followed after her.

"How did she get in?" Delgado asked, joining me to watch as Shayne and the guards sprinted along the corridor before veering to the left and out of view.

I handed him the car keys. "No idea. Can you grab the fingerprint kit from the trunk of Solomon's car? Shayne Winter just gave me a huge tip."

"I don't think she gets how to be a maid at all. She's supposed to take the tips," said Delgado and laughed.

"Not one bit," I agreed, hitting speed dial on my cell phone. Lucas picked up on the last ring before it clicked through to voicemail.

"Got something for me?" he asked.

"I do. And it really is an 'I do.' I need you to find out who Amelia Toren married last year."

CHAPTER TEN

"They're really going to shoot the video?" I asked.

Solomon nodded. "Joe called and told me that the decision was already made. B4U are going ahead as a trio."

"Doesn't the four in their name make that odd?" *B3U*, I decided, *made no sense whatsoever.* B4U, however, was catchy, but a B4U with only three members also made no sense. I wondered what the rationale was behind the decision and how far up the list the factor of money was positioned.

He shrugged. "Guess it doesn't matter if they're doing that cute text-speak thing."

I thought back to all of Solomon's perfectly spelled and punctuated texts. "You think that's cute?"

"In an annoying sense."

We were sitting in Solomon's office, two cups of hot take-out coffee on the desk between us. My feet were resting on the desk, which wasn't especially ladylike, but it did enable me to admire my new sneakers. Paired with my ankle-skimming jeans, they looked particularly cute, in the best possible sense of the word. Solomon hadn't commented on them, but that didn't surprise me, although I knew he noticed everything. That he didn't tell me take my feet off his desk was another matter. He was distracted and it showed.

"What's going on?" I asked.

"Blackmail. Murder. Security breaches. Secret tunnels. Media everywhere. This case is a nightmare." Solomon sighed as he reached for his coffee, taking a long swallow.

"I already told you they were pains in the butt."

"I've heard you mention it a few times."

"I am surprised they're continuing as a trio, especially after they got the latest blackmail letter."

"Yeah about that," Solomon started, then stopped.

"What?"

"I have security all over the building. Although we didn't know about the passage previously, I had a guy stationed outside the service elevator downstairs. No one could have gotten into the suite. It's just not possible."

"Maybe there was a breach. Maybe one of the hotel staff was bribed."

"I checked. Not even housekeeping was on the floor when that letter arrived."

"So... who was?"

"Just the band and Joe, and those two goofs that sit by the elevator. My guys were posted on each elevator downstairs and they confirmed no one went up or down."

"Someone could have come through the tunnel much earlier. We didn't know when the letter arrived," I pointed out, feeling smart. I would have felt a lot smarter if I hadn't just widened the suspect pool again. "Maybe Maddox will get something off the fingerprints. If the blackmailer entered the suite that way, he or she might not have thought to wear gloves."

Solomon reached for the phone, punching the buttons before putting the receiver to his ear. "It's Solomon," he said, "How's it going with the fingerprints from the secret passageway?"

"Maddox?" I mouthed and Solomon gave a brief nod. I sank back in my chair and waited, listening to one half of the conversation.

"You found something? Good. Any matches in the system? Huh. Can you tell me where the prints were found? Okay. The blackmail letter? Yeah, I've got my guys checking it. I'll send you copies. No problem." Solomon hung up.

"And?" I prompted.

"Yes, to the fingerprints. Several sets that matched were found by the elevator, the doorways and the control panels. Maddox says the hotel has fingerprints of the staff on file and he's identified more than a dozen prints as those of the housekeeping staff. When they went through the system, however, they came up clean. There're a couple sets that haven't been identified yet;

and he found one unknown that matches the prints from the elevator and outside Katya's suite. Definitely not a hotel employee, so he's still digging."

"And you're sending him the blackmail letters?" I asked, wondering if Maddox hadn't yet received the copies I emailed as my share of our deal.

"Copies," corrected Solomon. "I've had them analyzed at the lab, but I doubt there will be anything to work with in fingerprints or DNA once I compare the prints to samples from the band. The blackmailer was careful. Mass marketed paper, the printer is generic, the envelope wasn't even licked, and there's no indication any of it was actually touched, so the perp thought ahead enough to wear a pair of gloves."

"Dead ends." I tried not to reveal my dejection with my voice as Solomon listed all the problems I'd already encountered.

"Dead ends," Solomon agreed.

"At least, you're playing nice with the FBI," I said as the image of the hotel reservations popped into my head again. I didn't ask Maddox and he didn't say, but I still wondered.

"It always pays to play nice with the FBI."

"We need Lucas to get us that bank account information." Just as I said it, the desk phone rang. Solomon grabbed it. I heard Lucas's muffled voice, then Solomon hit the speaker button.

"I got something," said Lucas, sounding excited. "And you're going to love me forever."

Solomon raised his eyebrows.

"Fine, you'll probably pay my salary a while longer," said Lucas as if he could see Solomon's facial movements.

"Get to it," said Solomon.

"First thing, I found out who owns the blackmailer's bank account."

Solomon and I both sat bolt upright.

"Who?" I asked.

"Just a sec," said Lucas. "There're two things. You wanted to know who Amelia Toren married?"

"Yes. Did you find out?"

"I'm emailing the certificate to your phones now."

Solomon and I both grabbed our phones. I gasped as the email attachment downloaded.

"Are you kidding me?" I asked.

"Am I a kidding man?" Lucas replied. "Now back to that bank account... I've got a name and photos of the account being opened in person. You won't believe who it's registered to."

~

Solomon and I were speeding towards the hotel. If I could have gotten us on a spaceship to get us there faster, I would have. With the two new pieces of information, that Lucas verified beyond any doubt, we needed to talk to the band.

"Why haven't transporters been invented yet?" I

asked.

Solomon glanced towards me. "What?"

"You know. Like *Star Trek*."

"*Star Trek*?"

"If we could get a beam-me-up thingy, life would be so much easier."

"Life is about to get much easier."

"Does this mean I'm going to get my bonus?" I asked, thinking about the bonus Solomon mentioned when he handed me the case. I could do a lot with the bonus. I could get a patio built in my backyard. Or go on a girls' weekend trip with Lily. I could buy some gorgeous shoes. With what B4U were paying, I could do all three and still have some money left in the bank. Even better, it would be great compensation for dealing with a few of the most obnoxious women I ever encountered.

"Looks that way," said Solomon, which sounded a lot like a yes to me.

We left the car in the employee parking lot and moved seamlessly past the security guards posted at intervals all along the way. At the elevator, we rode the car to the top floor. Solomon called ahead to see if Joe were in the building so he could ask him for the band's schedule that day, but he didn't tell him why, or even that we were visiting. Luckily for us, the band weren't scheduled to start shooting the video until later, so they were currently in their suites, apparently, lying low. The paparazzi swarmed around them every time the hotel doors opened. That was good news for us, because we needed to confront Amelia about her secret wedding.

Even more pressing, we could tell all of them who the blackmailer was.

"I don't get how she thought it could be kept secret for so long," I mused as we ascended. "It didn't take us long to get a hold of that certificate. Journalists would have found it too. Actually, one did."

"What are you talking about?"

"Um, so, I got the tip off about Amelia's marriage from a journalist."

"You didn't think to mention that before?"

"It didn't occur to me, but I just remembered she's going to break the story in tomorrow's edition."

"Oh, jeez!" Solomon rested a palm against his forehead. "Tomorrow's edition of what?"

"I didn't find out."

"Why not?"

"Because she ran from security, and by the time I knew they caught her, they'd already ejected her from the building."

"Who is the journalist?"

"Shayne Winter."

"Why does that name sound familiar?"

I thought back, one more mortifying time, to the humiliating story Shayne once printed. It ran with a huge photo of Lily and me dressed as a plush pony while working a case. I decided to feign ignorance rather than relive it. "No idea!"

Solomon took his cell phone out of his pocket in a flash. "Delgado. Find a journalist named Shayne Winter and squash her story about B4U. Yes, now!" He hung up and turned back to me. "Anything else you've forgotten to tell me?"

I pursed my lips, thinking. There was that awful, horrific moment in the strip club with the band singing and gyrating half-naked around stripper poles, but I not only handled it, I even buried it. "Nope," I lied.

"Good. They're paying us to keep everything discreet. We can't afford any leaks."

"I thought no news was bad news, and everything else was good news?"

"Not to this band. Their image is everything right now."

The elevator doors slid back and Large and Larger nodded to us as we stepped out.

"Do you two ever sleep?" I asked.

"Hmmph," said Large. Larger shook his head.

"Okay, then," I mumbled, wondering why I ever bothered speaking to the two men. I presumed they were employed primarily for their bulk, and not for their scintillating conversation.

"Where's Joe?" asked Solomon.

Large inclined his head towards Amelia's suite.

"Good to talk," I said with a wave as we stepped past them. Larger waved back and smiled.

Joe was sitting in his suite with the band, and for once, not one of them was screaming. Amelia was playing with her phone. Shelley was flipping through a magazine, and Lauren was doodling on a notepad. It was such a serene scene that I couldn't help glancing at Solomon to see if he were as suspicious as I. By the look on his face, he was.

"Solomon, Lexi." Joe stood, reaching a hand out. "I didn't know you were coming by."

"Last minute decision," said Solomon. "Have we interrupted something?"

"Nothing. The band and I are just hanging out after our conference call with management back home. I told you we're continuing with the video shoot? The girls are psyched."

The "girls" did not seem psyched at all. Shelley gave a small snort at Joe's words, Lauren ignored us entirely, and Amelia's brief glance told me she was pissed.

"Is there something I can help you with?" continued Joe. "Do you have a lead on the blackmail letter? We haven't paid... yet."

"We do have some news," I said, taking the lead and trying not to enjoy the moment. "We'd advise you not to pay."

"But they'll reveal our secrets!" said Amelia. "We have no choice."

"Actually, you do have a choice. Amelia, your secret is going to break in a high circulation newspaper tomorrow. We expect it'll be picked up nationwide." I didn't know that for sure, but it was an educated guess. Any scandal pertaining to B4U would be big news.

"Oh my God," Amelia groaned. "How did they find out?"

"I have no idea, but it wasn't hard for us to verify."

"They found out my real age," Amelia moaned. "The whole country will know I'm nearly thirty, and not a teen sensation! I'll be fired for sure now!"

"I think your age will probably be mentioned, but that's not your secret, Amelia." I pulled out my phone, bringing up the photo of the marriage certificate Lucas emailed. I stepped across to her, holding the phone out. She took it, frowning, and gasped, her mouth falling open. "You bitch! How did you find out? And who did you tell?"

"It doesn't really matter," I told her, pulling back my phone before she hurled it at me or the wall. "What matters is that everyone is going to know you and Joe got married last year."

"Joe who?" asked Shelley, jerking her head up and looking from me to Amelia, to Joe. "That Joe? Our Joe? You married Joe! Holy shizzle!"

"I'm screwed," said Joe, his head falling back.

"You're screwed? C'mon, Joe! I'm going to go from being the teen sensation everyone loves to an old married woman. My life is over!" Amelia wailed as she slapped the back of her hand against her forehead and sank against the pillows. "I'll be fired. We'll have to disband now for sure!"

"You married Joe?" Lauren gaped. "It was bad enough trying to airbrush your wrinkles from every magazine shoot, but now you've got a wedding ring too?"

"Shut up, you stupid cow. Your secret is way worse than mine!" screamed Amelia.

"Screw you!" Lauren yelled back.

"This is great!" Shelley clapped her hands. "I always thought Joe was gay!"

"He's not gay! He's my husband!" screamed Amelia.

Shelley sniffed, mumbling, "Doesn't prove anything. Might still be gay."

"Take. It. Back!"

"Without your wig, you kind of look like a boy," Shelley continued, apparently oblivious to Amelia's reddening face.

"Don't talk to my wife like that," said Joe, his loud voice cutting through the air.

"You didn't ask us to be bridesmaids?" said Lauren. "Amelia Toren, you're one mean bitch."

"It's Amelia Toren-Carter," replied Amelia.

"Where'd you get married? Vegas?" asked Shelley.

"Actually, yes," said Joe. He was rewarded with a screech of laughter from Shelley. She shut up when a candlestick hit her in the head. Leaping to her feet, she clenched her fists, her face filled with fury.

"Settle down," said Solomon, jumping between them. "The marriage thing isn't a big deal."

"Actually, it is," yelled Lauren. "We could lose our jobs! Katya's dead. This bitch married our manager. The band is done. Thanks, Amelia! Some of us needed the income, you know."

"I know why you need it," said Amelia. "I know all about your dirty, little secret!"

"You shut up!"

"No, you shut up!"

Lauren and Amelia faced each other angrily and I waited, frozen, wondering if I should jump in and add another body between the three remaining band members. Then I remembered I had bigger news. News that could make me the next target for a candle or vase, or whatever else lay within reach.

"Actually, we told you about the news of your marriage breaking as a courtesy," I informed the quiet, tense room. "We're trying to prevent it from getting out, but it's unlikely we'll succeed. As far as secrets go, I don't see it as one that's too damaging. With good PR, you could spin it easily."

"Great. Just great." Amelia crossed over to Joe and flopped next to him on the couch. He took her hand, raising it to his lips.

"I don't care, honey. I'm with you all the way."

"I love you, kissyface," said Amelia, puckering her lips before they kissed.

"I'm not convinced," said Shelley. "I still think he's gay."

Joe turned to her. "I'm not gay. Your gaydar is off."

"My gaydar is definitely on," said Shelley, "I told you that already. I'm not proud of hiding my past. It's just that no one needs to know about it."

"Lexi's right; we could stay together," said Lauren. "This might not be over yet. That will teach the blackmailer they can't mess with us!"

"You can do some damage control," Solomon agreed. "But our other news is not as easy to fix, and it might bust up the band."

"You discovered Lauren's secret too?" Amelia said. "Finally! There's no way to spin that story."

"Actually, no. We discovered your *other* secret."

Shelly's jaw dropped and her eyes widened. "Amelia has another secret! You sneaky bitch! I thought you were so freaking boring!"

"I don't have any other secrets," said Amelia, frowning. "What are you talking about?"

"This." I reached into my purse and pulled out the photo I had Lucas print before we left the agency. It was an eight-by-ten and Amelia's face was clearly turned to the security camera. Sure, the print was a little grainy, but it was definitely she.

"What is this?"

"This is a photo taken in the Cayman Islands when you opened a bank account."

"I never opened a bank account in the Caymans."

"Yes, you did," said Solomon, taking over. "This was taken eight months ago at the bank, and we also have flight records of you taking a plane out there and flying back the next day."

"You went to the Caymans without telling me?" Joe asked.

"No, they're talking crap," said Amelia, looking at us, a direct challenge in her eyes.

"Here're the flight manifests," replied Solomon, passing the printed sheets to Joe. He took them, and briefly perused them before looking up in confusion.

"So she spent a couple of days in the Caymans? So what?"

"Well, she opened an account while she was there and we've matched the account to the same one the blackmailer is using for the cash deposits demanded from the band."

"They're using Amelia's account to steal her money and the band's?" Joe asked, the strain on his face showing more than hope.

"No," I said slowly.

"What exactly are you saying then?" he asked, looking from me to Amelia.

"Don't do this," said Amelia, "Please, Lexi? Solomon?"

Joe sat forward, twisting towards his wife. "Honey, what's going on?"

"Oh, man, you're so dumb. I worked it out already," said Shelley. "Lexi, tell them."

"Oh!" said Lauren, her mouth dropping open in surprise as she stared at Amelia. "No way!"

"No," Amelia pleaded. "Please..."

"Amelia, you're the blackmailer," I confirmed.

"Amelia?" Joe's face screwed up as he gaped at her. "They've got this wrong. No, you've got this wrong.

Amelia's been set up. This must be... it's got to be some kind of mistake. Right, honey? I thought it could be but no... not you." Amelia remained silent. "Honey?"

"They're right," Amelia said softly. "I'm the blackmailer."

Solomon stepped forward and caught the candlestick that flew from Shelley's hand towards Amelia. Without a word, he placed it on the credenza. "Tell us everything," he said, "and we might be able to help you."

Amelia took a deep breath, and just when I thought she would clam up, the whole story emerged from her lips. "I hate being in the band. It was fun the first couple of years. We made a lot of money and the parties were great, and all the stuff people gave us. All that cool designer stuff and the fans everywhere..."

"It was just awful," said Lauren sarcastically.

"Shut up!" said Amelia.

"Yeah, let the bitch talk," said Shelley. "I'm gripped. Now, spill."

"I would if you'd just..."

Solomon cut in. "Quiet!" he yelled. "Amelia, keep talking. Everyone else, don't say a word!"

"I wanted to do other things. Write and perform new material, but management wouldn't let me. Everything had to fit the image they wanted for B4U and they said my lyrics wouldn't be used unless they were all cute and poppy. They stifled me creatively. I have all these amazing songs, and I can't even release them for free without getting my ass sued." She topped, breathing heavily. "And then they hired Joe and we got closer and closer..."

"She was so wonderful," said Joe. "But I couldn't get involved with her without losing my job. We tried to resist it, but I loved her so much."

Amelia clasped Joe's hand between hers. "My contract is virtually unbreakable unless I got fired and they would never do that. I write most of our material. Without me..."

"You're totally replaceable," said Shelley. "You think you're the only one who can write? Get over yourself!"

"Zip it!" Solomon waved Amelia to continue.

"Joe and I fell in love. Then last year, I got sick. I told management and they gave us all a few months' vacation..."

"And you told everyone that you were holed up, writing material for the new album," I said, vaguely remembering a report last year in an entertainment magazine.

"Yeah, except I was really having chemo. I had early stage leukemia. I was really lucky. One bout of chemo and I went into remission, but if finding Joe wasn't a huge wake-up call, this was! I overcame an early death, but I couldn't get out of this damn band. We started talking about getting married and having kids before it was too late, but I knew management would never let it happen. They want all of us to date boy bands, not our managers, or in Shelley's case, other chicks."

"So you decided to get out?" I guessed.

Amelia looked up and nodded. "Yeah. There was no clause for me to get out, but management had a whole bunch that allowed them to get rid of any one of us at their discretion. It was so unfair! We're just cash cows to them! They don't care about us! I knew if the band had huge issues, they would fire me at least. If I got released from my contract, I could get my life back."

"So you found out everyone's secrets and began to blackmail them, hoping the friction would be enough to destroy the band?"

"Yeah, or releasing our secrets."

"Why didn't you come to me?" asked Joe softly. "I could have helped you."

"No, you couldn't. We talked and talked about it. We went over every contract and there was no way out, except for me to get fired!"

"What about us?" asked Lauren, looking appalled. "Why didn't you tell us?"

"I don't know!"

"You stole our money and now we're all going to get fired," said Shelley. She reached for the open bottle of wine on the coffee table and poured a large glass, knocking it back almost as quickly.

"I didn't spend a cent, I swear. I'll get it back to you."

"You better!" said Lauren. "You have no idea what you've done."

"You'll get every penny! I'm so sorry, I..."

"Save it," Lauren snapped. "I don't want to hear how awful your life is. I'm sorry you got cancer, but you treated us all like shit. You knew our secrets and you used them against us while intending to ruin our lives. Don't protest! That's what it comes down to, isn't it, Amelia? You weren't just going to ruin your career, you intended to ruin ours too."

"Looks like she succeeded," added Shelley, raising her second glass. "Cheers, Amelia. I officially hate you more than I hate Katya now."

"Which brings us to the next thing," said Solomon. "We've been looking for a connection between the blackmail and Katya's murder..."

"Whoa, guys! Wait! Nuh-uh! I had nothing to do with Katya's murder!" Amelia wailed as Joe looked at her, shocked.

"Can you prove where you were at the time of Katya's murder? So far, we have no alibi for you," I told her.

Joe's shoulders dropped, relaxed. "Actually, that's not a problem. I can give her an alibi."

"We know where you were," I told him. "I saw you and I know you've been lying to us and the police."

"Yeah, I know, but I couldn't tell you who I was with. You accused me of kissing a girl and I had to make up a bullshit story about being in another place."

"Yeah, we knew that was a lie," said Solomon.

"You should have taken lessons from Amelia. She's

an awesome liar," said Lauren. "So who are you boning behind your wife's back?"

"It's not like that, Lauren. I made up my alibi because I couldn't tell you I was with Amelia. Like she said, I could be fired for having a relationship with her."

"You're married," I pointed out. "Plus, I saw you with a short-haired woman and Amelia was spotted downstairs prior to the murder."

"Oh hell," said Amelia, running a hand through her hair. In one swift tug, she pulled it off, revealing a cool, pixie crop. "My hair fell out and I've been wearing a wig while it grows back. I don't always wear it when I think no one's around. And yeah, I was downstairs but only for a few minutes. Joe and I steal any opportunity we can to be together."

"It suits you. It's the new you," said Joe, stroking his wife's hair, and they kissed.

"This just keeps getting better," said Shelley. "I knew it was a wig! Didn't I say that, Lauren? I said she wore a wig! I'm waiting for the moment you reveal your Adam's apple."

Amelia breathed hard through her nose. "For the last time, I'm not a..."

"Okay, move on. Lexi, does this look like the woman you saw?" Solomon asked.

I nodded as I assessed Amelia's surprising, new look. It suited Amelia far more than her long hairstyle did. In fact, the pixie crop accentuated her great cheekbones and widened her eyes. Even better for her and Joe, she was definitely the woman I saw him with. "Yeah."

"So you two have a solid alibi, thanks to Lexi," Solomon told them.

"But we're still going to get exposed in the press tomorrow," said Amelia. "At least, this is almost over."

"Think of it this way," I told her. "You're getting exactly you wanted. You're out of the band; and as for the rest of you, the blackmail letters stop and Amelia will return all the money she took."

"I am sorry," she said, looking at Shelley, then Lauren. "I hate the band, but I don't hate you two. I made a huge mistake in the blackmail and I'll make sure you get paid back. Within the hour, I promise. Maybe the band can go on with just you two?"

"B2U sounds stupid," said Shelley. "We're screwed. At least, I have an alibi. Did that asshole, Josh Alvarez, tell you he saw me at the warehouse? I forgot I left the hotel and got the car service. Like, a thousand people saw me. So we all have alibis except... oh!"

We all turned to look at Lauren.

"Oh shit," she whispered.

CHAPTER ELEVEN

"This is like a soap opera in our backyard!" Lily spooned another glob of ice cream into her mouth and stared, riveted, at the TV screen. We were watching the *E! News* anchors discussing Amelia and Joe's secret wedding. The segment began five minutes ago and already, we'd seen a montage of photographs starting from Amelia's first break, when she played a high schooler in the B4U TV series, to leaked photos from their quiet Vegas wedding.

"The dress is pretty," I said, as another shot of the happy couple flashed onto the screen.

"It's amazing how undiscovered photographs always seem to turn up for a story. How do they do that?"

"I think it begins with an 'm' and ends in a 'y'."

Lily screwed up her forehead. "Marry?"

"No! Money!"

"Oooh! Well, duh, sure. But you're right. The dress is lovely. How'd she get that on the quiet? That looks high-end."

"I have no idea."

"I thought you asked all the critical questions. What happened to, 'Who designed your dress?' or 'What kind of frosting did you get for the cake?'"

"Those things slipped my mind," I told her. I was remembering how the focus switched so swiftly from Amelia's confession and reasoning for the blackmail plot to the knowledge that Lauren was now the only band member who had no alibi for Katya's murder.

"Is that... Ohmygosh! It is! It's Shayne Winter from the *Gazette*. Look! Isn't that the band's hotel?"

We watched as the screen split from the studio to a location in Montgomery. Shayne was dressed up since the last time I saw her in the unshapely maid's uniform. Wearing a form-fitted, belted jacket and perfectly styled hair, she beamed at the camera. Lily grabbed the remote and turned up the volume before reaching for another cookie, which she mashed into her ice cream.

"Yes, hi everyone, we're here live in Montgomery where I first revealed the fascinating secret Amelia Toren has managed to conceal for the past year. B4U's biggest star married their manager last year in a super secret, and very chic ceremony in Vegas, away from the prying eyes of the paparazzi that follow B4U's every movement."

"Can you tell us if any members in the band were in attendance?" asked the anchor.

"I can confirm that they probably were not. In fact, we're not even sure they knew about the whirlwind romance and ensuing secret nuptials. It looks like Amelia and Joe had them all fooled!"

"Do you think our secret couple were involved with Katya's murder?" the anchor continued.

"I totally asked you that already!" yelled Lily. "Everyone wants to know the answer to that!"

Shayne ran a hand through her hair as the breeze caught it, whipping it slightly around her face. "I can't tell you that, but I can tell you this band had more than one huge secret they kept from each other, which are only starting to unfold now."

"What does she mean by that? What secrets?" asked Lily, turning to me.

"I want to know what she means by 'unfolding'," I said, wondering if I should have been more worried. The band had plenty of big secrets; and it was only a matter of time before the press dug deeper into their background. Stories about Katya's tragic life had already begun to appear. They ran a shot of Katya across the screen before flashing back to Shayne.

"What kind of secrets?" the anchor asked.

"I can only confirm that there is another secret Amelia has been keeping from the world," said Shayne, sounding ridiculously perky and obviously enjoying her brief moment in the spotlight.

"What's that, Shayne?" asked the anchor.

"Not only is Amelia married, but she's also several years older than was previously reported. That means Amelia was never a teen queen; and already in her early twenties when B4U's first TV series aired!"

"Thank you, Shayne, for joining us from Montgomery." The anchor turned her slender frame to the camera as the screen filled with the studio shot. "That was Shayne Winter, reporting on the dramatic turn of events in Montgomery where B4U are taking a mid-tour break in order to film their latest video. Of course, that video project is now, most likely, being shelved, due to the horrific murder of their beloved band mate, Katya Markova. So far, no arrests have been made, but we were informed there are private investigators on the scene, along with local police and the FBI! We'll return with more breaking news on the case. And now onto..."

I reached for the remote and switched off the TV. "I thought the media circus was already in town, but this was so much worse. They practically threw honey to all the buzzing reporters with the lure of hidden secrets."

"Yeah. Sucks to be you."

"I'm starting surveillance on Lauren tomorrow."

"Why? More importantly, can I come? Not too early though. Maybe starting at midday or something?"

I thought about it. Lily and I hadn't spent a lot of time together lately, and I missed her. It surprised me when she took no convincing to come over for the evening, but that could have been because I was lucky and she just finished work. I grabbed the bottle of wine from the table and offered her a glass, saying, "Actually, yeah, that would be great. Watching Lauren will be easier with two of us."

Lily waved away the wine. "No, thanks, I'm driving. I've been reading up on B4U. Did you know Lauren got her high school diploma a year early? Or that she plays four instruments, including piano at concert level?"

"I didn't know either of those things," I confessed. There was only so much digging into a person's background I could do. I knew some of her financial information. I knew she had a driving license, but no car, and I knew she had a killer wardrobe. Unfortunately, I didn't know if she was an actual killer. All those other little details that Lily knew were public information if anyone cared to dig far enough back. Despite all that I didn't know, I did know a couple of pertinent things. One, the outcome didn't look good for Lauren, since she didn't have an alibi; and two, I had direct access to her. I fully intended to use that while I investigated-slash-stalked her.

Immediately after Shelley drew attention to Lauren's missing alibi, Lauren clammed up and our meeting was over. After we agreed Joe's dejected request that we stay on the case, Solomon and I left. We agreed in unison that we needed to find out who Michael was, and what Lauren got up to when she thought no one was watching. While Joe groveled to his bosses, we needed to find out if Lauren was involved in Katya's death. Even I had to admit that despite the discovery of the secret passage, Lauren was still the only viable suspect.

"Have you ever heard the name Michael in relation to Lauren?" I asked, since Lily appeared to be the fountain of B4U knowledge.

"Michael? No, I don't think so. Why?"

"Just a name I heard mentioned."

"Okay. Well, I have to go home." Lily checked her watch before scooping the last of the ice cream into her mouth and grabbing another cookie. "I have one hour before Jord gets home."

"He's working late?"

"Yeah, a school got burgled and a bunch of their equipment was stolen so he's staying late to work the scene."

"That's awful."

"I know! Working late is rough."

"I meant the school."

"Oh. Nasty, isn't it? Stealing from a school? Some people! Anyway, when are we following Lauren? Does she do anything fun?"

"I've only known the band a few days. So far, I've seen one die, and found out another one was years older than everyone thought and secretly married, and learned that they have bitchy fights. Oh, yeah, and they go shopping."

"I like the shopping bit. Call me tomorrow?"

"First thing."

"So long as that means eleven. I want to sleep in."

I promised I would call at a reasonable time before walking Lily out, and watching her walk to her car. I waited while she buckled up and drove off before closing the door. I cleaned up our snacks, rinsed and washed the bowls, and dispensed the trash into the can while I thought about the case.

We had discussed the theory that the blackmailer and the murderer were separate people, but now that it was confirmed, I had to focus on the only clue we were left with. We cleaned up the blackmail plot, just like we were under contract to do; and extracted Amelia's promise she would not send any more blackmail letters and would return the money. So now where were we? We were left with Katya's murder, and one strong suspect, as well as several other minor ones.

Joe's request to keep us on to assist with the investigation was a relief in some ways. I was far too curious to find out who killed Katya and why to leave the case alone. Sure, the band girls were hard work, but one of them was murdered, and my persistent, natural curiosity needed to know why. Why did someone go to considerable effort to access a secret passageway to her room? Who else knew about it? And did Katya know about the secret entrances too? Did that mean Katya knew her murderer well enough to tell him or her about the passageway? Each time I thought of a question, I thought of another one that needed answering. Unfortunately, for Lauren my theories were all unproven, leading me back to square one: tailing Lauren.

I dried my hands and switched off the lights in the

kitchen, moving back to the living room and grabbing my phone. First, I dialed Garrett.

"Little sis, you been busy with that crazy ass band?" he asked, when his wife, Traci, passed over the phone.

"They're keeping me busy," I admitted, filling him in on my recent discovery about the blackmail.

"I'm guessing you're calling about the murder?"

"How did you know?"

"I've been waiting for your call. I can't tell you much, since it's an active investigation. Plus, your Special Agent ex is handling it since it's high profile."

"He told me. What can you tell me?"

"Probably not much more than you already know." I heard a door shut before Garrett continued. "The stab wound to the back was what killed her. It severed an artery and would have ended her life her very quickly."

"Isn't that an unusual way to be stabbed?"

"I thought so too. Usually, stab wounds go to the front areas of the body. The heart, the stomach, a limb. Accessible areas when there's a confrontation. Very rarely to the back, or in that position. I got the impression that the killer might have some medical knowledge."

"How did you come to that conclusion?"

"The kill stab was very precise. It wasn't a frenzied slash. You saw the room. There wasn't any struggle, and Katya didn't have any defensive wounds."

"Katya must have been comfortable with the killer to have turned her back. Do you think it was someone she knew?" I asked, knowing that was another mark against Lauren.

"I'd say it was likely to some extent, especially since she didn't scream when whoever it was entered. She could have been surprised though, or threatened into silence." Garrett paused.

"You don't think that's likely?"

"I just read the autopsy report. There was no sign that Katya attempted to strike her attacker or defended herself in any way. No DNA under her fingernails, no hair caught in her fingers, no ligature marks, or bruising to her wrists or ankles, and nothing in her mouth to keep her quiet."

"So, no sexual assault either?" I guessed, wondering when Maddox planned on sharing the report with me.

"Correct. All her clothing was in proper order and there was no evidence of any prior sexual activity."

"Okay. So she wasn't attacked and she wasn't defending herself. That suggests she either knew her attacker or at least, felt comfortable at allowing the creep into the room. Could you determine anything about him or her?"

"No. I can tell you that the strike went downwards, but the ME estimated that Katya was already on the floor. I think the killer straddled her, pinned her down, and delivered the fatal blow, killing her swiftly. It was pulled out and plunged in again just an inch under the first wound. The knife was still in her back when you found her."

I shuddered, and didn't need any reminding. "I thought that was strange. Didn't you?"

"If you'd stop interrupting, I would tell you that!"

"Sorry."

"No problem. The hilt was wiped clean, but the knife wasn't new. We matched it to a set from the hotel kitchen, but we already cleared it with the chef it belonged to. He reported his knife set was stolen a half hour before Katya was found. He was talking to the deputy manager during the kill, and that checked out."

"So the killer swiped it?"

"That would be my guess. He or she probably passed through the kitchen, grabbed the knife, and then accessed the suite. Not wanting to go through the annoyance of getting rid of the knife, the killer left it in situ. Removing the knife would have increased blood spatter too. However, we did get a small amount of DNA trace from the knife. We still don't know how the murderer got in and out."

That sounded positive for Lauren. I was sure she didn't have time to run down to the hotel kitchen, steal a knife, and quietly re-enter the suite. Also, she was famous. Someone would have seen her. "Maddox didn't tell you?"

"Tell me what?"

"We found a secret passageway that enables housekeeping to access the suites without being seen on the floor."

"No shit?"

"None at all. Maddox took some prints from the passageway and entryways. It looks like there were hidden entry points to every room. The killer could have gotten into Katya's room via any one of them and escaped again, unseen. It would explain why I didn't see anyone when I walked along that corridor on my way to interview Katya."

"I'll check into that angle. Tomorrow, I'm going to interview hotel staff and speak to the manager again. Like you said, housekeeping knew about that secret passageway and the murder weapon was a hotel knife. One of the staff could have done it."

"But why?"

"Hell if I know, Lexi. Hey, I saw Solomon earlier. He looked distracted. Everything okay?"

"He seemed okay when I last saw him," I told my brother.

"Must be the case getting to him. We could do without the press here, making everything harder by watching our every move."

"Tell me about it," I said, wondering how long it would take for the news about my run-in with Shayne to travel to my brother. I figured it wouldn't be long; and if I were really lucky, it might even come up at a family dinner.

"Okay, well, I'm going to be working extra hours on this case. At least, we have Maddox to liaise with. He might not be one of our own anymore, but it's nice we knew him as a cop."

I frowned. "He hasn't taken the case over?"

"Nope, not exactly. We're working it together as a joint op. Pretty decent of him. The FBI can easily call grabs on the case if they wanted to. High-profile cases like these are career builders."

I agreed it was decent of Maddox not to steal the case out from under MPD. I rang off after agreeing that we would make certain to catch up at the next family dinner. When that would be scheduled, I didn't know, but I was pretty sure my mother would want the case gossip soon, even though she had no idea who or what B4U were.

I checked my watch again before placing my next call, wondering if it was too late. I did have to tell Maddox to leave the blackmail letters alone; they were a dead end. If he looked for any answers there, he would simply be wasting vital time on the real case. After several attempts at picking up the phone and putting it down again, I dialed Maddox.

"Where did you get to?" he asked. "I went to take some fingerprints and you were gone."

I grimaced, but I shouldn't have been surprised. I took off after my run-in with Shayne and that was rude. "Sorry, I had to take care of other business. I heard you found usable prints?"

"You heard right. There were a lot belonging to hotel employees and a few unaccounted for."

"Garrett is looking at a hotel employee, thanks to the knife."

"Makes sense. Want to hear about the really fun print we got?"

"I think I can guess, but please surprise me."

"It was Katya's. On the console panel *inside* the passageway. I matched it to the sample print we took from her body."

"So she did know about the passageway!" I punched the air triumphantly, then lowered my arm as I realized all the possibilities that raised. If Katya knew, whom else did she tell?

"Looks that way. She might have been using the passage herself. I found her prints by the elevator too, and also outside the other suite the band were using."

"Joe's or Amelia's?"

"Amelia's. So, Katya wasn't accessing Joe's suite, and it doesn't look like Amelia or Joe were using the passageway either. Just a minute..." There was some rustling as Maddox got up and I heard footsteps before a door closed.

"Am I interrupting something?" I asked.

"No, it's fine. I was in a public area and with a case this high-profile, I need to be careful. Did you know some journalist got into the hotel before breaking the wedding story?"

"Gosh. I wonder how that happened." I pulled a face and picked up my notepad. "You definitely didn't find any prints from Lauren in the passageway?"

"None, but there were some prints that were too smudged to use. I couldn't see definitively that they weren't hers, just that I can't..."

"...find any evidence that they are," I concluded.

"That's correct. Why the interest in Lauren?"

"She's the only one in the band without an alibi."

"That is news to me. Spill."

"I'll trade you. Your information for my information."

"How did I know this wasn't a friendly chat? Okay, what do you want to know? I can still get you the autopsy report."

"Nope, got that. I just want to be kept in the loop, please. I'm working an angle and I need help," I admitted.

"No problem. Your turn."

"Okay. I saw Joe and Amelia together immediately prior to the murder. Neither of them could have killed Katya because they were too busy making out in the housekeeping closet at the other end of the floor. Shelley was in the hotel that day, but was witnessed across town by more than one person, including their security chief and the chauffeur for the car she took. No one can confirm where Lauren was. She isn't talking and that makes me suspicious. I'm starting surveillance on her tomorrow."

"The band decided to keep you on?"

"Yep. I wrapped up the blackmail case and told them it was Amelia. All she wanted was to get out of the band, and I think it just spiraled out of control. Solomon guessed Joe suspected her all along but didn't want to believe his wife was behind it. As Amelia definitely didn't kill Katya, it's unrelated; so those letters I sent you are a dead end. Joe asked us to stay on and look into Katya's murder."

"Are you sure?"

"Absolutely."

"He didn't need to keep you on for the murder inquiry. The FBI and MPD are working together."

"I know, but I've been given a job to do and I intend to do it. Joe's under a lot of pressure from his bosses."

"It's getting crazy. We have leads that take us in different directions, not to mention, psycho fans and journalists every time we turn around. The whole thing could get dangerous. Solomon shouldn't have put you right in the center of it."

I paused, thinking back to all the other dangerous situations I'd encountered, starting with the first body I found before getting dragged into the case. I survived each and every one of them... but it only took one bad turn to end all that. And only one wrong decision for me to become the victim. Even so, I wasn't about to back down now. Katya may have been nuts, but she needed someone on her team, someone who wouldn't stop looking for the truth, someone with an "in" with the band; and that person was me. "I'm there because I can get the job done," I told him. "And I need to know what Lauren is hiding."

"Honey, are you ready?" a woman's voice called.

The phone went muffled for Maddox's response

before he came back on the line. "I have to go," he said. "Let's meet tomorrow and we'll go over what we know about Lauren. Okay?"

"Okay?" I agreed as I ended the call, frowning. I didn't know who the voice belonged to, but I'd never heard it before. I also knew not a single one of his colleagues would have ever called him "honey." The image of the reservation for the romantic getaway flashed in front of me. Did that voice belong to Maddox's mystery woman?

Amid a case that was built on secrets and lies, why didn't he tell me about her just like any other friend would?

CHAPTER TWELVE

"Lexi Graves, get over yourself!"

Lily and I sat in my car outside the hotel, away from the circle of press camped out on the doorstep. Despite a cordon set up by the hotel to restrain them, the press crowd seemed to grow exponentially by the hour. The eager reporters and a heaving bank of photographers were all straining for a shot every time the door opened. From our vantage point, we had a clear view of the front door, and another of the side street through which the employee parking lot was accessed. Whichever way Lauren exited the building, we'd surely see her. Not that it mattered, I secretly attached a small tracking device to her favorite purse that morning while she was busy helping herself to coffee and breakfast from the cart set up in her suite. The tracker currently beeped on my app, reminding me that Lauren hadn't moved. Thanks to the little, red, flashing dot, wherever she went, we could follow inconspicuously, without depending on her obeying her agenda, or having to call

Joe to locate her. Solomon, Joe, and I agreed that was best: Lauren was upset enough about being our chief suspect, so we didn't need to dismay her further by letting her know she was being tailed. Despite the Michael mystery, I just hoped she would turn up clean.

"Pardon?"

"We've talked about your ex-boyfriend for the last thirty minutes! I thought you were over him? Or do you care that Adam Maddox might have a new girlfriend?"

"I don't mind!"

"So what's the problem? That he didn't tell you?"

"I don't know. Maybe." Did it matter? I wondered. I awoke thinking about Maddox and the mystery woman, and it needled me all morning. As soon as I picked up Lily, I told her everything. Everything took two minutes, since I knew nothing.

"Did you tell him about Solomon right after you dumped him?"

"No, but that was different. Maddox and I just split up, and I was really angry at him. I thought he was cheating on me!"

"Let's look at it from Maddox's perspective. His ex-girlfriend, who dumped him for cheating, took up with her boss while she was pretending to be married to him..."

"For a case!"

Lily continued, adding, "For a case, and then she consummated the fake marriage, and did it end there? No, his ex is still dating his former colleague, and they seem really happy. Meanwhile, Maddox might finally have found someone nice and hasn't told you, and you're upset about that?"

"I'm upset he didn't tell me."

"You didn't tell him about Solomon!"

"He figured it out before I got the chance; plus, I was mad at him at the time."

"And you figured this out. What did you think Maddox was going to do? Pine over you forever?"

I took a deep breath and mumbled, "Whose team are you on?"

"Yours, sweetie, always."

"I just wanted to talk about it."

"Okay. Talk."

I shrugged and pulled a face. "That was it."

"So what are you going to do now?"

A green blip appeared on my cell phone screen, signifying my mark was on the move. I pointed to the car pulling out of the service exit, with Lauren just visible in the rear seat as the driver's window rolled up. "Follow that car."

"I meant Maddox."

"I've given it a lot of thought, and thanks to our helpful chat... nothing."

"Hmmph," said Lily. "Back in the day, we would have stalked him until we knew the truth."

"Do you want to stalk him?"

"No, stalking B4U is way more fun. What does a superstar diva do on her time off? Drive, Lexi, drive!"

We followed the blacked out vehicle for several blocks. I didn't make much of an attempt at pretending not to follow, but traffic was with me that morning, and we blended in easily, following two or three cars behind. Lauren's vehicle turned through a set of gates and we drew to a halt outside.

"Ohmygosh they're going to do some kind of deal," gasped Lily. "Drugs? Could it all be down to drugs? Is Michael her dealer?"

"This is where the band are rehearsing for their video."

"Then why are we out here? I want to be in there." Lily jabbed her thumb at the warehouse before turning hopeful eyes on me. "Plus, how can we follow Lauren out here?"

"Good point."

I pulled a U-turn and followed the car through the gate, sliding into an empty space, far from the warehouse doors. Unlike the first time I visited, the small lot was almost full. I spotted a few people milling around the doors behind the security guards. Along with the security guard that Solomon and I interviewed previously, there were three other men in identical black coats and slacks, wearing headsets. One carried a clipboard.

Grabbing my phone, I placed a call to Solomon. "I'm following Lauren and she pulled into the warehouse," I told him.

"Okay... good?"

"Is there something going on here? Security has obviously been boosted."

"Rehearsals for the video. I'm with Joe now. He told me the management company got pretty angry at the band, but they're going ahead with the video and calling the band a trio. They've tweaked it so it's also serving as some sort of goodbye montage to Katya."

"Sounds grim."

"Schmaltzy is a better word."

"How about crass? I can count the days since her death on one hand."

"I'll see your 'crass' and throw in 'capitalism.' B4U are the hottest band in the States right now, and all these leaks are just making them even more interesting to the fans. Sales are up. They'd be fools to miss out on such an opportunity. Apparently, they stand to make big bucks."

"So Amelia and Joe's wedding didn't derail anything?"

"Apparently not. They're really happy and the press coverage swiftly moved from a dirty, little secret to an amazing, against-the-odds love story. Plus, it's keeping B4U in the press right now, so it's more positive than the Katya-getting-stabbed-in-the-back story."

I took a deep breath, thankful for never choosing the media career route. My worst career decisions began as a brief stint in the Army and extended to several years of temping. They both seemed better than running personal stories about public figures. "Okay. Am I on the list to get into the warehouse?"

"I'll check with Joe..." The phone went silent and I gave Lily an *I dunno* shrug while we waited. Solomon rejoined the line, saying, "You're on the list. If anyone gives you a problem, call Joe and he'll fix it."

"Thanks."

"Stay in the background, Lexi. It doesn't matter if Lauren spots you. She expects to see you, but don't approach her. Just watch what she does when she thinks no one is observing her."

"Got it." I hung up. "We're in."

"Yay!"

"My name's on the list," I told the clipboard-carrying security guard. "Lexi Graves."

"Me too," said Lily.

"You are?"

"Lily Shuler-Graves."

"You're not on the list."

"I am. I'm right there," said Lily, tapping the underside of the clipboard. It popped out of the guard's hands and flipped upside down, landing in a puddle. "Oh, shoot!" she exclaimed, sounding as insincere as she looked.

"She's my assistant," I said, giving him my *don't give me any trouble* look.

The security guard fished the clipboard from the puddle and wafted it in the air, sending dirty droplets flying at us. "Get a better one," he suggested.

"Great thinking!" I grabbed Lily's arm and propelled

her inside.

"I've never *not* been on a list before," she pouted.

"And I'm rarely ever on one. Today is a good day."

"And what was with the duck face back there?"

"That was my *don't mess with me* face!"

Lily paused. "I definitely wouldn't mess with that face."

We stopped a few feet into the warehouse, looking at the scene in front of us. There was activity every way we turned. Cameras were set up around stage sets at the far end of the warehouse, and camera operators and other black-clad people stood in small groups, talking and pointing. Off to one side I spotted the dance troupe, practicing hard. We watched one guy throw a petite woman into the air. She spun several times and dropped gracefully into his arms before being placed upright and tipping into a vertical split. Several other dancers moved in front of them, breaking into a routine as the choreographer called out instructions.

"Do you see Lauren?" I asked, looking away from them.

"Yeah, she's over there talking to... is that Shelley? Oh wow!" I followed the direction of Lily's pointing forefinger.

"Yeah, that's Shelley."

The two women were talking to Annabelle, the wardrobe mistress, but as I looked around, Amelia was nowhere in sight.

"Can you get her autograph?"

"What do you want an autograph for?"

"I have no idea, but that's what famous people are for... to sign autographs."

"Yeah, but what would you do with it if I got you one?"

"I have no idea. Frame it?"

"I'll see what I can do. Let's sit over there and try and look like we're not spying on everyone."

"We should have brought disguises. You want me to grab something from the wardrobe rack? We could blend in with the dancers."

"Can you do that?" I asked, pointing to half of the dancers doing splits on the floor. Meanwhile, the other half somersaulted over the tops of them before grabbing their partners and spinning them into a frenzied routine.

"Let's just sit."

We found plastic chairs at the periphery of the warehouse. They were partly shaded by the columns that stretched to the ceiling, and perfect for spying on Lauren as we camouflaged ourselves amidst a few other people. She spent some time with Shelley and Annabelle before they all walked over to the wardrobe racks and browsed through the clothing. Just as they finished, Amelia appeared amid a burst of applause from the dancers, shouting, "Congratulations!" She beamed at them, waving and blowing kisses.

"Look at the big star," muttered the guy closest to us. "Bye-bye, Katya, it's time for Amelia to shine." His friend simply nodded.

Lily leaned in, her voice soft enough for only me to hear. "If you hadn't told me Amelia was clean, I would say she was our biggest suspect right now. Katya would have hated all this attention centering on Amelia. I read that in a magazine. She hated anyone who she thought was more talented than her."

"Everything I hear about her says she wasn't a team player."

"Not even a little bit. I read she got into it with one of the backup singers at the start of the tour."

I glanced away from Lauren, towards Lily. "Where did you read that?"

"Same magazine."

"What else did the magazine say?"

"That Katya thought the backup singer was angling for her spot in the group, so she made sure to put her in her place. Her name was Clarissa. That's a pretty name, isn't it? I don't think I'd call a baby... oh wait, that's her! That's Clarissa! I recognize her from..."

"...The magazine?" I concluded.

"How did you know?" Lily frowned.

I shook my head. "Never mind. Let's talk to her. Maybe she's got something to say about Katya and the way she abused most people."

Sometimes, it's hard to start talking to a total stranger. Sometimes, however, they let you skip all the hard work and seem happy to let loose. Clarissa was the latter sort, I found out as we approached.

"Let me tell you," she started, after we introduced

ourselves. "If I were a cop, I'd look closely at me too, but I have an alibi. The other singers and I all went for lunch the day Katya was killed; and it was a long, boozy one, if you know what I mean."

"Where did you go?" I asked.

"A place downtown called Lily's Bar. Great cocktails."

"That's my bar!"

"Get out!" squealed Clarissa.

"Get in! It really is. Oh wow! I am so excited. Stars drink at my bar," Lily mouthed at me, her jaw dropping. "Also I have cameras everywhere, so I can probably prove that Clarissa is telling the truth."

"So there you have it. I wish I could say I killed her because it would have given me a lot of personal satisfaction, you know, but I didn't." Clarissa shrugged, like it was no big deal for her to have that desire or a good alibi.

"That's nice to know. Was it a regular occurrence for Katya to get nasty with crew members?"

Clarissa raised an eyebrow and gave me a *you really just asked me that?* look. "Regular? More like a daily occurrence. The bitch had attitude, ya know? There was nobody off limits that she didn't mind getting into it with."

"Why did she get into it with you?"

"She overheard me practicing with the band. I have a similar vocal range to Katya, so when she didn't show up for rehearsal, I stepped in to sing her part. She eventually arrived late and hit me with her purse, accusing me of trying to steal her part."

"What happened after that?"

"After that, she pulled a chunk of hair from the side of my head. Joe spoke to me privately, and apologized on Katya's behalf. Then he gave me a thousand bucks in cash to 'cheer myself up' he said, before reminding me of the 'no talk clause' in my contract."

"No talk clause?"

"Standard policy on a tour like this. No one wants a crew member selling stories, but I figure the band hired you, so I'm not breaking the rule by talking to you."

"You're exactly right. Wasn't a thousand bucks an insulting figure for suffering like that?" asked Lily.

"Not when Joe promised to put my demo in front of management after the tour was done. It's my big chance. I like working as a backup singer, but I've always wanted to record my own material. Amelia even wrote me a song."

"So all you have to do is stay on the tour, keeping mum about Katya's attack, and you can get your shot at stardom?"

"That's right, and I wouldn't do anything to jeopardize that."

"Like what?" I pressed.

Clarissa rolled her eyes. "Like killing Katya and ending the tour."

"Is the tour over?" I asked.

"Not so far as I know. I thought it might be, but

we're about to start shooting the video; and no one told me it was canceled, so it looks like it's going ahead."

"Killing Katya doesn't really fit in with your desire to not jeopardize anything," Lily said.

"Pretty big gamble to take," Clarissa agreed as someone yelled her name. She spun around, raising her hand. "Wardrobe. I need to get fitted for the shoot. Is there anything more?"

"Yes. Did anyone else get into it with Katya?" I asked.

Clarissa looked around. "Throw a rock, and you'll probably hit two or three people. All I know is: it wasn't me and I can prove it. Try talking to the dancers. They hung out with the band too."

"She seems too happy to be our killer," said Lily as we watched Clarissa walk over to wardrobe where the other backup singer waited.

"Should killers be miserable?"

"It would help. Come to think of it, I don't recall you having to deal with any miserable killers. They all seemed pretty happy. The thieves too. I might just become suspicious of happy people. They have a lot to hide."

I laughed and slipped my arm around Lily, giving her a quick squeeze. "Then you'll always be my number one suspect. Let's talk to the dancers. I spoke to them before and they seemed okay."

The dancers were taking a break, sprawled across their corner of the warehouse, in the same mish-mash of clothing I'd seen them wearing previously. I wasn't sure I'd seen outfits put together like that before, but figured it was hard to be fashionable, sporty, and warm all at the same time. It certainly seemed hard to coordinate.

"Isn't that your brother?" asked Lily as we crossed the warehouse towards the dancers. I paused mid-step when Garrett stepped inside the main doors and looked around.

"Yep," I replied, grabbing Lily's elbow and propelling her forwards until we reached the far wall. Turning around, we watched Garrett approaching Lauren before taking her to one side. "Can you keep an eye on Lauren while I talk to these guys?"

"I guess. What's up with your tracker?"

"By the time it says she's moving, she could be gone before we even got into the car."

"No problem. I could sidle closer and listen in."

"I think Garrett might recognize you."

"True. How will we ever know what they're talking about? A homicide detective interviewing your chief suspect sounds like something you might want to listen to."

"I'll call him later."

"You again," said Devon, looking past me. "Where's the hottie?"

"Practicing his pirouettes in front of the mirror," I quipped and Devon pushed my arm and laughed.

"You're a peach," he giggled. "What can I do for you? Anyone else been murdered? Did you make an arrest yet? Does your hot friend want to take me away in handcuffs?"

"Me? Sure, but only because you need arresting for having an ass that looks that good in jeans," Lily replied.

It was hard not to do an eye roll, but I just about managed it. "He means he wants to get arrested by Solomon," I explained.

"Good choice," said Lily without missing a beat while giving Devon a knowing nod.

"We're still looking into Katya's murder," I told him when they stopped giggling.

"When you find them, can you tell me so I can send a gift basket?"

"To Katya's family?" asked Lily.

"To the murderer," said Devon.

"Did you all spend much time at the hotel?" I asked, hoping the clear animosity between Devon and Katya might lead to something juicy.

"Not really. We have another hotel away from the divas. We only go over for a meeting or the after-show party."

"Are any of the dancers close to the band members?"

"Are any of you close to the band?" Devon shouted as he addressed the troupe, enunciating slowly, as the dancers blinked at him. "It's an easy question, morons!"

There were some shrugs and a couple of vaguely affirmative answers, while some said "kind of" and a few said "no."

"Didn't think so," he said. "We all get on pretty well, but this tour... well, there's a hierarchy when we're off the clock."

"Can you think of a reason why anyone would want to kill Katya?"

"I thought you were here about the blackmail? Do you get confused when that hot hunk of man love is around? I'd find it hard to keep my questions straight too. I know what my answers would all be: yes, please!" He stuck a hand on his hip and nodded vigorously.

"We came here about the blackmail, but now we're looking into the murder," I confirmed, glad that the outcome of the blackmail hadn't leaked to the crew. I figured it was only a matter of time.

"Like I told you the other day, honey, we were all at The New Montgomery Dance School downtown when Katya popped off this mortal coil."

"Except Don," said the closest dancer, sliding into splits.

"Except Don," I echoed, looking for Don. He gave me a wave. "You were at the hospital with a knee injury?"

"And I'm pretty sure I was on camera too," he said.

"Did any of you ever have an altercation with Katya? Or did she ever shout at or threaten anyone?" I asked.

Ten hands rose, including Don's. Devon raised his hand too.

"About anything in particular?" I asked and they all began to speak at once. "One at a time!" I called over the top of their indignant voices.

"She hated our outfits and wanted them changed."

"She didn't like our positions on stage."

"She thought I gave her a dirty look."

"Katya said I stole her shoes."

"She was mean to Don when he told us he was getting a divorce."

"She wanted me fired because I had the same purse."

"She said I made advances. I mean, really? I'm gay. And not lady gay."

"She was just a mean bitch."

"Did any of you like her?" I asked. Most of the dancers looked at their feet, but a couple shook their heads.

Devon crossed his arms. "None of them killed her, which is a shame."

"None of those reasons are motive enough to kill someone over. Did any of you see her getting really nasty with someone? Did you hear rumors about her threatening someone? Or someone threatening her?" Lily asked.

"I heard a rumor that she was boning one of the crew members, and also had a thing going on with someone else. She was planning to drop the poor jerk," said a very pretty redhead in a neon yellow crop top.

The blonde woman next to her nodded. "Yeah, I heard she picked up a crew guy on every tour, made him her bitch, and then tossed him to the curb when the tour ended."

The redhead continued. "It was like she was a big shot, business dude with an intern. Total cliché."

"I pity the douche that screwed the bitch," added the blonde.

"Anyone know who the guy is?" I asked, but they all shook their heads.

"Lauren's on the move," whispered Lily, nodding towards the place where Lauren and my brother were standing.

"Thanks guys. Sorry to take up your practice time," I added. Devon surprised me by hugging first me, then Lily.

"Every time you turn up, you make my day," he said. "I am loving this tour so much more now that Katya is dead. No stress, plenty of gossip, playing for the cameras at every turn. It's wonderful!"

I didn't know what to say that, and I was rarely lost for words, so I just let him squeeze me again before he turned back to the dancers, and screeched at them to get off the floor.

I lost sight of Lauren for a moment and when she reappeared after a few worrying minutes, during which I thought she slipped out the door, she was in full costume and flanked by Amelia and Shelley. Another couple of minutes, and I saw Garrett working his way through the crowd. He was moving towards the doors so Lily and I sank back into the shadows at the edges of the warehouse. The band, along with their backup singers and dancers, took their positions on the first set. Then the cameramen took their places while the rest of the crew began to move seamlessly, like they were being directed, themselves.

Slowly, they ran through the shot, adding bursts of music, checking camera angles, striking poses, and testing the lighting.

"All this for three-and-a-half minutes?" I whispered.

"And they haven't even started shooting. What's that screen for?" Lily asked as the band moved from the first set to a blank canvas wall. One-by-one, they stood next to the screen, looking up at it with mournful expressions while images of Katya flickered across the screen. "This must be the montage bit for the Katya tribute," Lily decided. New instructions were given and the band tried different stances, as well as different expressions. Finally, the three of them sat, their backs pressed against the wall, looking upwards.

"Amelia, can you do that tear again?" called the director. "You looked so sad."

"I'm bored," snapped Amelia.

"You look sad and that's perfect. Exactly what we want. That's right, girls. Okay, let's try a holding hands scene. I want you to join hands and look up at the screen."

"Even when she's dead, Katya gets the big spotlight," said Lily.

"Yeah. I wonder if they're pissed about that."

"Damn good actors. Hey, how much do dancers earn?"

"I don't know. Not much."

"Then how come Don is wearing a Rolex?"

"A Rolex?"

"It's a fancy pants watch."

"I know what it is! Are you sure?"

"Positive. My mom bought my dad the same model. It cost thousands."

"Maybe he saved for it?"

"Isn't he the only one of the dancers without an alibi?" Lily pressed.

"No, he was at the hospital but..."

"We should check into that."

"You know what? Yes, we should."

"We can't take his word for it," continued Lily.

"I'm going to check into it." The dancers moved away from the set, leaving the band to take up positions on podiums with the backup singers behind them, and I walked over to Don. Lily declined to follow, insisting she was watching Lauren and we couldn't do that if we both talked to Don.

"Do you have a minute?" I asked. He was by the water fountain, pouring a cup of water.

Looking up, he gave me a surprised look, then smiled. "Sure. What do you need?"

"I'm just confirming everyone's location at the time of the murder for my notes," I lied. "Can you remember the name of the doctor who took care of your knee?"

"Sure, but it was a nurse. She was really pretty and sweet, and I remember her name because it was my favorite childhood book, *Alice in Wonderland*. Her name was Alice. Alice Graves. She'll have my records, right?"

I smiled at the stroke of luck. "Yes, she will."

Don grinned. "Great."

"Do you have the time?"

"Sure." he held up his wrist, twisting to see the face of the watch. It was a Rolex, all right, and a real one. "It's quarter past the hour."

"Thanks."

"Let me know if you need anything else?"

"I will. How's the knee holding up?"

"Never better."

"Glad to hear it. Take care."

I walked back over to Lily, indicating for her to follow me to a quieter spot, away from any straining ears. "I need to make a couple of calls."

"Did you work out who did it already?"

"No, but I know that everyone we just spoke to has an alibi. How can everyone have an alibi except Lauren?"

"Maybe Lauren really is the only one who could have done it."

"Maybe." I dialed Lucas and he answered quickly.

"Hit me with it, Lexi, and make it hard."

"Sounds dirty," I replied, "and sorry, but this is easy stuff. Can you crosscheck a hospital admission? Don somebody. I have the surname somewhere, but I don't remember right now."

"What time span am I checking for?" Lucas asked.

"Around the time of Katya's murder."

"Got it. Don Kenley. Checked into Montgomery General at ten and was seen by the nurse... hey, he was seen by your sister-in-law... at twelve-fifteen and discharged with a prescription for a painkiller at twelve-twenty-six."

"That's a big gap in time."

"I'm looking at the manifest and it appears the ER was really busy that day. Lots of breaks, fractures and minor wounds from some kind of vehicle crash. I'm crosschecking against the same time period of the previous two weeks, and they were overloaded for this shift."

"That explains the long wait before he got seen."

"Anything else?"

"Can you check to see if B4U's dance crew ran a workshop at the dance studio downtown. Also at the same time as the murder?"

"I can do that without checking. My fiancée attended it."

"She dances?"

"Beautifully."

"Can you ask her what she remembers and get back to me if it's anything out of the ordinary?"

"No problem!"

"Look who's here," said Lily, nudging me as I hung

up. Maddox and another man were standing on the other side of the warehouse. Maddox was looking around as if searching for someone. Finally, he settled his gaze on me and waved as they both crossed over to join us.

"This is interesting. I've never seen a video filmed before," said Maddox.

"They're just practicing," I told him. "They've been at it a while."

"I know. I checked with the director and he says they'll be here a few more hours. How's the surveillance going?"

"Not much to see. Lauren walks from there to there and strikes a pose, then sits down and looks sad, then moves to another set and mimes. It's all for the video," I explained at Maddox's puzzled expression.

"How long have you been here?"

"A couple hours."

"Don't you have better stuff to do?"

"Not really."

"Take a break. Grab a coffee. We'll watch Lauren a while."

"You sure? I could use a coffee."

"I'm sure. Go. You have thirty minutes."

Lily and I walked over to the hospitality cart set up in the corner of the warehouse at the left of the main doors, before Maddox changed his mind. I poured both of us coffees and we helped ourselves to warm Danishes and fruit as the hospitality lady busied herself.

She kept her back to us and organized the cardboard cups and paper plates.

"You know, the band aren't as interesting as I hoped. I thought they'd be way more exciting," said Lily, reaching for a second pastry.

"How so?"

"I have no idea, but this looks like a lot of hard work, and it's like you said: move here, move there, sit there, now sing, and stop, and do it again. It's not how I imagined the life of a superstar would be," Lily confessed.

"They get up to the interesting stuff on their personal time," I confided. "Did I tell you Shelley's big blackmail secret was a sex tape she made a few years ago?"

"Get out!"

"Seriously."

"Who's the dude?"

"*Dudette.*"

"No! Way!" shrieked a voice, only it wasn't Lily's. The blood rushed from my face as the hospitality lady straightened up and turned around. My heart thumped and I suppressed the wail that rose in my throat.

"Shayne?"

CHAPTER THIRTEEN

"Teen queen lesbian!" Lily passed the newspaper to me and I reached for it reluctantly. "Could have been worse."

"Precisely... but how?" I muttered, unfolding the paper to read the screaming headline one more time. Below was what I could only describe as an absolutely stunning photo of Shelley. Unfortunately, the inset photo showed a very different story: somehow, Shayne Winter had managed to get hold of a terrible shot of Shelley. She was passed out drunk, her blouse half-unbuttoned, and lipstick smeared across one cheek. She was sprawled across a sofa with one hand still clutching the neck of an empty vodka bottle.

"I was trying to be nice," Lily replied, taking the newspaper and throwing it onto the back seat of her Mini. "There is no way this could possibly be worse."

"Did you read the bit about the unnamed source 'gleefully' outing Shelley?"

Lily nodded. "I figured that was you."

"I wasn't gleeful. I was gossiping... quietly."

"In front of a reporter."

"No, behind her, but I didn't know that. Oh man, when Solomon finds out!"

Lily slid a sideways look at me. "Do you think he'll spank you?"

"No, it'll be much worse."

"You should dress extra sexy for the next few days and hope it distracts him."

"Full on naked wouldn't work."

"Try full on naked, but add stockings and heels."

"That's not naked. And what's the point of the stockings?"

"I don't know, but ask any guy, they love them to the point of getting googly-eyed."

"Not enough to wear them themselves," I pointed out, although I was ninety-nine-point-nine percent grateful for that.

"We hope. Is that Lauren?"

I peered at the woman exiting the restaurant. "Nope. Similar coat and hairstyle, but not her."

"She's taking a long lunch. I wonder what she's having."

My stomach gave an ominous, little rumble that I hoped only I could hear. "I bet it isn't her words. I wish I could eat mine."

"Forget about it. What's done is done. Being gay isn't a big deal these days. In fact, it's kind of hot."

"Really?"

"Yeah, totally."

"You think Shelley won't mind being outed?" I winced.

Lily pursed her lips thoughtfully. "I think she'll kill you if she finds out it was you."

I slumped further into my seat. "That's what I thought."

"Then her manager will kill you."

"Oh, great."

"Finally, Solomon will kill you."

"I may as well paint a bull's eye on my head."

"You could do that for Halloween."

"Huh?"

"Dress as a bull's eye. It would be hilarious."

I let out a wail and covered my face with my hands. "How can this day get worse?"

"We could lose Lauren, and then you'd have to confess that too."

"Let's not," I decided, jumping as my phone began to ring. "It's Solomon."

"Don't answer. Avoid him."

"For how long?"

"Four to six months?"

"That conflicts with getting all sexy in seamed stockings to distract him."

"It does, doesn't it?" Lily shrugged. "You're in a sticky situation, and I don't mean in the naughty way."

Taking a deep breath, I answered the phone.

"Where are you?" asked Solomon.

"Outside Alessandro's where Lauren is having lunch."

"Is she alone?"

"No, two of the dancers are with her."

"Good. Don't lose her."

"Promise," I said, crossing my fingers ever so slightly.

"Have you read the news today?" asked Solomon.

I screwed up my face, so glad he couldn't see me. "No."

"Specifically... the entertainment section?"

I closed my eyes and pulled a face. "No," I lied.

"Someone leaked a story about Shelley's sexuality."

"No way?" I squeaked, hoping I sounded credible. "That's terrible. Who would do something like that?"

"Probably someone on the crew sold her out. I'm surprised it didn't come out before now."

I huffed a breath of relief. Solomon didn't think I was the culprit. "Is it a big story?" I asked.

"It just broke nationally," Solomon told me as I cringed. "Don't come to the hotel today. Shelley is ready to kill just about anyone who gets in her path. I hate to think what she'll do to the person who actually leaked the story."

"Is it really that big a deal?"

"Her sexuality? No! Who cares whom she chooses to bed? No one should care so long as it's legal. But her privacy? Yes, she has every right to that. That said, there's still a lot of homophobia, which is why so many stars choose to conceal their sexual preferences in case they challenge the old-fashioned ideal of 'normal'."

"Like George Clooney," whispered Lily.

"He's married and his wife is gorgeous and smart," I whispered back.

"What's that?" asked Solomon.

"Nothing, never mind. Lily is with me on a stakeout."

"Do I have to pay her?"

"No."

"Don't lose Lauren," Solomon warned before hanging up.

"The good news is: he doesn't know it was me. The bad news is: Shelley is pissed and the hotel is off limits again. They're trying to stop her from going homicidal."

"That decides it."

"Decides what?"

"You should definitely dress sexy." Lily leaned over, popping two buttons on my blouse before using both hands to give my boobs a boost.

"Lily!"

"What? You have double whammy sexy going on now. You could use this to your advantage on Solomon *and* Shelley! Distracting them both!"

"I never knew boobs could potentially save my life."

"If they were as big as mine, they'd potentially endanger your life on a regular basis too."

I looked at Lily's boobs. "They do look bigger than

usual. Did you get a new bra?"

"Hey, is that Lauren?" she asked, pointing again.

I returned my gaze to the restaurant doors, wishing I were inside, eating a slice of the tastiest lasagna known to Montgomery. "No, that's a man."

"Oops. Hey, is that..."

"That's her!"

"Oh, finally," sighed Lily. "I knew I'd get it right if I kept trying."

"Follow that car!" I shouted, restraining the temptation to point when Lauren and her two companions climbed into the huge, blacked-out SUV that drew to the curb in front of them.

"I love it when you say that; although I hope this doesn't turn into a high speed chase because I forgot to fill the tank and... oh, there they go!" We pulled into traffic several cars behind the SUV, but since the residents of Montgomery favored smaller, more inconspicuous cars, it wasn't hard to follow the behemoth. The journey didn't last long and the SUV pulled into the parking lot in front of the warehouse. It began spilling its occupants out in front of the doors as we pulled into a space. We watched Lauren and the dancers breeze inside, not waiting for the security guard to check their names.

"We have to go in. There are too many exits that she could slip out by."

"Yeah, and I bet there's paparazzi on every single one." Lily pointed to the four photographers leaning over the wall, their cameras pointed at Lauren and her mini entourage. "Do you think Shayne snuck inside again?"

"No, I think Solomon would have tightened security."

"Where do you think she's going to run to anyway? I still don't get why we're following her. She doesn't look like a murderer. She seems kind of nice, even pretty."

"I don't think she'll run anywhere. It's who she talks to, and what she does that interests me."

"Do you think she'll accidentally tell someone she killed Katya? Or do you think a murderer would be more careful?"

"I can't predict anything."

"Shame. I was going to give you some easy things to start off with before going big with the lottery numbers."

I laughed, my mood lightening. It was a good idea having Lily for company on surveillance, and she was more than ready to do it when I called to ask. I suspected a large part of it was unfettered glee at my idiocy the previous day, as well as curiosity about what happened during rehearsals and filming a music video.

As we exited the Mini, I caught sight of an SUV parked in the corner of the lot. It looked a lot like a vehicle I'd seen earlier, parked a block from Alessandro's, but I thought nothing of it until now. Two suited men exited the SUV, approaching the security guards ahead of us. They both flashed badges and entered. We followed them inside, moving easily past security and into the warehouse. I was surprised to see rehearsals had already started, but when I looked around for the two men, they were nowhere to be found.

"They just don't quit, do they?" said Lily as we looked around at the activity. The set was ready, and some of the dancers were seated at the hair and makeup stations while the remaining three band members stood with wardrobe. "Blackmail, murder, secret marriages, sex tape leaks... and here they are, ready to perform."

"They are true professionals," said a voice behind us.

Whipping around, I could only wonder whom we had opened our mouths in front of this time. I found Joe Carter standing there with his arms folded. He stepped forward, alongside us. His eyes had gray patches underneath them.

"Long night?" I asked.

"Never-ending," he said with a shake of his head. "You heard about the leak? The stuff about Shelley?"

"We knew nothing about it," said Lily quickly.

"Just what we saw in the paper," I added, since that was already public news.

"I may as well tell you since you're working for me... except you. Who are you?" Joe asked, noticing Lily.

"She's working with me," I told him.

Lily nodded furiously. "That's right, but I also own a bar that would be perfect for a wrap party."

"Have we met before?"

"Yes," said Lily. "Katya threw a vase at me."

"What were you going to tell us?" I prompted, before Joe asked Lily to narrow down the occasion.

"About the management company. We were this close to having the video canceled, thanks to that leak," Joe told us as he slid his thumb and forefinger close together. "The band would have been seriously penalized for the embarrassment it caused, and the tour could have totally failed, ensuring we all lost our jobs."

"It's kind of like the blackmail plot finally unveiling," said Lily. She squeaked when I pressed on her toe with my foot. It might have been what I was also thinking, but it wasn't a good idea to voice it, especially to the blackmailer's husband.

Joe didn't seem to notice as he continued. "Yeah, except Amelia wasn't the source of the leak. That blackmail stuff is history now that our marriage is out in the open. She's happy. I'm happy."

I wondered if Amelia really was happy. She may have been happy that I alibied her and Joe for Katya's murder, but the band remained together, which wasn't her objective when she started the blackmail plot. If I didn't know I was the accidental leak, I would have thought she was making one last attempt to embarrass the band into getting fired. Despite his assurance that they were happy, I wondered if Joe suspected Amelia of being the leak.

"You believe me, right?" Joe asked.

I nodded. "Absolutely."

"Good, thanks. I don't want anyone thinking Amelia did this. I talked for hours to the big bosses, and they were close to firing the whole band, but something amazing... hey, thanks," Joe said, pausing as a guy in a headset thrust a clipboard at him. Joe scribbled a signature and the guy hurried off.

"But something amazing happened?" I prompted.

"Yeah, our PR got some interest from a major publisher seeking the band's story. All this crazy stuff has made B4U super hot. There's going to be a bidding war for the tell-all story."

"That's great," enthused Lily.

"And Ellen DeGeneres called this morning and wants Shelley on her show tomorrow. She's flying in to do an on-set interview, and Giuliana called from *E!* and she wants to do an in-depth interview with the band on *Beyond Candid* and maybe do one of those hour-long biographies for the network chronicling their rise to the top. They're even talking about a reality show."

"That all sounds great," I said, wondering why Amelia was cooperating with everything. What happened to her wanting to get out so she could have a married life and solo career?

"This all sounds like money talking," said Lily.

"Money, money, money!" added Joe, grinning. "Management canned all the rumors about the band getting fired, thanks to all the renewed interest in them. B4U aren't just going to be huge, they'll be megastars." He held up his hand and I high-fived him since it seemed like the right thing to do.

"That sounds great," I said, despite the insincerity in my words.

"Yeah, there's just one problem," said Joe.

"What's that?"

"Can you please make sure Lauren isn't the murderer?"

"Will that hurt the deals?" I asked, thinking, yes, it would.

"Hell, no," he laughed. "We can probably up the price of everything. But I don't want that, I want Lauren to be okay. She's a nice kid. Probably the nicest of them all, and I mean no disrespect to my wife in saying that."

"I can't make any promises, but she's under twenty-four hour surveillance. If we can get the proof she didn't do it, we will," I assured him.

Joe breathed out. "I appreciate that."

"He won't appreciate the bill," Lily muttered.

Joe glanced at her. "I don't care what it takes, or how much it costs, if you prove Lauren didn't kill Katya. Since you're my alibi," he said, pointing his forefinger to me, "I don't mind saying Katya was a huge bitch and everyone hated her, but she didn't deserve to die; and if Lauren didn't do it, I don't want her going down for it."

"Like I said, I'll do what I can."

"Thanks." Someone yelled Joe's name from over near the video set and he looked up, raising a hand in recognition. "I have to go, but one more thing..."

"Yeah?"

"Did you find out who Michael is?"

I shook my head. "Not yet."

"I tried asking Lauren, but she clammed up and said she didn't want to talk about it. Maybe he's from her past, but if not, maybe this Michael guy can give her an alibi."

"He's right. Michael could be the key to Lauren's innocence," Lily said as we watched Joe walk away. I scanned the area designated for wardrobe as I looked for Lauren, my heart thumping briefly in the moments I couldn't see her. Then, it began beating with relief again as she reappeared in full costume. She, Amelia and Shelley all walked over to the set, and the crew broke out into applause. For the first time in the brief days since I'd known her, Shelley gave a shy smile and waved, taking a small bow.

"Let's get to work, people," she yelled. "Let's make beautiful music."

Lauren and Amelia cheered and high-fived her.

"I don't know who Michael is," I confessed. "I can't find any record of her ever knowing a Michael. He's not on her birth certificate, and she's not registered as being married. She doesn't have any brothers or cousins with that name. I even scoured her relationship history. No Michael."

"The guy has to exist somewhere."

"When Fletcher takes over the surveillance shift, I'm going to search deeper into her background. If he's there, I'll find him."

"What if he's here?"

I paused. The idea had already crossed my mind, but I only made a cursory effort at looking for him. "There are no Michaels in the crew. I already checked."

"What if he isn't with the crew?" Lily suggested. "What if he came to Montgomery too, but he's Lauren's big secret, right? They wouldn't announce it if it was a secret, romantic thing like Amelia and Joe. Maybe he'd stay at the hotel in a different room and have secret trysts with her?"

"I'll check the hotel registers."

Lily gasped. "What if he's married? That hussy! Maybe that's why it's such a big secret. She's a home wrecker!"

"Don't start anymore rumors!" I warned.

"You know who you should ask," Lily said, turning to the set and pointing. Beyond the cameras that were getting into position, and the dancers, now hurrying to their marked spots, were three stunning women who were taking their places on the podiums. "You should ask Amelia. She knows everyone's secrets."

~

Fletcher arrived midway through filming. "Your six

hours are up," he said, sidling, unnoticed, next to me and making me jump.

"Don't do that!" I hissed as a guy in a black shirt marked "crew" held a finger to his lips. He pointed to the neon *Quiet! Filming!* sign.

"Sorry. What's going on?"

"They've just started filming."

"I can see that. Bring me up to speed," said Fletcher.

While Lily watched the set, looking totally captivated, I whispered my surveillance report to my colleague. It was brief, since Lauren's day consisted of nothing more than leaving the hotel, collecting two dancers from their hotel, eating at Alessandro's while Lily and I waited with a pair of Butterfingers outside, and then straight back to the set. After several hours of full-costume rehearsals, the band finally began to film their first sequence. "According to the schedule Solomon emailed to my phone, they'll be here for another few hours before heading back to the hotel," I summarized. "There's no way you can lose Lauren."

Fletcher snorted. "Famous last words."

"Whose?" asked Lily.

Fletcher shrugged. "No one knows. Dude died before they got his name."

"Oh, that's sad," sighed Lily.

"Okay, we're going," I told him as he shook his head at Lily. "Is Lucas in the office? I might need help with some background research."

"Does the guy go anywhere else?"

"There are unconfirmed reports he has been spotted out in the open."

Lily added, "He's got a great tan for an agoraphobic."

"Do you think Lucas is agoraphobic?" I asked, stepping away and strongly urging Lily to follow me before Fletcher could listen to anymore.

"Nope. He came into the bar last week with a really pretty woman. He had his arm around her."

"That must be his fiancée. I think they've been together for years."

"Aww, that's nice. You know what else is nice? Your sister and Delgado came into the bar a couple of weeks ago. They had cocktails and Serena was really nice to the bar staff. None of them cried. Not once!"

"She's pretty nice to everyone since she and Delgado got together."

"Do you think they'll get married?"

"I don't know. I think Delgado wants to, but Serena's ex-husband has pretty much put her off marriage."

"Maybe they'll shack up together in unwedded bliss."

"I think she's still got those traditional values of placing marriage above living together."

"They'll make cute babies."

"Probably," I said in semi-agreement. My sister and co-worker getting married wasn't something I thought much about. But now that it was on my mind, I liked the idea of having Delgado as a brother-in-law. Given his predecessor, a cheating rat-bastard — which I confirmed when Serena asked me to tail him — the bar he had to hurdle over was not set very high.

"You and Solomon could make cute babies?"

"I try not to think about it," I told her as we got into her car.

"You must. You must imagine what it would be like sometimes."

"Okay, sometimes." Truthfully, I awoke that morning thinking about exactly what it would be like to marry Solomon and start a family with him. We skirted around the issue of a shared future occasionally, but neither of us ever said anything stronger than "I love you." Neither of us ever suggested that marriage was on the horizon, or a family. I wasn't sure if I were waiting for him to broach the subject, if he were waiting for me to, or if neither of us even thought that far ahead.

Lily and I discussed my future a few times and I was still trying to process my thoughts. As I considered it now, on our way out of the warehouse, I wondered if kids would be in my future. I believed I could be a good mother. I thought I would like to be a mom one day too, but right now, could I handle pushing a stroller and keeping up with my life of surveillance and solving crimes? Although my job was flexible, it would certainly be hard to combine the two. Before babies entered the picture, there was something else... could I see Solomon and me taking wedding vows? Would I sell my beloved buttercup yellow bungalow and move into his smart townhouse in Chilton? Or would Solomon move into my smaller, cuter pad? Could I see Solomon fathering our children? And the two of us taking turns at getting up in the night and pushing a stroller around the park?

Somewhere, deep inside me, my ovaries pinged.

"What's the sudden interest in everyone making babies?" I asked, thinking back to Solomon's mention of insisting his daughter keep her room tidy. Clearly, he saw himself as a dad one day.

"Just making small talk... Is that the time? I'll drop you off at the agency on my way downtown. I have an appointment."

"What for?" I asked, barely having enough time to buckle my seatbelt before Lily sped out of the lot.

"Dentist. Ouch!" She raised a hand to her jaw and winced unconvincingly.

"What happened?"

"I bit a... really big... um... nut?"

"You bit a really big nut?" I repeated.

"Super hard nut. Think I cracked a tooth."

"Shouldn't you be in a lot of pain?" I asked, my suspicion growing.

"I am! That's why I'm going to the dentist!"

"Your dentist is in West Montgomery. We're going..."

"Downtown, where your agency is. No need to thank me for being a brilliant friend. In fact, here's your agency now. Let me know when you find out who Michael is. Later!"

I was on the curb before I could ask Lily another thing. "My best friend is weird," I said to the empty sidewalk. Lily's Mini sped into the distance before turning a corner and disappearing. "Also, I don't have a ride home." My shoulders dropped as I turned and walked up the steps into the building that housed the agency. I greeted Jim, the doorman, and hopped into the waiting elevator, stepping onto our floor seconds later.

The agency was empty but for Solomon who sat in the small office in the corner, reading what looked like a magazine. The blinds were up and his door was open so I dropped my purse on the desk and walked over.

"How did surveillance go?" he asked, looking up and smiling as I entered.

"Fine. Lauren didn't do anything weird. She just followed her schedule. They started filming the video for their new song as Fletcher and I swapped places."

"She meet anyone out of the ordinary?"

"No. She hung out with two of the dance crew for lunch, then it was all crew on set."

"Hmm."

"I spoke with Joe. He wants us to clear Lauren rather than pinning Katya's murder on her."

"Reasonable request."

"But clearing her? What if she did it? So far, she's the prime suspect."

"Find the truth," Solomon said simply. "Even if our

client is wrong."

"Ok. Hey, I think I saw someone else observing her too," I told him, recalling the two men with badges.

"Yeah? Who would that be?"

"Could be MPD or FBI. I didn't recognize them, but they had that law enforcement look."

"I'll reach out and see who else has an interest in watching Lauren. Why are you in the office?"

"I want to try and trace Michael."

Solomon frowned. "Michael?"

"Lauren's big secret, remember? Hey, are you reading a mom and baby magazine?"

Solomon dropped the magazine. "No. It's a parenting magazine."

"How's that different?"

"It has a mom and dad on the cover and there's a column written by a dad on page seventeen."

"Okaaay."

"It's interesting stuff."

I paused, feeling confused. I'd seen Solomon reading a bunch of things from *Time* to the national newspapers, and a few books too, but the parenting magazine was a novelty. "Did Lily call you?" I asked, suspicion tingeing my voice.

"No. Why?"

"No reason."

"I think I'd make a good dad," said Solomon.

I froze, rooted to the spot. My day was getting weirder. "Okay."

"I mean, I'd get up in the night and change diapers. I don't even mind picking out strollers; and if a nursery has to be pink, so be it."

"Okay," I said again.

"I'd probably wear one of those sling things that you put the baby in so it's strapped to your chest."

I opened my mouth to say, "okay" again, but this time, nothing came out but air.

"Just saying," said Solomon, as he picked up the magazine again.

I remained standing, unsure of what to say. First, Lily asked if Solomon and I would have babies... now Solomon was telling me he'd be a great dad. All of a sudden, the rush of the future infiltrated my airspace and all I could do was allow my thoughts to spiral in every direction through my mind, as if my future life were flashing before my eyes. None of it was clear, but it was... possible. Wedding, marriage, baby, home, family... they were all there, waiting for me and all I had to do was grab them.

"There's something I need to tell you," I said without thinking first.

CHAPTER FOURTEEN

"Lexi!"

"I know! I know! I'm sorry!" Color flooded my face as the weight of Solomon's disapproval bore down on me, but I just couldn't keep it in any longer. Not when he was talking about babies and painting a nursery pink. I couldn't keep my secret to myself. I had to tell him about my rookie error, as well as my part in leaking the story to the media. "I didn't mean to speak in front of a journalist."

"It's too late for 'sorry.' You should never have opened your mouth."

"It won't happen again. I promise."

"I hope not. You're lucky this time, Graves. After the band and their management's initial reaction died down, they began to see the positive side of Shelley's story breaking."

I dropped into the chair. "Joe implied they stood to make a ton of cash if the various deals went through."

"Let's hope so." Solomon fixed me with a hard look.

"Is there anything else you want to tell me?" he asked.

"No."

"Let me rephrase that; is there anything you *need* to tell me?"

I thought about the awful impromptu stage performance at the strip club that I managed to quash. Spinning a story in B4U's favor was one thing; but that video would be hard to explain. Thankfully, I was certain I had the only copy. I vowed I would destroy it as soon as I could. "Nope."

"You sure?"

"One hundred percent."

"Okay. You said you had work to do?"

"Deeper background checks on Lauren, especially in relation to her secret man, Michael," I told him, again.

"Do you have a lead on this Michael?"

"No," I said, relieved that the conversation switched to more stable ground, "but I can't help thinking Michael is the key to Lauren's missing hours. She doesn't want us to know anything about him, and she is sticking to her story. She says that she was taking a nap when Katya was murdered. Lily thinks she might be secretly meeting him."

"She could be right. Did you ask Amelia what she knows?"

"No, she was surrounded by people all day, and I couldn't risk losing Lauren. I'm going to find her later when the video shooting wraps up."

"Get as much information as you can use to prompt

her. Amelia might not be as forthcoming, since she's been outed as a blackmailer, and Shelley and Lauren seem to have forgiven her. She might want to put it all behind her."

"I think they understood why she wanted out, but..."

Solomon picked up the desk phone. "But what?"

"Amelia hated the band so much that she wanted out, so why is she being so compliant now?"

"Does it matter? She narrowly escaped a blackmail charge and could have been implicated in a murder. She's probably relieved."

"Are we working on probables now?" I asked, knowing Solomon liked hunches, but he liked facts more.

"No, but the blackmail case is closed. We're not working on any other aspect of the case except surveillance on Lauren and finding the murderer. I only hope the two things aren't one and the same."

"I'm on it." Leaving Solomon's room, confused but relieved, I took my position at my desk, fired up my laptop, and started my search. It was great to finally have the time, and get away from all the craziness of the past few days. I wanted to conduct an in-depth research on one single band member.

While I had a stack of digital paperwork that combed through their most obvious records, including their drivers' licenses and dating histories — I suspected Shelley's was largely faked by management, given the volume of young actors and boy band members – as well as her limited financial records. Lucas slammed up against a virtual brick wall when it came to their bank accounts; but according to the report I now read, he located several properties registered in their names. Katya had a condo in LA, Shelley had an apartment in Santa Monica, and Amelia owned apartments in LA and New York. As I examined the records again, I expected to find similar properties for Lauren. She had an apartment near Katya, but also a house in the suburbs.

The house was an anomaly, so I entered the address in the search engine and called up a street image for it. It was a neat, single story with an unenclosed lawn and had a minivan parked in the driveway. The house looked tidy and well maintained, apart from the child's bike on the lawn. I looked through the paperwork Lucas handed me, searching for information. Finding it, I read quickly. The utilities were registered to a Josephine Young, whom I figured had to be Lauren's mother or sister. It made sense she would buy a house for a family member to live in.

"Lexi," Solomon called. I looked up, finding him in the doorway.

"Yeah?"

"I checked with MPD and FBI; our girl is being followed by both parties."

I wasn't surprised. "Did they say why?"

"No. Time for you to charm your relatives and get some answers."

"Great, my favorite activity." I reached for my

phone.

"I know what your favorite activity is, and it's not that." Solomon smiled.

"Sexual harassment in the workplace isn't okay," I told him primly.

"Just for that, I'll let you make all the moves later. I might need a lot of persuading."

I held back a laugh. "Doubt it." Dialing Garrett first, I ran through a few questions in my head. Was the police interest in Lauren the same as ours? What did they know that I didn't? Was Lauren their number one suspect in Katya's murder? Did they know who her mystery man was?

"Sis, this is not a surprise," said Garrett on answering. "I know why you're calling."

"You do?"

"Yup. It's about Mom and Dad's potluck dinner this Friday, and whether Traci is going to make her peach cobbler or not. The answer is yes."

Obviously, that wasn't why I was calling, but it was good news. My mouth watered at the thought of the hot peaches. "Will she make enough that I can have two helpings?"

"Most likely, since you're eating for... Oh, hey, what are you bringing?"

That had me stumped, especially since I didn't recall a word about any potluck dinner. "Umm..."

"You forgot, didn't you?"

"No!"

"You did!"

"I might have," I said, struggling to recall an invitation and drawing a blank. "Don't tell Mom."

"What if I tell Dad?"

"What if I tell Traci you sent me to buy her anniversary gift because you were too busy handling a suspect?"

"Okay, you win. Dinner is at seven. No need to thank me for saving your bacon with the parents."

"Thanks. Actually, since we're shooting the breeze, I saw your guys following Lauren Young."

"Shit. I knew I shouldn't have put those doofs on surveillance."

"Yeah, your bad. Why are you having Lauren followed?"

"She's my chief suspect in Katya Markova's murder!"

"How come?" I asked, my heart sinking. It was bad enough that I was heavily suspicious of Lauren, but worse that Garrett could actually arrest her.

"Let me go out on a limb here and say you saw my guys following her because you're also following her..."

"Yeah, but your guys didn't see me!"

"It's not a competition!" Garrett sighed. "You're also following her because she's your number one suspect too."

"Yeah, but I want to prove she didn't do it."

"I want to prove she did."

"Which do you think the FBI want to prove?"

"They're following her too? Jeez!"

"You didn't know?"

"I do now. We can't have three teams following her. She'll get wise."

"You want to compare notes?"

"Yes, but I don't have a report from my guys yet. What do you know?"

"I know I have access you guys don't. I have Lauren's schedule and I can get inside the warehouse where they're shooting their video, and the hotel, too."

"My guys just flash their badges. It's like a super cool, all-access pass," Garrett teased.

"Again, with the competition?!" I harrumphed my dissatisfaction with skirting around our mutual knowledge. "Okay, so far, Lauren hasn't done anything out of the ordinary. She's following her schedule. I haven't seen her do a single suspicious thing, but I have two problems that I need answers to."

"Is one her alibi at the time of Katya's murder?" Garret guessed.

"Correct."

"She told me she was taking a nap. Do you believe that?"

"Yes and no. It's a crappy excuse so it doesn't sound made up, but without someone witnessing her, in reality, she could have been anywhere."

"My money is on her being down the hall, holding a knife. What's the other thing?"

"I'm trying to find a guy called Michael. He was the

secret Lauren was trying to keep concealed when Amelia was blackmailing them."

"What's the connection to Lauren?"

"I don't know."

"What do you know about him? I can run him through a few databases, see if we get any hits."

"I only have his first name, so that's a no-go. Actually, I don't know anything about him at all. I hoped he might have come up in your investigation?"

"I've got the file on my desk, and I don't see anything. No close relatives called Michael. No husband. No boyfriend, past or present."

"Those are my findings too."

"I can't promise anything, but I'll look into it."

"Thanks."

"About the FBI..."

"I'll call Maddox," I decided. "Maybe we can set up a meeting and share resources?"

"They're already supposed to be sharing with MPD. We had a deal."

"You think he'll share with me? You are."

"Not officially, and you may as well try. No need to tell him I'm pissed at his surveillance team. I'll let him know."

I hung up after making a note in my phone's calendar about the family dinner. A cursory glance through my messages revealed my parents hadn't sent me a text or an email. I could only assume someone must have told me and I promptly forgot. At least, now

I had the opportunity to save the day, so long as I could either bake something, or buy something and put it in a dish, and pretend I made it. The latter was the lazy option, but participating in a daily surveillance slot hardly allowed time for baking. I doodled *Cookies?* on my desk pad and grabbed the phone again, this time, dialing Maddox.

"Hey, this is a nice surprise. Have you had lunch?"

My stomach clenched with sudden hunger. "No. I missed it."

"You should never miss lunch."

"I was busy watching your guys watching Lauren Young."

"Oh, crap. Were they that obvious?"

I grinned, enjoying Maddox's squirming. Truthfully, I'd only spotted one team watching Lauren, but it was fun to tell both Garrett and Maddox that it was their respective team that I caught. "Yeah. Can I pick your brains?"

"Sure. Meet me at the cafe on Century near my office in twenty minutes?"

"On my way."

Maddox was waiting at the counter by the time I walked the few blocks to the cafe. I slid onto the stool next to him. "Coffee?" he asked, leaning over to kiss my cheek in a friendly way.

"Please. Did you order?"

"No, thought I'd wait for you." He raised a hand, notifying the waitress to walk over. She poured me a coffee and refreshed Maddox's before telling us the day's specials.

"I'll take a salt beef sandwich and..." He looked across to me.

"Same for me," I said.

"So you wanted to pick my brains?"

"Yeah, about the case. Seems we have three teams watching Lauren."

"Sounds like two too many."

"That's what I figured."

"I can't call off my team."

"I'm not calling off mine."

"Your team is you!"

"Me and other people!"

"Think we can persuade MPD?"

I shook my head. "Probably not."

"I could pull rank. This is officially an FBI case."

"Do you want to piss my brother off?"

"No, I remember last time, and it wasn't pretty." We both thought back to the awful time my brothers gave Maddox when we all thought he was cheating on me while working undercover. Turns out, a large segment of MPD were not happy about the events, but things cooled down pretty quickly and returned to normal. I figured my brothers had something to do with settling the tension in the atmosphere once it turned out things weren't as I first thought. It was a huge shame and I tried not to think about it. I was just glad that Maddox and I could be friends now, even if there was a lingering attraction that we both did our best to ignore. Or, at least, I did. Maddox, I reminded myself, had recently booked a romantic trip for two. "What's on your mind?"

"Just the case," I lied quickly as I took a sip of the coffee. It was hot and nutty so I added a couple of sugars to sweeten it.

"How can I help?"

"I'm trying to find a guy called Michael. He's connected to Lauren somehow, but I don't know how."

"He hasn't come up during my investigation."

"That's what Garrett said."

"How did you get his name?"

"Michael was the threat used against Lauren in the blackmail plot."

"Ah. The one orchestrated by Amelia?"

"Yeah."

"Sounds like she should be the one you talk to."

"I plan on it. I just haven't had chance yet."

"There could be a reason you can't find him."

I shook my head as I held back a laugh. "I'm counting on it!"

"No, I mean, he could be our hit man."

For a moment, all I could do was stare. "You think Lauren hired a hit man to get rid of Katya?"

Maddox shrugged. "Could be. Let's look at the facts as Lauren knew them a few days ago. The band hated each other. She was being blackmailed by someone who knew about her mystery guy. She puts two and two together, gets the wrong number and figures it's Katya behind the blackmail, since she's always so nasty. To protect her guy, Lauren and this Michael guy get together and plan to kill Katya. They use the secret passage to access Katya's room, unseen, and she's later found stabbed to death. He exits the same way and leaves via the service elevator, simply walking out of the hotel, never to return, and Lauren waits in Amelia's suite, pretending she took a nap."

"How do they access the service elevator?" I asked, searching for flaws in Maddox's hypothesis.

"One of them steals an employee pass or keycard?"

"Could be. Did you check hotel records for access to the elevator?"

"Yes, but it services all floors, so there's too many people to eliminate."

"Fingerprints in the service passage?"

"Still some unknowns. Some I've matched to hotel employees, and they've been cleared."

"What about Lauren's alibi? If she planned a hit, wouldn't she give herself a rock solid alibi?" I asked, stating the most obvious problem with his theory.

"Yeah, I'm stuck on that too." We waited while the waitress placed our sandwiches in front of us. I took a large, hungry bite, sinking my teeth into soft bread, tangy pickle, and delicious salt beef.

"If you accessed her finances, perhaps you could find a payment to this Michael guy?" I suggested.

"If they're in on it together, it's unlikely she would

pay him; and definitely, not by bank transfer or check."

"If they've been together a long time, she could have made other payments to him? Or him to her? Maybe they went on vacation and he bank transferred his share?"

"Why would she accept that? She's rich."

"I don't think B4U are that rich. I mean, they make a lot of money, but I think the band are salaried."

"I'll look into it. Maybe see if she made any payments to menswear shops, or had gifts shipped to another address that we could match to him."

"Can you..."

"Keep you in the loop? Sure. And you'll give me a heads up after you've spoken to Amelia? It would be good to have something extra to go on when I dig into this further. Michael is a common name, you know."

"I'll let you know what I find out."

"You hear about that story that got leaked about Shelley?"

"Yeah."

"Some people are dumb," laughed Maddox as he stuffed the last of his sandwich into his mouth.

I swallowed. "Er, yeah."

"Who tells reporters that kind of stuff?"

"No idea," I lied. "Who knows how reporters get that stuff?"

Maddox lifted his wrist, and checked his watch. "I have a meeting to get to. Good to catch up. We should do this again, but for longer. Want to get dinner some time?" He dropped a few dollars on the table next to the receipt the waitress set down a moment ago. I noticed he covered the whole receipt.

"Sure, that would be nice. I have surveillance for who knows how long, and a family dinner on Friday, but maybe after that?"

"I'm out of town this weekend. Maybe, next week? I'll give you a call." Maddox pecked another kiss on my cheek, grabbed his jacket, and rushed out, leaving me with the remains of my sandwich and wondering not so much about Lauren's mystery man, but Maddox's mystery woman. Our friendship seemed to be edging out of the fledgling stage and back to an easy repartee, but it clearly hadn't yet gotten to the personal discussion point. He never asked me about Solomon. I never asked him about dating. It just wasn't something we were comfortable with. At least, not in the same way I could ask any other guy buddy. Now that I thought about it, did I discuss Maddox with anyone but Lily? Solomon never asked me about him, although I was sure he knew we met up from time to time, and I didn't usually bring up our meetings in conversation.

"Being an adult is weird," I muttered, as I pushed my plate away and swallowed the last of my coffee.

"Tell me about it," said the waitress, reaching for the cash Maddox left and pocketing it.

We laughed, I thanked her and grabbed my jacket, ready to hail a cab for the hotel, and wishing I hadn't agreed to Lily picking me up in her car this morning.

That gave me no other choice but to walk or take cabs. I could have gotten the bus, but Montgomery's public transit system wasn't the best, and I didn't have the time to take multiple buses across town to the hotel.

Ten long minutes, and one expense receipt later, the cab tossed me out in front of the hotel. I entered through the main entrance, the paparazzi ignoring me, thankfully, and crossed the lobby to the elevators. Solomon's security waited by the elevator to the penthouse suites and they admitted me without question.

Large and Larger waited in their usual seated positions in the corridor. "Hey," I said brightly as I stepped out. "I'm looking for Amelia." Large inclined his head to the right, which I took to mean she was in Joe's suite. I wondered if she moved in there permanently now that their marriage was out in the open. Fortunately, the door was ajar so I figured I wasn't interrupting anything that would cause me to want to bleach my eyes. All the same, I knocked loudly as I entered.

Amelia was alone, reading a magazine. Her wig was firmly in place which was a shame because I thought the short cut suited her better.

"How did the shooting go?" I asked.

She looked up. "We got the first ten seconds," she told me.

"But you were there for hours!"

"Only the last two hours were filmed. Didn't I see

you there? You and the blonde chick?"

"Yeah, we stopped by."

"You should come by later too, when we film the club scene. It's got a big dance number."

"I'd like that; thanks. Are you all finished for now? When do you have to be back?"

"Not until eight. Lauren and Shelley are filming their solo scenes now. I left early to take a break."

A toilet flushed in the next room and I looked up, expecting to see Joe. Instead, Don stepped out. "Hey, the private detective!" he said, looking unhappy. "Are you interrogating Amelia? Amelia, do you want me to call someone? Joe?"

"No, it's cool," Amelia replied as Don dropped onto the armchair and stretched his legs. She glanced at me again, frowning. "Unless you *are* here to interrogate me?"

"No, not at all. Can I sit?" I took the adjacent armchair when she nodded, and slid off my jacket, folding it over the arm. "Actually, I wanted to ask you something about the blackmail?"

Amelia sighed. "Didn't we wrap that all up? I returned the money and apologized."

"That's great. I'm glad you did, but it's about..." I looked at Don, who was studying his phone and pretending not to listen. "Can we talk privately?"

"Don knows everything. You don't have to worry about him."

"Are you sure?" I glanced over at him and he looked

up, giving me a sharp nod.

"Yeah, we've been friends since the tour started. We just clicked, right, Don?" She waited while he agreed, then continued, "Look I'm over all that blackmail crap. I won't do it again."

"That's okay. I just need to know how you knew about everyone's secrets?"

"We've been together years. I overheard stuff, or sometimes the girls drank too much and blabbed it out. I just paid attention."

"That's how you knew about Katya's past in Russia?"

"No, that came from a reporter."

"The reporter approached you?"

"No, he went to Joe with a big file about Katya. He had photos and certificates, all kinds of stuff, and not just from Russia, but her life here too. He even had a video of her fancy, private school music recital. She didn't learn to play piano by ear like she told everyone in her big rags-to-riches sob story. Her parents paid a concert pianist to teach her."

"You saw the file?"

"Yeah, I read it. Joe doesn't know."

"What happened to the file after that?"

"I don't know. I never asked. I assumed Joe paid off the reporter because the story never broke. Then Shelley ran into some PR girl who claimed to know Katya from way back. Honestly, I'm surprised it hasn't come out now that she's dead; but all the obituaries keep focusing on this terrible, sad life she was supposed to have had. If only they could have seen her in her prim, little, school uniform, or riding her twenty thousand-dollar pony."

"She really had everyone sucked in," said Don. "We all believed her story. I think even Katya believed it sometimes."

"None of you had any reason not to," I told them. "People lie so easily."

"Yeah, I bet you can see through them all?" Don put down his phone, as our conversation piqued his interest.

"Sometimes. Sometimes, it takes a while. None of you should feel bad about getting sucked in. Was Katya a friend of yours, Don?"

"I thought so, at first. The dancers, me, we all really clicked with B4U. I thought Katya and I clicked, but she was a nasty piece of work. She must have heard about all the awful things she did to people. If Lauren killed her... well, I'm not surprised," he said.

"No one deserved to die from a knife in her back," said Amelia, but she shrugged so I figured she wasn't all that devastated.

"How did you know Shelley's secret?" I asked, directing the conversation back to my main concern.

"She got really super drunk one night and it just came out." Amelia giggled. "Literally."

"And obviously you know your own secret, but what about Lauren?"

"Look, I don't know why you're asking all this, but

really, I'm over it. I don't want to talk about it anymore."

"I just need to know what you know about..."

"I said, I'm over it, okay? I don't want to talk about it anymore. I'm past all that. Ask Lauren. It's her deal." Amelia fixed me with a furious look. With her pursed lips and narrowed eyes, I figured I only had seconds before she shut down completely. Having Don back her up didn't help.

"Can I use your bathroom?" I asked, figuring I'd give us both a break and try again in another couple of minutes.

"Sure, it's over there." Amelia flashed a hand at the furthest door.

"Thanks." I walked over, shutting the bathroom door behind me. It was nice, far bigger than my bedroom, and beautifully appointed with marble countertops and a sink faucet that looked like it cost more than my whole bathroom. Since I didn't really need to be there, I opened the cabinet doors below the sink and took a look. There wasn't anything personal amongst the spare towels and extra toilet rolls, so I shut the doors and walked over to the shower cubicle. There were a couple of shower gels in the cubicle; his and hers. Besides that, nothing.

I counted to a hundred, then flushed the toilet, ran the water in the sink and mussed up the towel on the rack before I unlocked the door and stepped back into the room. Don was pouring tea from the large pot, and

Amelia had tossed her magazine onto the coffee table.

"Is this your last video?" I asked, starting a conversation that I hoped would make Amelia feel comfortable again.

She shrugged and sighed. "I don't know. Maybe. Management are still talking about the future."

"You don't want to continue with the band?" I asked, wondering why she was keeping up the charade after the lengths she'd gone to in order to get fired.

"I don't care. We could make a lot of money if we stick together."

"That's good news."

"Yeah, I guess."

"Listen, about Lauren..."

"I said, I don't want to talk about it! If you want to talk to Lauren, she's at the warehouse, filming. I'm not getting into anymore trouble for this shit and I'm not saying another word."

I tried several more approaches, but Lauren didn't want to talk and Don was looking increasingly agitated. Rather than risk one of them calling Joe and getting me into more trouble, all I could do was thank Amelia for her time and leave.

Stepping out of the hotel, I hailed a cab and climbed in, asking to be delivered to the warehouse. I was hoping Fletcher hadn't solved the case in the hours since he took over. What should have been a twenty-minute journey turned into over an hour as we got stuck in a traffic jam due to a collision on Century Street.

When I arrived, I was bored and frustrated, but I needn't have worried about Fletcher. I found him sitting on a plastic chair, his feet up on another, far away from the crew, and he didn't look happy.

"What's happenin'?" I asked.

"Nothing unless you enjoy this kind of stuff."

"I do. Are they still filming?"

"Yeah. Shelley is doing her thing now and Lauren is in makeup. She just finished. Amelia left a couple of hours ago."

"I know. I just spoke to her at the hotel. I need to talk to Lauren."

"Solomon called. He's looking for you."

"Why didn't he call me?"

"Said your phone is off."

I pulled my cell phone from my pocket and touched the screen. It was off. I pressed the reset button and it whirred silently to life. "Don't know how that happened," I said, puzzled as the battery indicator flashed almost full. Three text messages immediately popped onto the screen.

Two from Solomon timed thirty minutes ago and ten minutes ago read, *Call the office*. The third was from Lily and simply read, *OMG! You're on TV!*

"What the hell?" I asked the phone. To Fletcher, I asked, "Did Solomon say why he wanted me to call?"

"No, he just said, 'When you see Lexi, get her to call me right away'."

"Did he sound annoyed?" I asked, wondering what

Lily meant by *on TV.*

"He didn't sound happy. What did you do?"

"Nothing," I said. "I saw him this morning, then I went to talk to Amelia, but she clammed up so now I need to talk to Lauren." My phone rang and I jumped. Solomon. I answered it, my stomach tightening into a knot.

"Where are you?" asked Solomon.

"The warehouse. Amelia wouldn't talk so I came to ask Lauren directly..."

"Leave it for now. Get to the office. We have a crisis."

"What kind of..." But I didn't get to finish. Solomon already hung up.

CHAPTER FIFTEEN

To me, a crisis might mean a whole bunch of things. It might mean that my mother called and insisted on Solomon baking something for the potluck dinner. Or it could mean a major curveball was impeding our investigation... As I hailed yet another cab and made my way back to the agency, I was at least reassured that we hadn't lost Lauren, lest she go on a murderous rampage.

When I arrived in the office, thirty long minutes later, Solomon did not look like he received a call from my mom. He looked like he was about to go homicidal! Given that his facial expressions were limited at best, I quickly ran through my options. The one I chose was turning on my heel and hightailing it out of there, then hiding until whatever happened blew over. But sadly, I could not act on it.

"Explain this," said Solomon, jabbing a button on his laptop and turning it around so I could view the screen. "No, wait, let me increase the volume," he added, hitting another button.

My heart skipped a beat as a grainy video filled the screen. The picture might not have been HD or perfect, but the image was clear: three women stripping and singing on a small stage in a dark club in Montgomery. The same video I thought I scrubbed every image of as the bouncer and I checked everyone's cell phones. Clearly, we missed someone. I watched myself rushing across the screen, grabbing discarded items of clothing as I hurried towards the stage. With a sinking heart, I knew exactly where I saw this video before. The Blue Moon's doorman sent it to me with his assurance he deleted it from the phone on which he found it.

"Uh..." Did I delete it from mine? I couldn't remember. I closed my eyes, knowing I didn't want to see anymore and cringed.

"That's what I thought. Keep watching."

"I don't need to."

"Yeah, you know what happens next."

While I cowered and winced, a top flew off, landing on a vacant chair near the video version of me. I watched myself grabbing it.

"Remember earlier? When I asked if there was anything else you needed to tell me? Didn't you think I might have meant something like this?" Solomon's voice rose as he jabbed a finger at the screen.

"I thought I handled it!"

"You didn't see the guy holding the camera?"

"No, but it's probably a cell phone..."

"I worked that out already!"

"...And I was so busy making sure no one was filming..."

"Except this guy!"

"I'm really sorry!"

"Sorry isn't good enough on this one."

"Maybe we can speak to whomever emailed it to you? Get them to sign a..."

"Too late. This wasn't emailed to me. It's streaming on the biggest gossip blog in the world!"

Feeling faint, I whispered, "Oh, no!"

"And you know what's even worse than this video getting streamed to... let's see, nine hundred thousand people in the last hour?"

"Um, nothing?"

"No. I just got a call from Joe. He was asking me to explain why my employee is at a strip club where all three girls in the band were stripping and singing derogatory songs about their recently deceased band member. You know what makes that even worse? I had Lucas hack their network to find out where they got that video. You know what I discovered?"

"Someone local?" I guessed, thinking I needed to talk to Ray Domingo. Perhaps he realized selling the video was worth more than helping the sister of the man who once helped turn his life around. I had to admit, if I were in his position, I'd certainly feel tempted by the cash too.

"Your phone. This damn video came from *your*

phone!"

I paled. My stomach turned inside out as the shock hit me. "No. No way. It can't have!"

"Save it! This agency has never been so embarrassed. Do you know how hard it is to draw in lucrative contracts like this? Do you know how many times I've had to explain the agency's actions to Joe Carter? First, Shelley's leaked secret, then Amelia's secret wedding getting out..."

He didn't need to continue. I knew where he was going with it: it all came from me. The band may have screwed up, but I wasn't responsible for their actions. No, that was all on them. "Maybe if I talk to him..."

"No way! You're officially off the case. Take a short vacation. Chill out at home, and put your feet up or something."

"What? But I didn't do anything wrong!" I yelled, breathing heavily. My surprise and indignation from getting blamed for everything hit me. I didn't send the video; and I didn't know who might've hacked my phone, but clearly, Solomon was in no mood for another apology or explanation. "I've tried so hard on this case even when they threw things at me, and bitched and moaned, and even hit on you! I discovered Amelia was the blackmailer, and I also provided an alibi for Joe and her in the murder. I don't know who did this, but it wasn't me!"

"You're still off the case!"

I drew in a harsh breath and fought back furious

tears over the injustice of it all. "You know what? I'm done. I quit!" I exclaimed before turning around and walking out of the office. Naturally, I expected Solomon to call me back at any moment, but he didn't. As for me? I kept walking.

~

"You didn't accidentally send it to them? It's so easy to inadvertently hit a button?" asked Lily. I was perched on a bar stool in her bar, a Long Island iced tea in front of me. I asked her to hold the tea and replace it with more alcohol before I sobbed out the whole sordid story of B4U's embarrassing strip tape and how I caught all the blame. I didn't know how to prove I didn't mail the tape to a gossip blog, or if I even wanted to.

"No! I checked on the way over and it was in my sent file, but I didn't send it and there's no way I can prove it. The band girls probably think I got a payday out of it."

"Shame."

"What?"

"That you didn't get a payday. It would have softened the blow of taking the blame."

I took another long sip. "How can I ever get Solomon to believe it wasn't me?"

"By finding out who really sent it," replied Lily, the simplicity of her statement mind-blowing.

"That's just it, I don't know. My phone is always in

my purse, or my jacket. I never leave it alone."

"You don't have a purse today."

"I'm traveling light. I have my little wallet and phone in my jacket pocket, and I never even took it off except... oh no!" I thought back to my interview with Amelia. I took a fake bathroom break to give Amelia a moment to cool down, leaving my jacket folded over the arm of the chair. While I hoped she'd spend a few minutes trying to take it easy, she used them to search my phone, screw up my life and achieve her original objective: sinking the band once and for all, just to get out of her contract. "That bitch!"

"Who?"

"Amelia. It had to be her! She had access to my phone earlier. She could have gotten into it and emailed the video."

"Haven't you heard of pin protection?"

"Sure, but it's not hard to get past it if you know how. Maybe she looked over my shoulder one time and remembered it."

"You should tell Solomon that. He should be aware that Amelia might have set you up."

"I don't know. You should have seen him earlier. I've never seen him so mad."

"Did he get frown lines?"

I frowned automatically. "No."

"Did his face move at all?"

"He narrowed his eyes and yelled."

"Oh boy!"

"So I quit."

"You did what? Lexi!"

"The words just came out!"

"You can't quit! You're Lexi Graves, private investigator. Also, Solomon is your boyfriend, unless you quit him too?"

"I don't think so." I winced, wondering if Solomon considered my job resignation a rejection of him too. Since I was too mad at him to call, and figured he felt the same about me, I'd just have to assume he didn't believe it. "Do you think Solomon thinks that?"

"I'm not sure guys think, so probably not, no."

"Down on guys today?"

"No, just frustrated that Jord canceled date night; and left a note on the fridge to make something for potluck dinner at your mom's. What should I make?"

"No clue. I don't even know what I'm making. You know, I didn't even get an invite. Garrett told me."

"I bet I know what the dinner conversation will be. *You.*" Lily giggled and reached for another glass to wipe clean.

I dropped my head onto the bar and moaned while she patted me and asked me not to put off the other customers who were glancing in our direction.

"You know, you could still be a PI; just set up your own agency," she suggested.

"I don't have an office."

"Use the small room next to my office."

"I can't run a detective agency out of a bar. I can't

even run a business, period."

"Number one, sure you can. A detective agency run out of a bar scores major noir points; and two, I run a business. Your sister runs a business. So you can too."

"Thanks for the vote of confidence."

"You could always ask Solomon to rehire you."

I lifted my head briefly. "Never!"

"Then you'll have to go freelance. You have a mortgage to pay, remember?"

I dropped my head again, muttering, "And a fashion habit."

"You are never knowingly under-dressed."

"I have my standards."

"So, do you want that spare office? C'mon on, Lexi! It'll be fun. Your mom and I can help. We both passed Spy 101 at the adult ed center!"

The image of my mom and Lily sneaking around the library and following a mystery man popped into my head. "That's what you were doing at the library!"

"Uh... yeah. Our mark never suspected a thing. We graduated at the top of our class!"

"How many were in the class?"

Lily counted two on her fingers then tossed her hair. "I don't want to talk about it. So do you want the office, or not?"

"I'll think about it; thanks." I dragged myself upright, smoothing my hair as I checked my reflection in the mirrored back wall of the bar. I looked tired. At least, I held back my furious tears, thanks to a nonwaterproof mascara I wore that day. If I had a face painted like one of the Kiss members, I would have found it necessary to drag my sorry butt home.

"Lexi?" Hearing a female voice behind me, I looked over, my expression probably as sour as I felt. When I saw Lauren, I straightened up and tried to look less desolate. "Uh, hi. It took me a while to track you down."

"You tracked me down?" I frowned, utterly confused. "What are you doing here?"

Lauren slid onto the bar stool next to me. "Can I get a hot tea?" she asked Lily.

"You can, but that's so boring. Don't you want a real drink?"

"Yeah, but maybe later." Lauren smiled shyly. "Do you talk all to your customers like that?"

"Only the fun ones," said Lily. "I'll get your tea."

We watched Lily as she moved to the other end of the bar where the coffee and tea machine were located. Finally, my curiosity got the better of me. "Why were you looking for me?" I asked.

"I heard you got fired."

"I quit!"

"Because of the video?"

"Yeah."

"I'm sorry."

"Seriously?" I raised my eyebrows.

"Truthfully? No, I'm not sorry about what we did, just that we got caught. And I am sorry you lost your job over it."

I drained my drink. "At least, you're honest."

"I'm glad you think so. I want to hire you."

"Yay, your first client," said Lily, placing a teacup in front of Lauren. "Told you! Working out of a bar is smart. Are you paying?"

Lauren nodded quickly. "Yes."

"Good," said Lily, holding up a camera. "Smile!" Lauren immediately plastered a smile on her face and Lily snapped the shot. A photo slid out of the old-fashioned Polaroid camera and she stuck it on the mirrored wall. "I'm starting a wall of fame," she told us.

"There's only one photo," pointed out Lauren, "and it's me."

"You're a trend-setter," Lily told her.

"What do you want to hire me for?" I asked, feeling more than puzzled.

"I want you to keep on doing what you were doing."

"And what was that?"

"Following me."

"Okaay," I said, wondering if I should mention the other teams that were also following her.

"Okay, well, not follow me exactly. I want you to do the other thing you were doing... I want you to prove I didn't kill Katya."

"What makes you think I want to help you now? You and your band have been nothing but pains in the ass since I joined the case," I said, not concealing how bitter I felt.

"I know and I'm sorry, but you need a job and I need your help. You believe in me. I know the police are following me since I'm their only suspect. I need you to prove to everyone that I didn't hurt Katya. I didn't kill her."

"Why don't you tell them where you really were when she was murdered?"

"I..." Lauren paused, pinching her lips together. "I can't do that."

Somehow, I wasn't surprised that Lauren really was somewhere else, but I was glad she came close to admitting it. "Then how am I supposed to help you?"

"By finding the real killer."

"It would be a lot easier if you would told me your alibi. Then I can tell the police, let them verify it and boom! You are immediately eliminated from the suspect pool."

"I comprise the entire suspect pool, and believe me, I would if I could, but I can't. Look, it's not simple, okay?"

"You're protecting someone," I guessed, waiting for any sign that I was right. Lauren's face remained impassive. "That Michael guy?" She blinked in surprise and I grabbed onto it. "I knew it! Tell the police you were with him and get him to verify it."

"No."

"Then I don't think I can help you." I turned away, but kept watching her out of the corner of my eye. For a few seconds, Lauren did nothing. As she reached for her purse, I thought she would simply get up and walk away, but instead, she pulled out a checkbook and opened it. A moment later, she slid a check over to me. "How about now?" she asked.

"Are you serious?" I squeaked, looking at the figure.

Lily plucked the check from my hand, her eyes widening. "Are you?" she demanded.

"Yes. I would say deadly serious, but I don't think that would help." Lauren restrained a smile, but Lily just laughed and stuck out her hand. Taking it, Lauren shook it, looking confused.

"Congratulations," said Lily, giving her hand a final pump. "You hired a PI and you get your tea on the house since this is also Lexi's new office."

"In a bar?"

"She said with condescension, the same woman who was recently caught taking her top off on video," Lily mocked.

"I like you," said Lauren, her smile the most genuine I'd ever seen on her. "I like you too, Lexi. I'm glad you're going to help me."

"I didn't say I would," I pointed out as Lily wafted the check under my nose. I sighed. Since my salary was now between nothing and zero, and I did have grownup bills to pay, Lily was right. I had to earn money somehow and the fat check from Lauren would certainly come in very useful.

"What about if I tell you I think you were set up?"

Lauren asked.

That snatched my attention. "What are you talking about?"

"I know you supposedly leaked the video, but I'm pretty sure it wasn't you."

"It wasn't!"

"I know you went to visit Amelia and one of the dancers."

"Yeah, I spoke with her earlier at the hotel and Don was there. I think Amelia still wants to get out of her contract."

Lauren's next words surprised me. Instead of agreeing, she said, "It's not common knowledge, but Don and Katya had a thing going on. Did you know that?"

I sat upright. "No. Really?"

"Yeah, I saw him sneaking out of her room a couple of times during the tour and that was before he told everyone he was getting a divorce. He didn't know I saw him. I know Katya bought him some expensive stuff too. I think he might have leaked the video, not Amelia."

That conflicted with my theory that Amelia did it to get the band fired once and for all. "Why would he do that?"

"I don't know, but I don't trust him."

"Do you trust Amelia more?"

Lauren paused. "I'm not sure. I just know that Don doesn't seem all that cut up about Katya. If you were having a thing with someone, wouldn't you be at least a little bit upset that they died? And would you immediately find another dancer to get it on with?"

"He has an alibi," I reminded her.

"Yeah, I heard he was at the hospital."

"Say someone did set me up by releasing the video, why? What's the point?"

"Maybe you were getting too close to the truth. Everywhere you go, the truth just seems to follow you."

Lily snorted. "Yeah, and usually the national media, as well."

I gave her a sharp look before refocusing on Lauren. I had to admit she had my undivided attention. She was right about one thing: I was framed for leaking the video; and whether setting me up to take the fall was intentional or not, I was still without a job. In Lauren's favor, however, I truly didn't believe she killed Katya and now I knew her alibi confirmed that. Well, so long as Michael wasn't her secret hit man. "Okay, fine. I will try to clear your name, but I wish you would just tell me who Michael is and save me some time."

"There's one other thing," said Lauren. "You have to promise to leave Michael alone. He had nothing to do with any of this."

"I was starting to work on a theory that he was your hit man."

"I can tell you, one hundred percent, that Michael had nothing to do with Katya's death. Listen, the crew on this tour have more leaks than a rusty bucket.

Shelley's secret got out, then Amelia's. It's only a matter of time before the press flip over Katya's sad death; especially after they realize she was nothing more than a fake; and now here's this stupid video. I don't need the hassle." Lauren checked her watch and sighed, sliding off her stool. Her tea remained untouched on the bar. "I have to go. I'm meeting my lawyer back at the hotel."

"Your lawyer?" asked Lily before I could.

"Yeah. In case you didn't notice, the police and the FBI are both following me."

"They're following you?" I asked, playing dumb.

"Yeah, I saw you, which was cool because you're working for us, but I saw them too. They all think I'm some kind of idiot bimbo who only notices people's shoes, and spends all day in hair and makeup; but I notice lots of stuff."

I thought about Katya and Don. "I'm getting the impression you do."

"So I saw an SUV with the FBI guys. I recognized one of them. And then there were two other guys in some beat-up Crown Victoria. What a cliché!" Lily and I made agreeable noises as Lauren continued. "I figure, if they're following me, I'm their number one suspect; so it's only a matter of time before they bring me in for questioning. Do you think talking to my lawyer will make them even more suspicious?"

"I think you're a smart cookie," said Lily. "And you *should* speak to your lawyer."

I gave a nod of agreement. "Me, too. Listen, if they arrest you, or ask you to go down to the station, call your lawyer first, then call me. Meantime, I'll see what I can do to get them to back off."

"You can do that?"

"Lexi can do anything," said Lily. "You won't regret hiring her."

"I hope not."

"Let me get a new plan together based on what you've told me," I added, standing up to shake her hand. I was suddenly feeling professional again, thanks to Lauren's faith in me, as well as Lily's support, and not least of all, the check I intended to deposit as fast as I could get to the bank.

"What are you going to do now?" asked Lily as we watched Lauren leave. She walked past a couple of photographers before climbing into the backseat of the blacked-out SUV that took her everywhere.

"Prove my client's case," I said, pushing my glass away. I came there to get drunk, but I had no time for cocktails now. I had a case to solve. So, it was the same case as before, but there would be a certain unique satisfaction in beating Solomon to the finish line.

"You just want to beat Solomon."

"And prove Lauren's innocent!"

"Since you think Amelia set you up, I kind of wish you could pin the murder on her."

"I'd try, if I weren't her alibi."

"She still tried to shaft you... or that other guy.

What's his name?"

"Don, but why would he want to break up the band?" I paused, thinking about what Lauren said. Someone did set me up. Did Don have a reason for getting me away from the band and the case? We barely crossed paths, but as far as I knew, I was the only person who interviewed him. Had I gotten too close to something and not seen it? What Lauren told me about his relationships was interesting; Katya one moment, another girl the next. She was right in that he didn't appear cut up about Katya's death at all. "I need to look into the Don angle and find out what was going on there."

"About him screwing Katya?"

"I'd like to know if there's some truth to that. So far, I only have Lauren's word for it, and she's get a hell of a lot to lose. It helps her case, however, if suspicion falls on someone else."

"I've got another idea," said Lily.

"Does it involve me going to Solomon and telling him about this?"

"Duh. No. You're running your own agency now, and it's not like you even poached his client. Lauren tracked you down and approached you."

"Okay. What's the idea?"

"Lauren could be the real victim in all of this?"

"Katya's dead," I reminded her.

"Yeah, and everyone hated her, but does someone hate Lauren enough to want to see her in prison? Is there anyone who would benefit from getting rid of them both?"

~

I thought about Lily's words as I stepped through the doors of Montgomery General, but couldn't come up with any reason for Lauren being set up, other than because she was a convenient patsy. At the main reception desk, I asked for my sister-in-law, Alice, whom I knew was on shift. I'd just called my brother, Daniel, to confirm that when she didn't pick up her cell phone. The receptionist directed me towards the emergency room. As I walked through the sliding doors, I expected it to find the room bustling with bleeding wounds and people moaning in pain. Instead, there were a few bored-looking people and a little kid scooting a car around while making engine noises.

It didn't take me long to find Alice as she emerged into the waiting area, smiling in surprise as I waved.

"Are you hurt?" she asked.

"Not physically."

"Then you're probably in the wrong room. Do you need the mental unit?"

"Ha-ha. Actually, I need a favor. I'm investigating a case and a person of interest was in the ER recently. I wonder if you saw him?"

"I'm taking my break. Come with me," said Alice, and I followed her out of the waiting room. As we navigated the corridors to the empty break room, I told her about Don, his injury, and why I needed to make sure he was in the ER as he reported.

"I was on shift that day, but I don't recall him. However, you know, people I treated this morning could walk by and I wouldn't recognize them. What I can do is take you to Herb in security. We have cameras in ER, thanks to the damn fools who think they can get violent and beat on the nurses."

"That happens?"

Alice shrugged. "Occasionally."

"I'd appreciate talking to Herb, but a video of my guy would be even better."

"Is this anything to do with that band? Did you see their video?"

I cringed. "Unfortunately."

"I haven't seen it, but I heard the nurses talking about it. It's crazy what fame does to a person. Those girls were so young when they hit it big, and look at them now. They're all screwed up and one of them was even murdered."

"I don't think Katya intended to get killed."

"Someone intended for her to be," Alice pointed out, albeit, unhelpfully. "Did your suspect, this guy, did he do it?"

"That's why I'm checking his alibi. I can't tell you anymore about it."

"I'm glad you can't. It's a nasty business." She paused at a door, knocked once, then opened it. "Herb?

I've got someone to see you. Lexi, come in, meet Herb."

Herb was a short, portly man with a lovely smile and a thick sweep of pale brown hair and eyebrows to match. "Hi, Lexi," he said, looking up from his bank of screens.

"Lexi's my sister-in-law. She needs to look at some security tapes. Can you set her up?"

"It's not exactly hospital policy," started Herb, then stopped as he beamed at Alice. "But since it's you, sweet pea, I'll do it." He pulled over the spare wheeled chair and waved me into it as Alice propped herself against the filing cabinet. "Whatcha looking for, Lexi?"

"I need to see a recording from the ER waiting room. Do you still have those tapes?" I asked, giving him the date and time.

"Sure, everything is backed up digitally to our servers here, and we only purge them once a month, so we still have them. Do you want to look over them now?"

"Some of it, yes, but I'd appreciate it if I could get a copy for evidence."

"So long as you don't say you got it from me."

"Not a word. My sources are protected like gold," I assured him.

Herb grinned and tapped a few keys. The screen in front of me went blank before a new image popped up. The date was in the bottom corner of the screen, along with a timestamp, the seconds running. "What time did you want to look at?"

"About an hour ahead."

"Okay, let's speed it along." Herb clicked a few more keys and the tape sped forward faster.

"Whoa! Stop and back up."

"You see your guy?" asked Alice.

"I think so. Yeah, that's him," I said as Don walked into the shot, wearing a navy, zip-up jacket and a red cap. He took off his cap and looked around, glancing up directly at the camera. He stood still for a couple of seconds, looking around like he was waiting for someone.

"He's cute," said Alice. "What exactly did he do?"

"Nothing, I hope."

"Look, there's me!" We watched Alice walking past Don and then out of shot. Don looked up at the camera again and Herb hit *pause*, freezing his picture.

"You really don't remember him?" I asked Alice.

"Nope."

"Okay, Herb, can you play it again?" We leaned in as Don stepped to the left, limping on one leg, turned around and sat down, leaving only his lower legs and feet in the shot. He stayed seated for the next few minutes, occasionally moving one foot or the other. "Can you run this at double-speed?" I asked.

"Sure."

We watched Don's legs doing nothing at a faster pace until I conceded defeat. "He was definitely there," I said.

"You know, I remember that was a really busy day," said Alice as I turned around. "I think there were a lot of patients waiting to be seen. It might have been the day when a minibus overturned. We had a whole bunch of kids with broken bones, and all kinds of scrapes and traumatic injuries."

Lucas already told me about that when he confirmed Don's visit, so I nodded. "That would explain why he said he was in the ER so long."

"I can check the charts from that day."

"I'd appreciate that. Do you know who the other nurses were on duty during that shift?"

"I can find out for certain. I doubt any of them will remember him though. Faces kind of run together in this job, but I'll get you their names anyway. We all switch to an earlier shift tomorrow so I'll ask everyone then."

"Do you want to go through anymore tapes?" asked Herb. "I don't recall any incident report from that day, so I don't think he got into any trouble here, if that's what you're looking for?"

"Oh no, I just needed to confirm he was definitely at the hospital." I sighed, disheartened that I verified Don's alibi. So much for his affair with Katya, which gave him a motive. Perhaps Lauren interpreted what she saw. Perhaps she just needed someone else to be guilty. "Can you transfer this onto a disk for me?"

"Sure," agreed Herb, tapping his keyboard again. He pulled a disk from a drawer under his desk, stuck it in a drive, and we waited.

I left with Herb smiling, and a disk in my hand. "I think he's sweet on you," I told Alice and she laughed.

"Herb? No. I helped his wife deliver twins in the parking lot last year. One of them was breech. He still thanks me for it every day."

"Aww. Thanks for this—" I held up the disk "—I'm really stuck on this case. I don't know what to do next."

"You'll figure it out," said Alice as someone yelled her name while running past. "You always do. Just believe in yourself. I better go see what that's all about." She was gone before I could say goodbye.

Stepping into the parking lot, I fastened my jacket and looked around for my car before realizing that I didn't have it. But I still needed to get home. After I checked my wallet for cash, I sighed, dialing the cab company and waiting in the cold for the car to arrive.

CHAPTER SIXTEEN

There was a lot to be said for working freelance. With Lauren's check safely deposited in the bank, I covered my body in my very best bird-print pajamas, and with a notepad in my lap, I felt free to pursue the case anyway I pleased. Unfortunately, I didn't get any further than setting the coffee machine on and slathering my toast with butter. Beside me, my phone lay silently on the couch. So far, I counted zero missed calls from Solomon, three from my mom, one from Maddox, and two text messages from Lily, asking me if I solved the case yet. I didn't answer any of them and I was still peeved that Solomon didn't attempt to make any contact. That gave me one very worrying thing to think about: were Solomon and I history?

Pushing the thought to the back of my mind, I picked up the disk Herb gave me the day before. The images of Don, standing stationary, while other people moved around the ER kept playing through my mind all night. Something that I couldn't quite put my finger on bothered me. Getting up, I walked over to the DVD player and slid the disk inside before retreating to the kitchen to refresh my coffee. Returning to the couch, I grabbed the remote control and settled in for the dullest few hours of my life as I hit *play*.

Fast-forwarding to the moment Don stepped into shot, I studied him carefully. I watched him glance at the camera, standing solidly in view for a minute or two before taking a seat. It was almost as if he wanted to make sure he was seen, I thought, making note of it.

After he sat down, all I could see were the jeans on his legs and his sneakers. His feet occasionally moved, and sometimes, there was a hand on his leg. It was tempting to watch at double speed, but I had a feeling I was missing something, something crucial, so I watched even more closely.

Ten minutes after he sat down, there was a commotion and nurses jogged through the ER. That had to be the bus crash Alice mentioned, the one that caused delays in the patients' treatments that day. I continued watching Don's feet. At around the fifteen-minute mark, his feet moved out of shot, returning again less than a minute later. Then, for the next two hours, Don's feet shuffled occasionally until they popped out of shot once more, returning to view again a minute later. Finally, he got up, raising his hand and limping forwards. I watched him briefly halt, and turn his head towards the camera before running a hand through his hair. A nurse approached him, sliding his arm over her shoulders and helping him toward the swinging doors.

I clicked off the video and leaned back, still puzzled over what I'd seen.

My eyes brightened. *It was so obvious!* Why didn't I understand it before?

Jogging upstairs, I undressed quickly. I showered and blew dry my hair before dressing in tight jeans, a striped sweater, and heeled boots. I added the barest hint of makeup. I might have been a novice at freelance PI, but that didn't mean I had to dress like I was down-and-out, by wearing pajamas and feeling sorry for myself.

Before I left the house, I powered up my laptop and swapped the disk from the DVD player, putting it into the laptop's disk drive. I took a screenshot of Don's face as he looked up at the camera and sent it to my home printer. Minutes later, I flew out the door, armed with my photo and a surge of renewed enthusiasm.

I knew how the murder happened! I thought I knew why.

And I thought I knew who the killer was.

All I had to do now was prove it.

~

The hospital was as quiet as it was yesterday; and I had no problem finding Alice. She was standing at the information desk in her scrubs.

"Two visits in two days. I'm either lucky or a

possible suspect," she laughed.

"Actually, I hoped I could show my suspect's photo to your colleagues, and see if anybody recognized him."

"Sure, go ahead, but like I said yesterday, all faces blend together after a while."

Alice took me around to her colleagues while it was quiet, and introduced me to her co-workers as her "cool, PI sister-in-law." It warmed my heart that she thought I was cool; and I was glad word hadn't yet gotten around to her about my precarious job status. *Cut it out,* I told myself, as I produced the photo one more time. *You are a professional. You have been employed to do a job and you're doing it. That makes you a PI and a damn good one.*

"Do you recognize this guy?" I asked another nurse, my fifth interviewee. I threw in the date as well as the information about the bus crash to help her remember and pinpoint exactly, right down to the hour, whom I was asking about.

"Yeah, I saw him. He was cute and he winked at me."

"Are you sure?" I asked, both pleased and surprised that someone actually recognized Don.

"Yeah, absolutely. Made my day."

"Do you recall how long he was in the waiting room?"

"Let's see... Not long. I saw him before those crash kids came in. I think he went away, and then he came back later. Probably saw how long the wait was."

"You definitely don't remember him sitting and waiting? He was seated just over there," I said, pointing to the vending machine across the room.

"He definitely wasn't waiting. I kind of looked out for him, and he definitely wasn't there. I remember well because after his name was called, I treated him."

"You did? Can you remember what happened?"

"I can't tell you any medical details. That's against hospital policy."

"How about a brief overview?"

The nurse glanced at Alice, who nodded. "He said he twisted his knee earlier that day and was worried he might've torn a ligament, but I checked him over and his knee was fine. Not even any swelling. I told him to just take it easy for a couple of days and gave him a prescription for a painkiller. What did he do?"

"I'm not sure yet."

"Is he in trouble?"

"Maybe."

"Then I'm glad I didn't try to get his number. I've had enough bad boys. I'm holding out for a good one."

"I'll keep on the lookout," I promised and she laughed.

"I think you spoke to all the nurses. Can I help you with anything else?" Alice asked.

I thanked her and said no, and we briefly discussed the upcoming family dinner before I left. I walked to my VW, which was parked in the nearest lot. Inside, I set the timer on my phone and drove over to the hotel, parking about a street away. Picking up my phone, I timed the drive, which was twelve minutes, and I made a note that there was light traffic.

Looking over toward the hotel, I watched the increasing hordes of paparazzi filling the sidewalk. They sprang into action any time there was movement around the doors. In the duration that I was parked there, the band didn't make any appearances.

While I watched, I wondered about the surveillance I'd seen, and mentally reconnected the dots I'd joined together. I was sure I caught Don in a lie. The nurse remembering that he left and returned later fully supported my theory. I was reasonably sure Don switched places with someone else in the two minutes his feet temporarily disappeared from the screen. With the rest of his body in a blank spot, and someone else dressed in the same jeans and sneakers, Don could have easily made it appear on the hospital security tapes that he waited in the ER for a few hours. I only saw his face for less than a couple of minutes at the very start and the very end of the footage. Everything in the middle showed only his legs and feet, which could have belonged to anyone. However, proving in court that he actually made a switch might present a problem.

"If security footage can tell lies at the hospital, maybe it can tell the truth at the hotel," I said out loud. I was gazing up at the hotel I no longer had any access to, despite it being full of my ex-boss's staff.

Grabbing my phone, I dialed the private number

Lauren gave me. She answered after a couple of rings.

"How's it going?" she asked.

"I've found something interesting," I told her, "but I need your help to verify it."

"Shoot."

"I need to get into the hotel to see the security tapes. Can you help me get access?"

"Why don't you just walk in?"

"Because Solomon's guys are all over the building, and I don't want them to see me."

"Oh, right. I'm still at the hotel. I can get you in."

"Where're Amelia and Shelley?"

"They've gone shopping to get new outfits for interviews."

"What about Joe?"

"He's with them. He and Amelia are being all kissy-kissy. It's gross."

"What about security?"

"Just those two big dudes in front of the elevator. All the other security are downstairs."

"Okay, I need to get into the building and as far as I know, every exit is covered."

"Not the kitchen."

"The kitchen?"

"You know, where they make the food and stuff. I had to get out of the hotel that way yesterday because some fans got through the service doors. No one is guarding the kitchen doors because they only open from the inside. I can let you in that way."

"Okay, I think I know where you mean. Meet you there in ten minutes?"

"Sure, but how do I get away from all the security?"

"Don't worry about them. Just say you're hungry and pitch some kind of diva fit as you storm off. Oh, and scream a lot. If that doesn't scare them, cry. That makes all men uncomfortable."

"Got it."

I got out of the car before losing my nerve and walked away from the hotel, circling back a block later and taking a side road. It led me out of sight of the paparazzi and towards the west side of the employee parking lot that bordered the small garden for hotel residents' use. I had to climb onto a dumpster and sling my leg over the wall to drop into the walled garden, something that, surprisingly, didn't occur to any of the crazed fans yet. Or maybe it did. I dropped to a crouch behind a fragrant bush when I spotted a security guard strolling past. With less than two yards between us, I had to hold my breath as I waited for him to pass by. When he stepped through an arch and behind a hedge, I took off for the employee gate at the other end of the garden. I hurried through it without being stopped, pulling the gate closed. I hastily walked around the narrow, paved path until I reached the kitchen doors. Just as I got there, one popped open and Lauren stuck her head around.

"I thought you'd never get here," she said. "Do you know how many people I had to scream at? I even had to pop an extra button for Josh!"

I suppressed a smile as I stepped through, closing the door behind me. "Thanks."

"Where to now?"

"I need to get to the security suite. It's on the second floor."

"Let's go."

"You've gotten me this far; you don't need to do anything else."

Lauren squared her shoulders. "Oh, please! I got you in and I want to know what you got."

"I don't want to get you into any trouble."

"Yeah?" she scoffed. "Like the murder I'm going to get charged with? Like a little B and E counts?"

"It's not B and E because you let me in as your guest."

"Whatever. I'm paying you, so I'm coming."

"Uh..." I paused, unable to find a reason to argue with her.

"You need me. What if someone catches you?" Lauren pointed out. "You just got fired and it'd be so embarrassing to be thrown out of the hotel on your ass."

"I quit!"

"Same difference. I'm your boss now, so let's go."

I preferred the Lauren I met yesterday; the Lauren who was scared and needed help. However, if this Lauren were bound and determined to be my sidekick, truthfully, she could have been useful to have around. If anyone challenged me, I was pretty sure she could distract them long enough for me to achieve my objective. I had to find out if Don was on any cameras in the hotel around the time of Katya's murder.

"Okay," I conceded. "Let's go. We'll take the service stairs."

The security suite was at the end of a long corridor. With all the security concentrating on the areas the paparazzi and fans might try to break into, we had no problem reaching the suite uninterrupted and virtually unnoticed.

I knocked on the door and went in after a man barked, "Enter!"

"Hi," I told him, improvising on the spot. "I'm with B4U's security detail..."

"The divas on the top floor? My little girls love them," he said. "Every second word in my house is B4U. B4U this, B4U tha... Oh my gosh." He scrambled to his feet as Lauren stepped inside and bumped the door shut with her butt.

"I bet they'd love tickets to our show," she said.

He gaped at her before stuttering, "We couldn't get them. They sold out too fast. Wait until I tell my girls I actually met you! They'll be so thrilled!"

Lauren reached into her pocket and pulled out a clutch of tickets that she waved at him. "How do four tickets sound for our biggest fans?" she asked.

"Unbelievable," said the guard.

"Listen, AJ," I said, reading the nametag on his shirt. "We need your help. We need to review some security footage from the day Katya was murdered."

"I'm not supposed to show anyone that stuff," he said.

"Yeah? Well, I'm not supposed to hand out these free tickets," said Lauren.

"We won't take long," I told him. "I just need to confirm something; then we'll be gone. Plus, I'm with Lauren's security...""

AJ nodded. "Okay, I got the memo about the detective agency being allowed access to our footage. You're with those guys, right?"

"Yes, she is," said Lauren.

That seemed good enough for him. "Okay, tell me what you need."

The three of us sat in front of the monitors and I reconsidered pursuing a nice, safe career as a mall cop, sitting behind a nice, safe bank of security monitors full time, while we scrolled through the footage. "Stop; go back," I said, pointing to the top right of the screen. "Focus on this segment."

"Got it." The segment filled the screen and we watched a man walking through the employee entrance, his face hidden under a cap as he kept his head down. A maid bumped him with a cart and he jumped to the side, looking up and giving the camera an excellent view of his face.

"That's Don," said Lauren.

"And that's exactly what we need. Can you find out where he went from here?" I asked, and AJ began to punch some buttons.

"Maybe. We recently installed a face-reading algorithm... If I set it to run his face to this specific time window... there. Got him. That's him walking through the kitchen... here he appears again by the service elevator, and here he is, exiting it, thirty minutes later. We can follow him back to the employee entrance."

We watched, totally rapt as Don appeared on screen again and exited the service elevator. This time, his jacket was wadded in his hand, but he still wore his cap. "Can I get a copy of that?" I asked.

"Sure. I can email it to you now."

I gave him my personal email address and brought up the email program on my phone. A moment later, I got a notification saying the email had arrived.

"Thank you so much," said Lauren, giving AJ a bright smile as she counted off four tickets and passed them to him.

"My girls are going to be thrilled. These seats are amazing."

"Do you always carry tickets around with you?" I asked as we moved towards the door.

"Sure, they're great currency."

"That's smart." I leaned in, adding quietly, "You know what would be smarter? Telling me who Michael is."

"You know what's smarter than that? You proving to everyone I'm not the murderer." Lauren paused as her cell phone rang. "Adios! Gotta go!" she said as she clicked off her call. "I'm being called to set early. They probably want me to finish filming before I get arrested."

"Don't forget..."

"Call a lawyer, then call you, if that happens."

"That's right, and don't worry. I know you didn't do this. This video should prove that."

Lauren surprised me by stopping to give me a quick hug as we paused at the door. "Thank you for believing in me. Can you get out by yourself?"

"No problem," I assured her. I watched her rounding the corner before I did an about face and stepped back into the security suite, closing the door.

"Hey, thanks again for these tickets," said AJ, looking up. "I just called my wife and she screamed with joy. I haven't heard her scream like that since I proposed."

"You're welcome. Actually, I hoped you might be able to help me with something else."

"Sure. Anything."

"Can you run Lauren's face through your facial recognition program?"

"Yeah, I can run anyone's face."

"Can you limit it to a specific time window?"

"Sure."

I gave him the date and he looked up, alarmed. "That's when her friend was killed. You think she and this guy were in on it together?"

"No!"

"Is she a suspect?"

"Oh no," I said, grasping for a valid reason to see the footage. "I just wanted to test the software, and it was the first time I could think of."

"Right. Okay. Here's the first sighting of her in that time frame," said AJ, pointing to a screen as he called up the digital video file. We watched Lauren exiting the elevator.

"Where is she there? That doesn't look like the lobby or the penthouse suites."

"It's the sixth floor."

I frowned, wondering what business she had up there. The camera followed her as she walked along the corridor, apparently entirely unconcerned. She knocked on a room at the end. The door opened and she stepped inside.

"Can we skip ahead to the next time her face is recognized by the software?"

"Sure." AJ tapped his keys and the tape sped ahead, slowing down as Lauren reappeared on the screen. The time stamp read an hour later.

"Was she in that room for the whole hour?"

"Yeah, looks that way. The software would have picked up her face if she were anywhere else."

"Do you know whose room it is?"

"Nah. I don't have access to that kind of stuff. I just get to watch guests making out in the elevators; and check that the maids aren't stealing the robes. You can try the reception desk downstairs. They'll know who booked the room."

I thanked AJ again for his help and left. I was pleased at discovering something else that could help me prove Lauren definitely wasn't in on the murder. So far, my freelance PI career was going great! I knew where Lauren was at the time Katya died, and I knew someone else was in the room to alibi her. I also had a much better suspect; one I could tie to being seen at the hotel during the time he was supposed to have been at the hospital. Unfortunately, what I didn't have was any direct evidence to link him to Katya at the moment of her death. His visit to the kitchen, prior to taking the service elevator, was something. I figured he could have grabbed the knife then, concealing it in his jacket on the way down.

I paused at the corridor junction. I was wondering if I should take the stairs up to the sixth floor, and knock on the mystery room's door, or head downstairs and get out of the hotel before my luck ran out. *What if I happened to run into Solomon or Joe Carter?* Just then, my cell phone rang, causing me to jump.

Solomon.

I groaned inwardly and hit *reject*. I just couldn't deal with him now. I was too angry. I was angry that he took me off the case after I was set up, angry that he couldn't see that, angry that I quit my job, and angry that he let me. I was also really pissed off that he took so long to call. I felt undervalued and mistrusted and I wasn't in the mood to talk to him. I had to solve a case.

My decision made, I headed downstairs toward the kitchen, stopping short as I spotted Solomon and Josh Alvarez crossing the corridor, also heading in the direction of the kitchen.

"Damn it," I muttered, realizing my path was blocked. Peering around the corridor, I searched for another route. Delgado was posted at the end of the corridor, next to the employee entrance. At the other end of the corridor stood two more men; I knew they were Solomon's guys, but I didn't know them personally. The way I saw it, I had two choices: 1) go back the way I came, and wait for a chance to exit unseen via the kitchen, however long that might take; or 2), walk past Delgado and rely on family loyalty. He wasn't family exactly, but I thought he might become so soon. Crossing my fingers, I walked quickly towards him.

He glanced up as I approached and after blinking, narrowed his eyes. Clearly he knew.

"Two babysitting evenings, and one a weekend night," I said without breaking my stride.

"You got it and I didn't see you," he agreed as I kept walking. Just as the doors slid open, he looked over his shoulder and said, "You better not be in trouble."

"Nope. Later!" I waved, as I rounded the edge of the hotel, unchallenged, before exiting through the gates. I power-walked all the way back to my car. Setting my phone's timer to *start*, I drove back to the hospital, parking and checking my time. I made it back in eleven minutes, which was faster than driving from the hospital to the hotel.

"Katya treated her flings like crap. Don was her latest, and he had plenty of time to get to the hotel, go up to Katya's suite, kill her, and return back to the hotel," I said out loud, tapping my pen against my notepad. "But how did the knife get into his hand?" What I needed, I decided, was to speak to the guy personally.

I called Lauren's private number again. "I'm on my way to the set," she said. "What's up?"

"Do you know if all the dancers will be there?"

"Yeah, I think so. Let me check the shooting schedule. Uh, let's see. Yes. We're scheduled to film a scene with all of them. It's supposed to be a club ambience scene where they all break into this cool routine. It's going to..."

I cut in. "Can you get me into the warehouse?"

"Sure, I'll leave your name at the door."

"No, not mine. Solomon will know."

"Whose, then?"

I scrambled for a name, remembering whom I last visited the set with. "Lily Shuler-Graves."

"Kind of complicated for a made-up name."

"It's not made-up. You met Lily."

"Oh. Okay. Whatever. I'll leave that name at the door and say you're my guest."

"Thanks."

"Does this mean you-know-who did it?" she whispered. "Did we discover the right stuff?"

"I don't know, but I'm going to find out."

"Cool. See you there."

"Hey, Lauren," I called, worried that she'd hang up before I could warn her. "Be careful, okay? I don't want Don to know we're onto him. Don't do anything out of the ordinary. Don't go anywhere alone with him. If he suspects we know as much as we do, we could both be in trouble."

"What exactly do we know?" Lauren asked, sounding intrigued.

"Right now, not enough to tie him to the crime. Without more hard evidence, he could claim he was in the hotel for any reason."

"So get more hard evidence," said Lauren unhelpfully.

"I plan to. See you on set."

CHAPTER SEVENTEEN

The problem with identifying a murderer is no one ever really looks like one. There were exceptions of course, but as I watched Don lifting a dancer high into the air, tossing her and catching her again, I had to admit he looked like an average guy. An average guy with perfectly defined pecs, bulging biceps, and what looked like an eight pack. I could take a wild guess at what Katya saw in him. But I needed to confirm that Lauren's suspicion was true. Did Don and Katya actually have an affair?

"Cut," yelled the director and the dancers collapsed in a heap - dramatically, of course, with arched limbs and plenty of high-fives.

"Amazing, aren't they?" said the woman next to me. A small group huddled together on the edges of the set to watch the filming. I steadily edged my way closer, figuring I was more likely to be taken for a crew member if I physically aligned myself with them. Despite that I could prove I was Lauren's guest, I preferred not to have to explain myself. As for the few people I already introduced myself to, I just hoped they would keep assuming I still worked for Solomon. When it came to Solomon, I hoped he remained at the hotel so I wouldn't run into him. Once again, I looked around to see who was keeping an eye on Lauren, but I didn't see anyone familiar. I figured Solomon probably replaced me with one of his new guys and that the FBI and MPD had backed off.

"Amazing," I agreed. "Janette, right? From wardrobe?"

"Yeah, that's me," she confirmed, seemingly pleased that I recognized her. She didn't ask who I was so I didn't volunteer. I hoped she simply assumed I belonged in the building with everyone else. "They just keep going. They're like robots."

"What take are we on?"

"Seven. I don't know how they do it. I'm out of breath just watching them."

"That guy's really strong." I pointed to Don. "Did you see how he just threw the girl in the air?"

"Yeah, like she was a rag doll."

"It's great how he can keep going after everything he's been through," I said, waiting for my chatty, new friend to take the bait.

"What do you mean?"

"You know, getting divorced, and everything."

"Oh." She nodded knowingly. "He's really cut up about it."

"I bet he's got a whole bunch of girls waiting for his phone number," I said, tossing out more bait.

"Oh, yeah, the girls went nuts when they found out he was single again. Do you see how many abs he has? That's an eight pack! Who has an eight pack? I'm lucky if I can get a guy with a two pack."

"I bet he's seeing someone already. Guys like that don't wait around long," I told her, making my voice as conspiratorial as I could. After all, we were just two women gossiping as far as Janette was concerned.

"I heard that. And that he was getting it on with someone, but whoever it is, I don't think it's serious." We watched Don sling his arm around his dancing partner, pulling her in close and dropping a kiss on her forehead.

"That her?"

"Cynthia? No. She's been hooking up with Landon for like, two years or something. That's Landon," she said, pointing to a less muscled, but equally handsome guy. He'd probably have looked even better if he weren't glowering in Don's direction. "Cute, isn't he?"

"Totally," I agreed again, and it wasn't even a lie. "I wonder who Don was seeing? Do you think it was another dancer?"

"Nah."

"Oh my God, was it you?" I asked, my eyes widening.

She giggled and swatted my arm. "No, silly. I heard a rumor that he was with..." She looked around then mouthed, "Katya."

"Get out! For real?"

"Yeah, I walked in on them once and she went crazy, saying if I ever mentioned it to anyone, she'd have me fired."

"What a bitch," I murmured, adding every gram of concern I could. "How awful for you."

"Yeah, but I didn't take it personally. She was like that with everyone. She used to threaten to fire everyone at least once a day. I'd say it's hard getting used to being without her, but truthfully, it's not. Everyone is happier."

"Even Don," I added, but I wasn't sure if that were an observation or a question.

"Yeah."

"Hey, when did you see this thing between them? Was it before or after he said he was getting a divorce?"

"I don't know. It was only a week ago so... after that? I don't know. I'm not that close with either of them."

"I bet you hear all kinds of stuff in fittings."

"Yeah, they're not exactly discreet."

Neither are you, I thought, but didn't say it. "Anyone accidentally confess to the murder in front of you?" I asked, nudging her jokingly.

She swatted my arm again as someone called her name. "Oh, you are so funny! That's me. I bet someone ripped their pants again. I guess I have to sew whomever it is into their seams!"

"Saving the day again?" I faux-laughed, waving as she giggled and hurried away, leaving me some free time to observe Don. Although he didn't look like a murderer, he didn't act like one either. There was no creepy skulking in dark corners, no weapons hanging from his belt, and no blood on his hands in the visible sense. It made my life so much harder that he looked so damn normal. Happy, even. Lauren was right. Don didn't seem upset at all.

I turned, watching Don move into position on the next set as the director barked orders, flinching when I saw Solomon making his way towards me.

No, not towards me; towards the band's security chief, I realized, as he raised his chin in greeting. While he approached Josh, I stepped backwards, looking for somewhere to hide. Spying a pillar, I swiftly retreated behind it.

"Positions, people!" shouted the director. "Final run-through before we start taping."

I peeked around the pillar, watching Don grabbing the hand of his next dance partner, a lithe redhead with impossibly toned calves. She jumped up gracefully, colliding with him, her hand rushing to her mouth as she bit her lip in the most insincerely coy manner I'd seen since Lily realized my brother actually had the hots for her. Instead of stepping away, or setting her straight, Don stroked a hand down her arm until it came to a rest on her hip. She batted her eyelashes and he said something that made her gasp. She stepped out of his grip, circling around him, her hand trailing across his taut stomach as he turned to follow her.

Something told me they weren't just dance partners. For a man with a divorce going ahead, and a dead fling, he sure moved on fast.

My phone rang, startling me as I pulled my head back behind the pillar. *Solomon.*

I made a noise that sounded somewhere between "meep!" and "argh!" when my ring tone sounded in the near vicinity. Instead of canceling the call, I hit *answer,* cursing myself as I lifted the phone to my ear.

"Yeah?" I said, hoping I sounded more sullen than petrified. What if he'd seen me? Or heard my phone?

"Where are you?" he asked.

"Out," I squeaked.

"Did you remember I'm picking you up at seven?" he asked, not sounding at all worried or heartbroken.

"Seven? What for?"

"Dinner at your parents."

I pulled a face at the phone. "Oh. Is that it?"

There was a moment of silence, then, "Why did you think I was calling?"

"I don't know," I said, pretty sure I definitely sounded sullen now.

"So, seven?"

"Sure."

"Where are you?"

"Just... out."

"What are you doing?"

"Nothing."

"You're out doing nothing?"

"Yes."

A longer silence this time. "Did you really quit? For real?"

"Yes." I wanted to add more. I wanted to explain how hard this case was because of our hellish clientele, and the awful twist it took, not to mention the leaks. Sure, they were partly my fault, but it wasn't intentional. I wanted him to get that without me having to explain it.

"Huh."

"Yeah," I said to cover the sound of someone yelling a name, right behind me.

"Did you hear that?"

"Hear what?" My heart thumping, I wondered.

"Nothing. Must be an echo on the line."

"Where are you? It sounds loud."

"Working the case."

"Do you have a lead?"

"I can't talk about the case."

My turn for silence. Finally, when I was wondering if Solomon hung up — and I didn't dare peek around the pillar to find out — he said again, "So, seven?"

"Seven."

"What did you bake?"

"Oh shoot!" I yelled. Despite reminders, I totally forgot. Now I would have to factor in a visit to the market or bakery to buy something I could pretend was home-made.

"Where are you again?" he asked, "You sound really close."

"I just got home," I lied. "Okay, gotta go. See you at seven."

"Okay, are you resting up?"

"Uh, yeah, that's exactly what I'm doing."

"Maybe have a snack or something if you're extra hungry. Then take a nap."

I frowned. "Great idea! I think I'll do that and have a nap."

"Do you need extra vitamins?"

"Uh..."

"I'll get you extra vitamins. You can't have enough. Your health is important. Bye." He hung up and I glared at the phone, wondering what that little bit of weirdness was about. How could he be so concerned about my health when he thought I was jobless? Was it because I no longer had a health plan? The thought of that made me want to tap my phone against my forehead in annoyance. A good health plan was hard to find. On the plus side, since I was now freelance, maybe I wouldn't have to worry about getting shot, stabbed, or injured anymore?

Checking my watch, I did a double take. How had it gotten to be six-ten without me noticing? Solomon thought I was home, taking a nap before he picked me up. Meanwhile, I had barely fifty minutes in which to catch Don doing something suspect, buy some kind of baked goods, drive home, and get changed into something Mom-approved. I groaned, wondering how I could manage it.

With my phone in my hand, I sneaked a look around the pillar. First, I looked for Solomon. I found him just as he and the guy he was speaking to began to walk to the far side of the warehouse, their backs turned to me. Second, I looked for Don. Apparently, while we were on the phone, the dancers completed their rehearsal and he had his arm slung around the redhead. I held up my phone and snapped a photo of them. Tucking it into my pocket, I pulled up the collar of my jacket, pushed my chin down and jogged to the exit. I hated to leave Lauren, but I figured with her under constant watch anytime she left the hotel, she would be safe enough.

My VW was hidden behind a large truck, blocking it from view of Solomon's SUV, but I wasted no time in pulling out of the lot and aiming for home. Twenty minutes of light traffic, one tray of cookies, and no driving violations later, I pulled into my driveway. I ran into the house, checking my watch every few minutes as I made my way around, shucking clothes so I could shower. I put on a blue maxi dress with minutes to spare. Just as I heard Solomon's SUV park out front, I pulled my hair out of its band, ran my fingers through it, and added a last slick of lip gloss. Making my way downstairs, I stepped into the entryway as Solomon entered via the front door. He stopped dead, his eyes running over me and I felt that familiar tingle through my veins. Yeah, I was mad at him, but I loved him too. Not only that, but I lusted after him like crazy, which only exacerbated my annoyance even more.

"Are you ready to go?" he asked, not taking a step further.

"Yes." What I should have said was 'let's talk' or 'can I have my job back?" but nothing came out. All I could do was look at him and feel utterly confused. He wasn't my boss; but he seemed to still be my boyfriend. I wanted to be mad at him; and I wanted to have a relaxing evening with my family during which I wouldn't have to think about our crazy case. I wanted to tell him I thought I had a huge breakthrough, and that I knew who Katya's killer was, but I couldn't prove it beyond probable doubt, except I wanted to win something more. I wanted to solve this case alone, prove I was a good investigator, so instead of all the things I could have said, I said nothing.

We rode to my parents silently, the tray of cookies in my lap. When he pulled in front of the house, he shut off the engine but didn't open the door.

"Are we okay?" he asked simply.

I shrugged, looking out of the window.

"Lexi?" He reached for my hand. "Lexi, I know you're mad at me. I don't know if it's the case, or your hormones, but I want to talk."

"We can't talk." *Hormones?* I wondered.

"Sure, we can. We can talk anytime."

"No, I mean, my mom's peeking out from behind the

curtains."

"Oh. We should talk though, before we go in."

"I haven't told them."

"About..."

"Work."

"Oh! I thought you meant..."

"What did you think I meant?"

"Nothing! If you're not ready to..."

"Now my dad's there too," I said, looking past him, wondering what on earth Solomon was hedging about.

Solomon shifted in his seat to look at the house. "They must be waiting for us."

"I'm surprised my mom hasn't called my... oh." I stopped as my phone rang. "Hi, Mom!"

"Why are you sitting outside in the cold?" Mom yelled.

"It's not cold, the heater is still..."

"Do you not care about the environment?"

"Well, I..."

"Turn off the engine and come inside."

"The engine is..."

"We're all waiting."

"We're not late!"

"You're not early either," said Mom with a sigh. "You weren't even early for your birth."

"Isn't that a good thing?"

"Birth?" mouthed Solomon, looking puzzled.

"My mom's complaining I wasn't early for my birth."

"Kind of late to complain."

"Good point. Mom, Solomon says it's too late to complain about that."

"I'm putting your father on," said Mom.

"Lexi, this is your father," said Dad.

"I know. We've met."

"Can you come inside please?"

"Yes, we'll be right there."

"But we're waiting!"

"I know. Just start without us. We'll be two..."

"Lexi!"

"Fine! Okay, we're coming. And don't let Mom call again if I'm walking too slow on the path."

"Okay, just make sure Solomon helps you."

"What?" I said, but he hung up. The last time I needed help on a path, I was eleven months old and learning to walk. "My parents are weird. We have to go in now," I told him as Lily and Jord pulled into the space next to the curb in front of us. We all got out at the same time.

"Did Mom just call you?" asked Jord as Lily and I hugged quickly.

"Yeah, and she's been curtain peeking."

"She told me to hurry up and get here before you. What did you do?" Jord continued.

"Nothing! Solomon!" I turned to my boyfriend as I took a deep, frustrated breath. "What did you tell them about work? Did you tell my mom?"

"I didn't say anything; I promise," he said, looking

just as puzzled.

"I've just got to get the cake I baked," said Lily. "Go ahead. Be right with you. Jord, honey? Can you reach the cake?"

"How big is it?" I asked, laughing as Lily stuck out her tongue.

"I know you're mad at me," Solomon said as we walked along the path to the white house in which I grew up, "but that could be a good thing. Let's forget about yesterday. Come back to work, take the desk for a while. Forget all about this case, you don't need the stress. The desk is non-stressful. You could do background research. Maybe do a few phoners."

"I don't want to work the desk. I want to work cases like everyone else, and I don't want to get punished for one simple mistake... okay, a couple of bad mistakes," I corrected myself.

"You know B4U's album is set to make number one, thanks to the latest leak. It didn't turn out so bad after all. People love their sexy side!"

"Then why are you punishing me by offering me a desk job instead of my real job as a PI?"

"You're not being punished."

"Then why do you want me to take the desk?" I persisted.

"Just until the..." Solomon stopped as the door was thrown open and my mother held her arms out, grabbing me and pulling me close.

"My baby!" she wailed.

"Help me," I said, my voice muffled against her sweater. A wave of warmth rushed over me. My mother had the central heating on; there was definitely something afoot.

"Oh, my baby!" Mom wailed even louder as she released me to a shower of paper streamers flying over my head.

"What is this?" I asked, brushing pink and blue ribbons from my hair.

"Surprise! We know all about it! We're so excited. I can't believe you didn't tell me. Oh, my baby!" Mom pulled me in again. I peeked over her shoulder at my father beaming behind her. Beyond him, the entryway was crowded with my relatives, who were all applauding. "My baby is having a baby!" she yelled and everyone cheered.

"Baby?" I whispered, looking up at Solomon. He never looked so thrilled. "Baby?" I asked again.

"I found the stick in the trash," he said, smiling.

"Stick? Trash? What?"

"Sweetheart, I know you're pregnant. Baby, you've made me the happiest man alive." My family erupted into another round of cheers as we were pulled inside.

"Hold on! Hold on!" I waved my hands at everyone, trying to quiet them down. When they didn't respond, I yelled, "I'm not pregnant!"

Solomon frowned. "You are. I checked the lines against the directions on the wrapper. You're definitely..."

"I never took a test!

"I found it at my place," said Solomon, blinking. "I'm not pregnant, so it has to be you!"

"It's not mine!" I yelled even louder.

"No," said a voice behind me. "It's mine."

CHAPTER EIGHTEEN

Amid the sea of pink and blue balloons crowding the ceiling, and the ribbons trailing over our heads, everyone was talking. It seemed the whole family turned out for the pregnancy announcement party they were throwing for me. However, despite the congratulations being shouted, and the feel of my niece, Chloe's, hands gently patting my stomach, was an air of confusion.

"You're pregnant!" I yelled, turning to see Lily behind me.

"You're not pregnant!" said Solomon.

"I'm not pregnant!" I yelled back.

"You're pregnant?" Solomon asked, also addressing Lily.

She smiled and waved. "Definitely pregnant," she said. "You too?"

"Definitely not," I told her, wondering how I could convey that message to everyone else. I started by taking Chloe's hands and placing them on Lily's belly.

"You'll have better luck finding a baby over there," I told her.

"Then how did a positive test stick get into my house?" asked Solomon.

Lily raised a hand. "Me again."

"Hold on, hold on," Mom yelled over the puzzled voices. "Quiet, everyone!" When my siblings, in-laws, and nieces and nephews, filling the entryway quieted, she asked. "Which one of you is pregnant?"

"Lily!" yelled Solomon.

"No need to shout," Mom muttered. "Lexi, are you pregnant?"

"No! I keep trying to tell you that! I. Am. Not. Pregnant!"

"Solomon said you were pregnant."

"Solomon found Lily's test stick in the trash at his place and assumed it was mine."

"Why were you peeing on a stick at my place?" Solomon asked Lily. "Couldn't you do it at your own place?"

She shrugged as Jord wrapped an arm around her. "At least, I used your bathroom."

"John Solomon, did you get Lily pregnant?" yelled my mom, steaming towards him. What she thought she would do, I had no idea, but I got in between them just in case.

"No, Mom. He didn't!"

"Then who did?"

"Me, Mom," said Jord. "You know, Lily's husband."

Mom turned on her heel, launching herself at Lily and Jord. "I'm so thrilled. I'm going to be a grandma!"

"You're already a grandma," said Chloe, her hand sliding under Lily's sweater. "Where is it? Where's the baby? Can I play with it?"

Mom kissed Lily on both cheeks and hugged her again. "You're really not pregnant?" she asked me again, this time, giving me an extra suspicious look.

"No!"

"Is Solomon misfiring?" she asked, loud enough for the entire street to hear. "Can he not fire straight?"

"Yes!" I wailed.

"Is he firing those things? What do they call them? Blanks? Is Solomon firing blanks?"

I groaned and stuck my head in my hands as Solomon muttered, "I'm right here!"

"It's okay, honey," my mother said soothingly. "We don't judge here. Plus, you can always adopt."

"Oooh," I cried into my hands. "Please stop!"

"Maybe they can't swim," Mom continued, unabashed. "Maybe they need help."

"They don't need help. I'm very manly," said Solomon.

"He is." I nodded enthusiastically. "We're just not trying to have a baby. Look! Lily's pregnant. Yay! I need a drink." A large glass was pressed into my hand and my father gave me the weariest, most sympathetic look. It went perfectly with his "My daughter's going to be a mom!" t-shirt. He turned around and shuffled away. The back of his t-shirt read "Who's the Grandpa?!"

"My swimmers are like torpedoes," said Jord before my mother cuffed him.

"Can we please go inside?" I asked, edging forwards. "Lily needs to sit. I need to drink."

"Why are you all standing there? Come in! We have a gorgeous celebration dinner. I made cake! It's pink and blue. Traci made cobbler. What did you bring? Oh, cookies. Well done for trying, darling," said Mom as she relieved me of the cookie tray.

Somehow, I got elbowed out of the way in my mother's hurry to drag Lily inside and talk non-stop about pregnancy and swollen ankles, and pink or blue, leaving me pressed against Solomon.

"So, you're not pregnant?" he said softly when the entryway emptied, my family having followed Lily into the house, treating her like she was made of rare china.

"I'm really not pregnant. Oh, jeez, is that why you keep telling me to take naps and get vitamins and asking about my health all the time?"

"Yes."

"And the baby magazines?"

"Yes."

"And the talks about the future?"

Solomon nodded.

"Oh, wow."

"I thought you were pregnant."

"Didn't you think I would have told you?"

"I thought, maybe, you were waiting for three months or something?"

"Really? C'mon! Did you see my family? They can sense a pregnancy test within city limits. Wait; how did they know all this?"

"I ran into your mom when I was in the pharmacy, looking for prenatal vitamins, and she guessed. I made her promise not to tell even though she was really excited."

I looked over toward the living area, hearing the loud chatter carrying through to the entryway. "Do you think she paid any attention?"

Solomon smiled. "I guess there must be someone she didn't tell."

"Apparently, she didn't tell Lily."

"I don't think Lily minds. She's getting a surprise party."

"Did you know about the party?"

"No, I swear I didn't know a thing. I just knew I had to get you here on time or your mother was going to move in with us after the birth."

I swallowed the rest of the drink my father pressed into my hand and coughed. *Brandy.* "I think I need another one of these."

"Me too."

"Since I'm not pregnant, I could probably drink seven."

"Don't do that," said my sister-in-law, Traci, as she stuck her head around the door. "That's how I got babies two and three. Dinner is ready and no one thinks you're firing blanks, Solomon." She retreated and I snuck a glance at Solomon, sucking in my cheeks so I wouldn't laugh. Sure, it was horrible, but at least, I wasn't being blamed for the miscommunication. I figured since it was only a matter of time, I would enjoy the brief reprise while I could.

Solomon and I squeezed into the last two remaining chairs, and my mother waited until everyone was settled before she stood. "We were going to celebrate my youngest baby's pregnancy today," she announced, "but unfortunately, Lexi isn't pregnant."

"Isn't Aunt Lexi too old to get pregnant?" asked my nephew, Sam.

"I am not!"

"Grandma said all your eggs will dry up and die in a couple years."

"Really?" I narrowed my eyes at my mother. She started playing with the servingware.

"Loads of times. Do you want me to crack one?" Sam continued. "Are they in your purse? I didn't see a grocery bag."

"No, but thanks, Sam."

"What are firing blanks?" asked Sam. "My dad doesn't fire blanks. He said he's always locked and loaded."

"Oh, jeez," said Garrett as Daniel slapped him on the back. "Thanks, son."

"Maybe Solomon can borrow some of my dad's

bullets?"

"No, thanks," said Solomon and Garrett at the same time.

"Probably a good idea. It doesn't seem a nice way to have a baby. Usually, when you shoot someone, they die, but I guess it works different with ladies. Mom, can I have juice, please?"

"Yes, here, drink it all," said Traci, pouring him a large glass. "Just keep drinking. Don't stop."

"You always tell Daddy not to stop too."

"Huh?" frowned Traci.

"I guess he was pouring you a lot of juice last night when you kept saying, 'Don't stop, don't stop!'" Sam went on, oblivious to the giggles spreading around the room.

"Drink more!" yelled Traci.

Mom clinked her spoon against her glass. "As I was saying," she started loudly, "Lexi isn't pregnant."

"We know!" shouted everyone.

"And we mustn't make her feel bad about that. Pregnancy isn't for everyone and that's okay. Some people aren't meant to be parents; and if Lexi wants to be child-free, that's okay," she continued.

"Who said anything about being child-free?" I asked, only to be ignored.

"Plenty of people are child-free," Mon continued. "Maybe Lexi will get a nice pet, like a cat. Or take a lot of vacations."

"Things will stay where you put them," added Traci.

"And you won't have to change diapers," added Alice.

"Maybe I want to lose stuff and change diapers!"

"It's a shame though. Mixed race babies are fashionable. Kim Kardashian has one."

"Seriously?" said Solomon, very unseriously.

Mom nodded. "With Kanye."

"I might want a baby," I said quietly.

"But it's okay if you don't! Being in your thirties, you're a modern woman. You don't have to. You have a choice. You have a career!" said Mom, applauding her own statement. "And you can still have s-e-x. No one's judging."

"S-e-x," said Sam. "What?"

"Drink!" said Traci.

My dad made a strangled noise and stuck his fist in his mouth, appearing to bite it, as he closed his eyes.

"We might have a baby one day," I said, looking at Solomon.

"We might," he agreed, smiling slightly.

"Yay!" Lily yelled. "I'm pregnant! Hurrah! Hurrah for me and Jord!"

Mom turned from me. "I was just getting to that! We thought we were here to celebrate Alexandra and John's baby, but since they can't be bothered to produce one because they have very busy lives, and aren't thinking about the rest of us who would like to know what they're doing with their lives..."

"They're not even married," whimpered Dad. "They

have to get married first."

Mom ignored him. "So, we're even more grateful for Lily and Jord's special news! Congratulations!"

"Yay!" said Lily and clapped loudly.

"To Lily and Jord!" I yelled before my mother could continue with anymore of her mortifying speech, and raised my glass. "Congratulations!"

With all the dishes on the table, dinner was a feast. I had a spoonful of everything, and with conversations overlapping, my heart rate finally calmed down enough that I was able to talk to Lily.

"That's why you've been so weird," I said.

"What do you mean? I've been totally cool."

"You're always busy when I call you, or you hang up really fast..."

"I didn't think you'd want to hear me throwing up."

"If I'd known, I would have come over and held your hair back."

"Oh, like the old days," she said, hugging me quickly.

"Now I know why you were drinking so much tea, too. Why didn't you tell me? My boyfriend found out before I did."

"Only he thought it was you, soooo really, he didn't find out," argued Lily, "but I'm glad he's still your boyfriend. Did he give you your job back?"

"He tried to give me a desk job since he thought I was pregnant and I passed on it."

"You could have surfed the desk for another few

months until he noticed you weren't with child."

"Hmm, maybe. No, wait, no! I've changed! No more slacking like when I temped. Now I work hard."

"Speaking of working hard, how is..."

I held a finger to my lips. "Shh!"

"Oh, right." She pulled a face. "I forgot. Can I claim pregnancy brain this early?"

"Yes."

"But you're still doing the thing for... thing?"

I nodded. "And I found something?"

"The murder weapon?" Lily gasped, mouthing the words as the members of law enforcement surrounding us obliviously carried on with their conversations..

"No, we found that in Katya's back."

"Oh. What was it doing there?"

I raised my eyebrows. "Really?"

"Pregnancy brain!"

I wanted to tell Lily about Lauren and her secret visit to the mystery hotel room, but Solomon looked over at that moment. He reached for the dish next to me, passing it to Garrett before they continued their conversation. I couldn't risk him overhearing my discovery, not when I was working for Lauren. She wasn't exactly his competitor, but I wasn't stupid enough to think he would be pleased that I was still actively working on the investigation he kicked me off. I bristled about that all the way to my parents, but those thoughts were pushed to the back of my mind when the pregnancy party surprised me, not to mention

Solomon's apparently willingness to have a baby with me. In the past hour, I forgot how angry I was with him, and fantasized about a beautiful future.

"I'll tell you later," I told her.

"Is it juicy?"

"Major juice potential."

"I can't wait."

Several cell phones began to ring. I slid my fork back onto my plate and grabbed my cell phone.

"I don't know why you all have these things at the table," sighed Mom.

"I save people," said Garrett as he answered his.

"You're a homicide detective. Your people are dead," I said as I checked the screen. *Lauren.* "I have to take this," I announced, standing at the same time as Solomon.

"I have to get this too," he said, holding the phone to his ear and walking towards the front door.

I squeezed around the table and headed into the kitchen.

"Hey," I said, "I'm glad you called. I need to..."

"Lexi! Ohmygosh! I'm getting arrested!" screamed Lauren. In the background, I heard someone asking her to put down the phone and place her hands behind her back.

"What do you mean you're getting arrested?" I asked quietly so as not to be overheard.

"Just that! They're reading me my rights. Oh, shut up already! I'm talking to my detective," she said, her voice briefly distant. "They say I killed Katya. That bitch just keeps laughing at me, even when she's dead."

"Don't say anything else," I warned her. "I know you didn't kill Katya. I know where you really were."

"You do?" she asked slowly.

"Yes, I do. Where are you? Can you stall?"

"At the warehouse. That FBI guy just turned up. The one from the hotel."

"Agent Maddox?"

"Yeah, I think that's him."

"Tell him I'm coming."

"Do you think he'll care?"

I scowled at the phone. "Yes! Tell him I'm on my way and stay put. I'll be there as fast as I can. Do anything you can to stall."

"I will," she agreed. "Hurry! Please, Lexi. Hurry!"

"I need to go," I said, stepping back into the room just as Solomon did, saying the same thing.

"Where are you going?" he asked, suspicion edging his voice.

"Where are you going?" I repeated.

"The warehouse. It's about the case."

"That's what I meant," I covered quickly. "You're my ride home. I'm coming with you."

"You'll have to stay in the car."

"No problem," I agreed, crossing my fingers behind my back. "Promise."

"I gotta go," said Garrett, stepping into the room with a sigh. "New development in the case."

"B4U?" asked Solomon.

"Yeah, my guys are making an arrest."

"Did you order that?" I asked, turning to my brother.

"Yeah, but they weren't supposed to make the arrest right now. I have to get over there."

"Me too," said Solomon.

"Me too, but only because I need a ride home," I added, flashing my eyes at Lily.

"I can't give her a ride home," said Lily. "I'm pregnant."

"Let's go. Thanks for dinner, Matilda, Steve. Sorry I didn't impregnate your daughter," said Solomon. My dad sighed and nodded. My mother simply offered to bag up some food. We declined since it probably came with life advice, but I did grab a cookie on the way out.

"What a night," Solomon said as he opened the car door for me.

"One to remember," I agreed.

We were quiet as we sped towards the warehouse. For me, I was working out how I could get into the warehouse, and talk to Lauren before she went down to the station. I couldn't figure out what was going on in Solomon's head. I just had to be glad he was distracted enough not to argue about me catching a ride. As he drove, I took advantage of the time to grab my cell phone and fire a text to Maddox. *DON'T ARREST LAUREN,* I typed. *ON MY WAY.*

Why not? I got back within seconds.

She didn't do it, I fired back.

Gee, okay.

She didn't! I can prove it! I typed.

She's in handcuffs. MPD are waiting to transfer her to a squad car, he replied.

Unarrest her! Stall, I typed as fast as I could. *I'll the there in a couple minutes.*

"Who are you texting?" asked Solomon.

"Lily."

"We only just left."

"We're talking girl stuff."

"Forget I asked," he said, driving the car into the lot and parking next to a squad car with its sirens flashing. He switched off the engine and fixed me with a long look. "Are you going to stay put?" he asked.

"I said I would."

"You know, I had to take you off the case. I didn't have a choice."

"Okay."

"Are you still mad at me?"

"Yes."

"Will you come back to work?"

"Nope."

"Will you think about it?"

"Yes." *Right after I solved the case,* I decided.

"I want to continue talking about this, but I have to get inside. It doesn't look good. I may as well tell you. Lauren just got arrested."

Glancing at the flashing lights, I had to agree. It didn't look good at all. "Gosh, really? Aren't you supposed to be finding the real killer?"

"According to MPD, that's Lauren, and I don't have any evidence to prove otherwise. Your surveillance turned up nothing."

I wanted to say that I did have evidence, that I knew something that could prove it wasn't her, that I even had evidence that could help us find the real killer, but Solomon wasn't my employer, so I wasn't obliged to. Maybe it was petty, but Lauren hired me to look out for her interests and I planned on doing just that.

"I'll be right back," he said, leaning over to kiss me softly. "Please come back to work after this is all over."

I gave him twenty seconds to clear the lot before I got out of the car and followed him inside, bypassing the distracted security guard with ease. I found Lauren amidst a crowd of arguing people. She sat on a plastic chair, alternating between heaving tears and screaming her lungs out. She ceased both the moment she saw me.

"This is my PI," she said, pointing to me just as Maddox turned around. "Tell them I didn't do it."

"I don't think she did," I said.

"Okay guys, let's let her go," said Maddox. "I am so relieved you arrived and told us that evidence-less bit of information."

"Take it easy, guys," I said, stepping closer, wondering where Solomon was and why Maddox was being so snarky.

"What are you doing here?" asked Garrett, flashing his badge as he pushed his way through the crowd. "I thought you were waiting in Solomon's car?"

"You knew Solomon was coming," I pointed out.

"Yeah. And?"

"Then you should have worked out I wouldn't be staying put," I said smartly.

"Do you all know each other, or what?" sniffed Lauren.

"Brother," I said, pointing to Garrett then to Maddox. "Ex-uh."

"Friend," said Maddox.

"Ex-friend?" asked Lauren.

"No, definitely a friend," I confirmed.

"Boyfriend," said Solomon, his breath tickling the back of my ear and making me shiver. Great.

"I thought you're her boyfriend? Whatever. Small towns are weird. Lexi is my employee," said Lauren.

"What?" asked the guys together.

"Huh?" said Josh looking past me to Solomon. "We asked you to take her off the case."

Behind me, Solomon remained silent.

"You heard me! I hired Lexi to be my PI and she's gonna prove that I didn't kill the bitch! Then my lawyer is going to give you a talking-to like you've never heard before! And then I'm going to complain to your captain!"

"Lexi?" asked Solomon.

"She's right. I work for her and I do have proof that Lauren has an alibi for the time when Katya was killed."

"But you can't tell anyone," said Lauren.

I ignored her. "I also know who killed Katya," I said, looking around for Don. I spied him in the middle of the crowd. The cute redheaded dancer was still pressed to his side, but her attention was riveted on us.

"Start talking," said Maddox.

"'Cause I ain't walking!" added Lauren. "Tell them I didn't do it."

"I found evidence of Lauren in the hotel at the time of Katya's murder, but she wasn't on her own. She went to a room on the sixth floor and remained there until after the time ME confirmed Katya died. She wasn't on her..."

"That's enough!" Lauren cut in. "See!? I told you idiots I didn't do it!"

Maddox turned to her. "You said you were on your own in Amelia's suite."

"I was, but in that hotel room, not the suite."

"Was she alone, Lexi?"

"No, someone opened the door to her. There was at least one other person in that room."

"Please, don't," Lauren pleaded.

"Okay, so if Lauren was with someone who can give her an alibi, how did the killer get to Katya?" Garrett asked.

"He was able to bypass the band's surveillance detail by entering the hotel via the employee entrance. Then he rode the service elevator up to the band's floor and used the secret passageway to enter Katya's room unseen. He knew no one would see him so long as he was careful."

"Sounds pretty convoluted to me," said one of the cops at Lauren's side.

"It is," I agreed, "but it wasn't his first time. He used the passageway before while conducting an affair with Katya so he was already familiar with getting in and out without being seen. I believe he killed her when she broke it off with him. Maddox, you should be able to match his fingerprints to the ones you found in the passage; and I'm sure you can match the DNA on the knife to him."

"I need a name," said Maddox.

"Don. Don Kenley," I said, turning to point to him, but he was gone. "He was right here."

"Well done, Poirot! You lost him!" yelled Lauren.

"Go find him," Garrett instructed the uniforms. "Have you got any more evidence to prove he was in Katya's room when she was murdered?"

"Find Don Kenley!" yelled Josh Alvarez, puffing up his chest and waving his arms. "I want all eyes looking for him."

I ignored Josh barking orders as I focused on Garrett. "Yes. I can disprove his alibi, and I have hotel footage of him entering the hotel in the time window for the murder; plus, there's footage of him in the kitchen, where the knife used to kill her was stolen."

"Good work." Garrett patted me on the back. "Also, did you quit or get fired?"

"So who were you with?" Solomon asked Lauren as the uniformed cops broke from the crowd, fanning out. "What's the big secret?"

"Michael," I said, softly. "Tell them about Michael." I was bluffing, I didn't know who he was or what he was to her, but Lauren didn't know that. I needed her to confess she'd been with her mystery guy because so far, I was only guessing that he was the one she was secretly visiting.

"You know, don't you?" Lauren whispered as shouts for Don sounded across the warehouse. I nodded. "And you don't care?"

"Should I?" I countered. "Tell them, Lauren. It'll be better if it comes from you."

A tear trickled down her cheek and she sniffed hard. "Michael," she started, hiccupping, "Michael is my son. He's nine years old."

CHAPTER NINETEEN

I would have thought Lauren's bombshell could have stunned the warehouse into silence; but instead, it seemed to have the opposite effect. Garrett was shouting at his men to find Don while he uncuffed Lauren. Joe was shouting at Lauren, and Amelia had her arms around her friend. Maddox was on his phone, also shouting at someone. The uniforms fanning across the warehouse were quiet, their torchlights flashing in the darkest corners. Solomon was probably shouting in his head, but I didn't turn around to find out. I could tell he was still standing behind me; and his presence made my skin tingle, despite his silence. And me? I was gaping in surprise.

Taking higher priority on my list of problems was the now empty spot where Don was standing only moments before. The cute, little dancer chick also disappeared. At Garrett's prompting, I tried to explain to everyone how Don managed to dupe the hospital surveillance cameras into providing him with an alibi should he need it, while he walked into the hotel and grabbed a knife. Meanwhile, Don used Lauren's distraction as the perfect opportunity to escape. That wonderful, smart feeling I had only a minute ago vanished, and now I felt like a huge idiot. Had I been more thoughtful, and less intent on winning over Solomon, I would have texted Garrett or Maddox and advised them to fan their men around the crowd, ready to catch Don before he could make any break. If Don escaped now, I would have been totally responsible. Again.

It was a good job I'd already quit; otherwise, I'd probably have to fire myself.

"What do you mean you can't find him?" Garrett said into his radio. "He can't have gone far. Find him! You! Boss man! What kind of vehicle does Don drive?"

Joe paused from his tirade to frown. "How should I know?"

One of the dancers raised a hand. "He drives a red Toyota. I saw it in the lot on my way in."

Garrett grabbed his radio. "Look for a red Toyota in the parking lot."

"In sight," came the crackling reply. "It's empty."

"Check inside."

"Clear, and the hood's cold. This vehicle hasn't moved in a while."

"Shit. Keep looking." Garrett glanced up from the radio. "Any of you missing any car keys?" he asked. The cast and crew began to pat their pockets, frowning.

Garrett clicked his radio again. "Never mind. Post a uniform on the gates while I send security to lock them. Where the hell is security?" he yelled.

"He won't try to go out the front," I said. "He knows his escape route is blocked out front. Besides, he's too smart to escape in a car that's registered to him."

"She's right." Garrett glanced at us. "I got here to supervise the arrest, not to make a search. I don't have enough men to cover the whole warehouse, along with the rear area beyond the warehouse. He's already got a five-minute head start."

"Have your men take the front," Solomon instructed. "I have another guy here. With Maddox, we can start checking the interior. He might not have left yet."

"And me," I added. "Solomon's right. The warehouse is huge. He could be hiding until we all leave, and then just slip away."

"No way," said Solomon. "You're not on the case; plus, this guy is dangerous."

"She's on the case because I'm paying her and she just solved it," yelled Lauren.

"Thank you!" I gave her a grateful smile, but her face soured.

"I'm still mad at you," she said.

"Why? Because you have a kid? So what?" I asked.

"Duh. Do the math," said Amelia.

"Huh?"

Amelia looked at me like I was an idiot, which didn't help my current self-annoyance. "She had him when she was barely sixteen."

"Oh. So?"

"No one likes a teen mom," wailed Lauren.

"You're not a teen anymore; and you've done really well for yourself," I told her, momentarily distracted. Shaking my head, I realized the clues about Michael had been there all along. The house in Lauren's name that I assumed her mom lived in... with the kid's bike in the yard. The bike must have been his. As for the secret hotel room she rented, I guessed we'd soon find evidence that Lauren wanted to keep her son close by as she toured with the band. "I'm really impressed that you could become a single parent, even when you were so young, and you're crazy talented. That's quite admirable."

Lauren blinked back surprise. "You think so?"

"Sure. You're an inspiration to any young parent, single or not."

Lauren wiped her tears with a tissue. "Okay," she said, sounding confused. "Maybe."

"Can you find the asshole who murdered Katya now?" asked Amelia. "Or are you going to give a pep talk to anyone else?"

Maddox stepped forwards. "We'll team up. Lexi and I will take the east side. Solomon, you and your guy take the west. We'll work our way into the middle."

Solomon fixed me with an impenetrable look. Finally, he asked, "Are you armed?"

"Only with my knife," I replied, patting my pocket,

and momentarily happy at feeling the cool lump within. I had a gun, and a concealed carry permit, but I rarely took it from the house. The knife was better. Smaller, effective, not to mention, it made removing clothing labels on impromptu shopping trips easier. I was forced to use it to defend myself before, but I preferred using it as a deterrent, rather than as a weapon.

"Take this," said Solomon, removing a small pistol from his ankle holster and handing it to me. "Don't use all the bullets at once."

I checked to make sure the safety was off before tucking it into my waistband. I was pretty sure Don wasn't armed, but it didn't pay to guess wrong about that. If he were capable of stabbing one woman to death, he was surely capable of committing another murder.

"Let's go," said Maddox, placing a hand on my shoulder. I nodded to Solomon, and was glad when he didn't bar my way. Without his encouragement and his job offer, I might have never become a private investigator, or found my most fulfilling job. At times, he played my mentor and teacher, and he rarely stood in my way, except for this case. I was fairly sure he would have handcuffed me to a chair if I were actually pregnant, and I felt glad he knew me well enough that he could depend on me seeing the case through. Instead of arguing, he simply armed me.

"Be safe," Solomon mouthed as I turned away.

The crew and everyone else, drawn together by the

commotion of Lauren's arrest, were corralled near the wardrobe area, leaving the rest of the warehouse empty. From the corner of my eye, I watched Solomon and his guy, a man I vaguely recognized from the risk management team, jogging across the floor, and receding into the shadows. Maddox and I did the same, with Maddox leading in front by a couple of yards, with his gun drawn.

"Maddox," I hissed.

"Yeah."

"Don was standing with a woman. One of the dancers."

"Yeah?"

"I couldn't see her. She might be with him."

Maddox stopped so fast, I almost collided with him.

"Didn't you think about mentioning that back there?"

"I was distracted!"

"Pregnancy brain?" he asked, glancing at me, his face blank.

"Not you too! I'm not pregnant! Lily is!"

Maddox broke into a huge smile. "Oh! Awesome!"

"I know!"

"Text Solomon, tell him about the woman so we don't accidentally shoot her. What does she look like?"

"Petite, red hair, great calves."

"Could you be more descriptive? What about a name? Does she drive?"

"I don't know to both," I said, tapping a message to

Solomon before tucking my phone away.

"Let's keep going."

We ducked into tight corners, and checked behind pillars, all the while, trying to avoid tripping over the thick cables that snaked across the floor. With the shadows invading the dusty corners, and the warehouse becoming darker and darker the further we delved into the corners of the cavernous space, the more my heart rate picked up.

Hearing a footstep, out of rhythm with Maddox's and mine, my muscles tensed. I knew Maddox heard it too when he halted, holding a hand up for me to stop. We paused behind a pillar, waiting as the footsteps got closer. A hunched figure scrambled past us and Maddox let out a yell before launching himself at the person, knocking the intruder to the ground.

"Help!" screamed a female voice as Maddox wrestled her flat.

"Who are you?" Maddox hissed.

"Carlotta. Get off me!" She flinched, and began blinking as I shone the flashlight in her eyes.

"It's her, the woman with Don," I told him. "Where's Don?"

"I don't know. He grabbed me when you were all talking and said we had to go, except he wanted to go out this way, out the back exit. I didn't want to go, but he made me and then someone started shouting his name. He hurt my arm. What's going on?"

I ran the flashlight over her and saw the reddening

fingerprints on her upper arm. Her fear and confusion were palpable.

"Where'd he go?" I asked.

"That way." She nodded to the back of the warehouse. "He stole my car keys."

"Where's your car."

"Out front, in the lot."

"He might circle back," said Maddox, relaxing his grip slightly.

"He knows we're looking for him. He knows we'd stumble across Carlotta and he thinks taking away her keys will make us think he circled back."

"You're right. Out front is covered. You stay here," said Maddox, grabbing handcuffs from his waistband. He slapped one cuff over Carlotta's wrist and attached the other to a ring embedded in the pillar.

"You can't leave me here," she whined. "It's dark."

"I can't let you go wandering around. You could get shot." Carlotta whimpered and Maddox sighed. "I'm sending a text so someone will come for you, okay? Just stay quiet for now. Lexi, let's go."

We continued on, despite Carlotta's protests, and tried to stay low as we made our way darker and deeper. Our feet shuffling through the debris, we had to keep our footfalls as quiet as possible. By the time Maddox edged closer, tapping me on the wrist, I nearly screamed from my raw nerves alone. "Door," he whispered, pointing at a stream of dusty light in the corner. "I don't see any other exits and it's open a little bit. Don could have exited through there."

"You go first," I said.

"Why me?"

"I'm learning."

"To be a PI?"

"No, not to get shot first."

Maddox laughed softly. "Fine. I'll go first. Cover me." I knelt, raising my weapon and surveying the area as he jogged forwards. With his body hunched down low, he raced towards the door. No one shot from the shadows when he grasped the handle. He pushed it further open, and the door gave a long squeal as more light flooded in, pooling around him in a heavenly glow. He stepped outside, but no further than where I could still see him, and turned around, giving me the thumbs-up.

"Don't move," whispered a male voice next to my ear. I froze as something pressed into the small of my back, which, I was sure, wasn't a banana. An arm reached around and politely relieved me of Solomon's gun.

"Lexi, come over here," Maddox said, waving a hand, beckoning me.

I remained motionless.

"Lexi," he called, a little louder.

"Get up," said the man.

"Don?" I whispered.

"Yeah, it's me."

"Don, don't do this."

"Too late."

"It isn't. It's me, Lexi. I can help you," I said, trying to establish a connection with him, anything that would make him less likely to shoot me.

"I know who you are; and all I care about is getting out of here. Get up."

I rose slowly, the barrel still poking into my back as Don wrapped an arm around my neck. I realized the exact moment when Maddox discovered I wasn't alone; I could tell by the stiffness in his shoulders, his rigid posture, and the fear in his eyes.

"You think you've got it all figured out," said Don, nudging me forwards. I shuffled as Maddox remained still. "I can't believe you're even here. You should have got fired."

"You did leak the video?" I gasped, my jaw stiff.

"Yeah. Listen, don't try anything stupid, or I'll put a bullet in you."

"I'm not going to try anything, Don. Let's talk about this."

"That's what Katya said right before I killed her."

"But you're not going to kill me. We're not enemies, Don."

"I'll kill you if I have to. Call your friend there. Tell him to put his weapon and keys on the ground. Do it."

"Maddox," I called. "Don wants you to put your gun and keys on the ground."

"Okay." Maddox reached into his pocket slowly and tossed the car keys onto the floor. He bent at the knees and lowered his gun, placing it on the floor in front of him before rising. "They're on the ground. Now let Lexi go."

"Move away from the door. That way. That's right," Don said, as Maddox sidestepped away from his weapon, as well as the exit.

"Where do you think you're going?" I asked him. "There are cops everywhere."

"Yeah, watching my car out front, or waiting for me to steal Carlotta's. I've got this all planned out."

"Did you plan me too?"

"No, you were a curveball."

"Did you plan to kill Katya?"

Don paused and I could feel the heat of his breath on my neck. I wanted to shiver with disgust, but I forced myself to remain calm. I needed for Don to talk to me. I needed to stall him.

"I went to talk to her after she dumped me."

"But you killed her."

"She wouldn't shut up. She said all kinds of nasty stuff about me... about my wife. She always was a mean bitch."

"Everyone hated her."

"Yeah."

"Why did you hate her? I thought you loved her," I guessed.

"I did."

"You left your wife for her."

"Yeah. And you know what she did when I said I

told my wife about us? She laughed and called me a sucker."

"That's horrible."

"Like I said, she always was a mean bitch."

"So you stabbed her."

"Not then. I went to talk to her that day. I told her she didn't mean what she said about us being over. We had a connection, you know? I told her we'd be okay and we could work on our relationship."

"Sounds like you really cared about her."

"I did. I loved her so much. I was crazy about her. We talked about it, and we had everything planned out. I was going to tell my wife and get a divorce so we would get married, but it was... it was just a game to Katya. She just wanted to see if she could wreck my life. She actually told me that! She just wanted the satisfaction of knowing I'd do anything she asked, and when I told her I'd done it, and left Amanda she... she laughed in my face."

"That must have hurt."

"She wouldn't stop laughing. She said I was a major loser and I should never have thought she would lower herself to be with someone like me. She just wanted to see if she could make me do anything she wanted. I tried to reason with her, and tell her it's not okay to mess with me, and that we could make it work. She told me to get out."

"Then what?"

"Then I stabbed her. It was perfect. No one knew it

was me. She told me about the secret passage, and how we could come and go as we pleased without the rest of those bitches interfering. No one would have ever known."

"Except we caught you. The evidence is solid."

"Nah, you didn't catch me. I caught you. You and I are going to walk out this door and as soon as we're a safe enough distance away, I'll cut you loose. Any funny stuff and I'll shoot. Got it?"

The cool air brushed against me as Don began to pull me backwards towards the door. A light flickered in my eye, unnatural and dark, and I followed it as it moved down.

"Don, we have a little problem."

"Tell me about it."

"No, a new one. See this little red dot on my chest?"

Don's cheek brushed mine as he looked over my shoulder. "Yeah?"

"See how it's moving up? And now it's gone?"

"Yeah? What of it?"

"It's a sniper light. Snipers use it to mark their targets. It moved off me, which means it's on you."

"What the..."

Before he could finish his sentence, I grabbed the knife from my pocket, flicked out the blade, and jabbed it into his thigh. I dropped and rolled, using Don's weight as leverage to push myself away as he hit the doorframe. The bullet missed me by inches before it slammed into Don's chest, knocking him backwards.

He staggered against the wall, dropping to his knees.

"Lexi, are you okay?" Hands grabbed me, hauling me back. "Are you injured?" Maddox flashed his light over me. "You're bleeding."

"Not mine. Don's. I stabbed him." I dropped the knife onto the floor, breathing hard. "Who shot him?"

Maddox turned the flashlight on Don, or at least, what we could see of Don. Two guys were on him and he was screaming and wriggling. Somehow, they all seemed to organize themselves into some semblance of order and peeled apart. The guy who jumped Don first was Solomon's partner. His shirt was splattered with blood. Solomon barely looked ruffled as he rolled off.

"Caught him," said Solomon, standing as running footsteps approached us. "Let's go."

"You okay?" I asked Maddox.

"Just hurt my pride," he said, dusting off his suit with both hands. "I didn't see him. I'm so sorry."

"You couldn't have known he was behind us."

"You did really good," he said as my brother ran into sight. "I'll catch up with you both for the debriefing. Right now, I'm going to enjoy Detective Graves reading this jerk his rights."

"You shot me," wailed Don. "I might be dying."

"The bullet didn't hit anything crucial," I pointed out as they pulled him onto his feet. A wound just below his shoulder bled. A few more inches down and it would have been a fatal shot.

"It could have. This is police brutality!"

"I shot you and I'm not the police," said Solomon.

"Then I'll sue you."

"Go ahead. We'll see how far you get when I explain to the police you had a gun in my girlfriend's ribs."

"Plus, you're going to jail anyway," I added, rubbing it in slightly.

"It was heat of the moment! It was self-defense. She attacked me."

"I did not!" I squeaked indignantly, wondering if it was okay for me to kick him. It would probably have been wrong to kick a gunshot man, but I was really tempted. "You took my gun!"

"Not you! Katya!" Don slumped his chin onto his chest as someone pressed a wad of cloth against his wound and Garrett handcuffed him. "She attacked me. I had to defend myself. I can't go to prison. I'm too good-looking!"

"Shut up so I can read you your rights," said Garrett. "And when I say shut up, I mean shut up. You just hurt my sister."

Don fixed me with an angry look. "Do you know everyone?"

"Yes, obviously." I grabbed Solomon's proffered hand and stood upright. My jeans were smeared with Don's blood and my skin felt dusty and dirty. I needed to shower pronto; then I needed another glass of brandy. "Listen, Don, there's no way you can claim self-defense for Katya's murder. I have you on camera walking through the employee area at the hotel; and we know the knife came from their kitchen. It doesn't take a genius to work out you grabbed the knife from there, on your way up. You sneaked through concealed passageways and gave yourself an elaborate alibi at the hospital that I can also disprove, suggesting Katya's murder was pre-meditated."

"Someone should give me a medal for getting rid of the bitch," muttered Don, wincing as he was shoved forwards.

"How about twenty-five to life?" said Garrett as the paramedics passed me, stopping to attend to Don's wound as he began to wail.

"Good shot," I told Solomon when we moved away, leaving Garrett to deal with him.

"Good you moved when you did. I didn't have a clear shot until then."

"Teamwork." I smiled as Solomon put his arm around my shoulders, pulling me closer.

"Teamwork," he agreed. "Don't quit. I want us to keep working together. I like it. We're good together."

"Love you," I said, reaching up to kiss his lips, my decision made. I did love him, but the moment he thought I was in danger, and he had more to lose than just me, he benched me. Not only that, but he pulled me off the case that I solved. Yes, I screwed up, but I fixed it. I wanted to feel confident. Maybe it would be a good idea if we concentrated on our romantic relationship for a while, rather than our working relationship. "I love you more than I can put into words, but I've chosen to freelance."

CHAPTER TWENTY

The credits rolled by on the hour-long B4U documentary we just finished watching. It charted all the band members' careers, from their early beginnings as four eager "teens" to their final farewell video with just the three remaining members singing. Instead of being a misery fest, dedicated to Katya, the video was re-shot as an upbeat end to what was formerly a stellar career.

"The video was awesome. I wish we got to see the re-shoot," said Lily. She stuck her spoon in the ice cream and pulled out a huge glob that barely managed to fit into her mouth. The carton was resting on her growing bump. I wanted to pat the bump and see if it did anything yet, but I was afraid Lily would think I was attempting to eat some of the ice cream and stab me with her spoon.

"Me too. Shame they decided on a closed set."

"It's actually kind of nice without all those background dancers and all those set changes."

"Lauren called yesterday when the video was released. She said the management decided it wasn't really a farewell to Katya, but a farewell to their fans; so simple worked best."

"How's she taking the band getting fired?"

"Pretty well. She just signed for a TV reality show to film her life with Michael and her solo career."

"He's a cute kid."

"Really sweet. You know, Lauren spent so long being afraid of what people would think that it never occurred to her that her fans might be impressed by her dedication to Michael. As it turned out, she became a poster child for success as a single parent. She proves teen moms aren't bad; they just need some help to succeed."

"Just goes to show that sometimes, kids are the best mistake you can ever make."

I nodded, not adding it was great that Michael and his grandmother were both able to give Lauren a rock solid alibi for her secret visit. She told me that they often quietly joined her when she worked away from home and she'd visited with them as often as she could. She seemed like a good mother and I was happy that she could live freely now without fear of her secret being blown wide open. "She told me she and Michael are launching a fashion line for kids. Really cool boys' and girls' wear. Look what she sent me." I pushed the blanket off my legs and crossed the room, reaching for the parcel Lauren sent in the mail. Pulling out the little items, I passed them to Lily and we cooed over the miniature pants and t-shirts. "This is just the baby wear. When I told her you were pregnant, she said I could give it all to you."

"Adorable. I'm glad for her. What happened to everyone else after they got fired? Did Lauren tell you?"

"Amelia's retired from the music business for now. She and Joe bought a house in Orange County and they're trying for a baby. Lauren said Amelia might try to launch a solo career. She wrote the lyrics for the song currently at number one in the charts."

"Awesome. She had the best voice," said Lily, pulling an OMG face at the little green shirt she held up. "What happened to Shelley?"

"Rehab."

"Figures."

"She gets out next week, just in time to start shooting a movie, *Kissing in Action*. She got the female lead with that super hot actor. The one with the Italian name who does all those action movies."

"Get out!"

"Serious. The movie is going to be huge."

"Shelley's interview, the segment right at the end of the documentary, was really cool. I like how she didn't apologize for being gay. She seemed really honest. So like herself. Kids can relate to that. Maybe some of them won't struggle so much in coming out now since they have a positive role model like Shelley."

"Revealing their secrets seems to have worked out well but the band finishing seems like the best thing that could happen to them."

"Except Katya," Lily pointed out as she dug into the ice cream again.

"Except Katya," I agreed.

"I've been following the Don Kenley media circus. His life was a mess. Do you think he'll be convicted?"

"Yes, without a doubt." I handed over all the evidence I found to Garrett, pointing out Don's jacket when he left the hotel was missing by the time he was treated at the hospital, where he was caught on camera for his alibi. In a series of long interviews with Don and his lawyer, all the evidence was laid out in front of him. Maddox added fingerprints and DNA evidence from the knife that directly linked Don to the murder. After a long and arduous search, they even found his bloodied jacket, thrown into a dumpster at the hospital, and located the guy he'd paid to sit in his place while he left the hospital. Garrett had a full confession before he even got further evidence of Don checking out cameras at the hotel and hospital several days before the murder.

My hunch paid off; Don simply couldn't handle throwing his life — and wife — away for Katya, only for her to reject him. Instead of moving on, he killed her. He hoped Lauren would take the rap so he could continue his life as if nothing ever happened. His arrogance would have astounded me if I hadn't previously closed a number of cases with guys just like him.

The chief of police was happy. Joe Carter was happy and got a huge pay off, as well as a wife, and the continuing career as manager of a rock band to keep him busy. Amelia, Shelley, and Lauren were happy in their new careers. It seemed like everyone was pleased with the outcome. I wasn't sure what Solomon thought about it, since it never came up in conversation, except for a week after the arrest when he quietly handed me my bonus check for completing the case.

"What's going on with you and Solomon?" asked Lily.

"We're happy."

"No, I mean, really? What's going on? It's been two months and you're still working out of the back room of my bar. You are working, right?"

"Sure, a little bit." That was true. I took a few small jobs, the kinds of things Solomon would have turned down. They were mom and pop cases, nothing particularly intriguing or taxing on my brain cells, but I figured I had to start somewhere. With Lauren's money and Solomon's bonus check fattening my bank account, I didn't have to worry too much about the income yet, but I figured I would sometime soon.

"Don't you think you should go back to the agency?"

I spilled the uncomfortable truth. "Solomon hasn't asked me again." I thought he would, but he hadn't. Not once. It puzzled me. I wondered if it worried him that I never asked to return. I thought about asking, but didn't. I didn't know if it was pride that held me back, or if I were still angry somewhere deep inside that was hard to reach and forget about.

"How's your relationship?"

"What is this? Twenty questions?"

"Kinda."

"Our relationship is fine. Really, it is." Work might have brought us together, but it wasn't what kept us together. That was a pleasant revelation although I hoped, even felt, it was the case. Now, work was off the table, and we were talking about so much more. I missed working with him, but I liked the softer side of our relationship. I liked finding out more about the man I spent so much time with talking shop. Working alone gave me more time with my thoughts too. Without seeing Solomon so often, I could dedicate more time to thinking about us. Not just our future, but my future. Even though he never raised the baby topic again, it was easy to recall how attentive he became when he thought I was pregnant, and how eager he seemed at the prospect of becoming a dad. The more I thought about it, the more I saw how my future could be.

"I hope so. I like Solomon."

"Me too. Hey, you know who else is happy?"

"Who?"

"Maddox." Lily looked up and frowned, so I explained, "I saw him a couple of days ago. He was on a date and I think it was the woman he took to Lake

Pierce a while back. She seemed nice."

"Actually, I met her already."

"You never said!"

"I forgot! You're right, she's nice. Do we like her?"

I nodded. "We like her."

"Oh good. I find it so hard to stay pissed at people I don't know."

"Me too. Plus, this is a good thing, right? Maddox is moving on."

"Yup."

"Good."

We were silent except for the sounds of Lily enjoying the ice cream. "Ugh, it's all gone," she moaned pushing the carton away. "You need to buy bigger tubs."

"I would, but I don't want my niece or nephew to be born looking like Olaf, the snowman."

Lily giggled. She reached across and grabbed my hand. "We're properly related now thanks to the baby."

"Forever and ever," I agreed and squeezed her hand.

Lexi Graves returns in
TRIGGER SNAPPY
Out now in paperback and ebook!

When private investigator, Lexi Graves, quit her job, she never thought working freelance would be so hard. Struggling to make a name for herself as a solo investigator, she's intrigued when a wealthy, new client claims she's being stalked and chooses Lexi as her last hope for help.

Without any evidence, the police don't believe Juliet Hart is being victimized, and her boyfriend and best friend are also both skeptical. Yet, Juliet is convinced she is being watched and someone is playing tricks on her. Is she simply paranoid, or is there something more sinister at play?

Initially, the case appears easy: tail the client and find out if someone else is watching her too. Yet before Lexi can make serious headway, her client is arrested for a crime she claims she didn't commit. Now Lexi's case collides with her boyfriend's, her ex-boss, Solomon, putting them on opposite teams.

The more evidence Lexi finds, the more convinced she becomes that her client's stalker is not only very real, but has nefarious motives. Way in over her head, Lexi urgently needs to find out why her client is being stalked, and by whom, before it costs Juliet not only her freedom, but everything she values and holds dear.

About the author

Author and journalist Camilla Chafer writes for newspapers, magazines and websites throughout the world. Along with the Lexi Graves Mysteries, she is the author of the Stella Mayweather urban fantasy series as well as author/ editor of several non-fiction books. She lives in London, UK.

Visit Camilla online at www.camillachafer.com to sign up to her newsletter, find out more about her, plus news on upcoming books and fun stuff including an exclusive short story, deleted scenes and giveaways.

You can also find Camilla on Twitter @camillawrites and Facebook at https://www.facebook.com/CamillaChafer.

Made in the USA
San Bernardino, CA
27 September 2018